SEDUCED BY A
BILLIONAIRE

THE CAROLINA SERIES BOOK ONE

JILL DOWNEY

The Carolina Series
Book 1

by
Jill Downey

Cover Design Copyright © 2020 Maria @ Steamy Designs
Editing April Bennett @theeditingsoprano
Interior book design Julie Hopkins

DEDICATION

To my lifelong friend Sandy, who has always believed in me and been by my side cheering me on. Your love patience and encouragement mean everything...Thank you!

BOOKS BY JILL DOWNEY

Books by Jill Downey

The Heartland Series:

More Than A Boss

More Than A Memory

More Than A Fling

The Carolina Series:

Seduced by a Billionaire

Secret Billionaire

Playboy Billionaire

A Billionaire's Christmas

The Triple C Series:

Cowboy Magic

Cowboy Surprise

Cowboy Heat

Cowboy Confidential

PROLOGUE

"I don't give two fucks what their excuse is, if those financial documents aren't on my desk first thing tomorrow morning, I'll proceed with filing a subpoena. Have I made myself perfectly clear Elenore?" Kyle Bennett said to his assistant while maneuvering through traffic.

"Yes sir."

"Good. I'll see you in the morning." He disconnected abruptly, frustrated by the delay.

He pressed his foot down on the accelerator as he reached the open road, enjoying the sense of power afforded by the V8 engine of his Ferrari. He confidently rounded a sharp curve, his strong tanned hands relaxed on the steering wheel. He let his mind wander away from the heavy caseload of his law practice. *Finn.* As if he didn't have enough on his plate to worry about, he had just received the nanny's two-week notice yesterday. *Dammit!* His son had experienced enough change to last a lifetime. Now this.

"What the fuck!" A truck ran a stop sign and right into his path. He slammed on the brakes, but there was nothing there, no pressure—the pedal went all the way to the floor. Then the sound of scraping metal and shattering glass as his car was tossed in the air like a tin can. The last thing that flashed through Kyle Bennett's mind was an image of his late wife holding their newborn son. Then his world went blank.

1

---

*A*fter securing her hair in a ponytail, Ella Palmer leaned down to tie her running shoes. Her cat Daisy pounced on the laces. Snagging one shoestring she rolled onto her side and hung on with claws extended, then used her back feet to make sure her prey didn't escape. Apparently, she'd decided it was play time.

"Ow! You scratched me you little twit." Daisy ignored her and bit the toe of her shoe. Ella tried to extricate her foot from the cat's nails and teeth, finally succeeding by plucking one claw off at a time. Foiled, the calico flounced off.

After finishing her warm-up, Ella strapped on a waist pack to carry her water and headed for the door. Glancing down at her watch, she called over her shoulder, "Guard the house killer."

Daisy stared unblinkingly.

"Don't then," Ella responded. She loved her fiery

ball of fur, Daisy, a stray kitten she'd stumbled upon on one of her runs. A tiny, ruffled ball of fur with a big mouth. She'd demanded to be rescued and, in the end, they'd rescued each other. "See you later Daisy."

The first quarter mile was torture; her legs felt like lead until she hit her comfortable stride. The scenic bike path that ran along the Atlantic shoreline was a few short minutes from her condo and she invariably headed there. She ran through a charming residential area with Cape Cod beach styled houses. It was a gorgeous sunny day; the sky was baby blue with white puffy clouds scattered across the horizon. Bonus... she pretty much had the trail to herself since it was a weekday and well before tourist season.

The sound of waves crashing to the shore soothed the tension from her shoulders. The gulls squawked in flight and the smell of the sea assailed her nostrils as she watched pelicans dive bomb into the water. Her mouth curved into a smile. As she relaxed her thoughts began to wander. She had been feeling somewhat restless lately and couldn't quite put her finger on it.

She didn't think the problem stemmed from her job, although after six years working as a registered nurse, she thought she'd pretty much seen it all. She worked in the ICU, which was never dull, requiring an analytic mind and quick thinking. Her inquisitive nature didn't hurt either as she often had to problem-solve in tight spots.

She liked her colleagues for the most part, barring her supervisor, Deloris Henry, who had it in for Ella and tried to make her life miserable whenever an opportunity presented itself. Her co-worker, Deb

Richards, had become her best friend and honestly kept her from losing her mind some days. The doctors on staff were generally okay. A few had the God complex, but most were respectful and easy to get along with.

She hated this unsettled feeling. *Am I bored? Could be the long drought since my last relationship. Maybe I do need a little romance in my life. Whatever. If it happens, it happens.* She *was* a bit attracted to Andy Thompson, one of the docs who'd been in pursuit, but she had sworn to herself she would never date a doctor again.

Reaching the halfway point of her run, she pivoted and headed back the way she'd come. Her ponytail bounced in rhythm with her footsteps and breath, by now all synchronized like a well-tuned instrument.

She made it back just in time to jump in the shower and dress quickly for work. With her hair still damp she did a French twist and secured it with a claw clip. Hastily slipping on her Dansko clogs she raced out the door.

2

*E*lla listened attentively as her colleague Kari brought her up to date. "It was a little hairy last night, but I feel more confident that Mr. Bennett's going to pull through. His vitals are less erratic. Arrived by squad early last evening, they had to pry him out of the vehicle. One emergency surgery to repair a torn femoral artery in his right leg, another to set the broken bones. Internal bleeding was stemmed. Multiple contusions, three fractured ribs, all on the right side, compound fractures of his right Radius and Ulna bones, swollen left wrist, not fractured, probably a sprain. Mild concussion."

"Is he communicative?"

"A few words, but not really, he's been pretty out of it. It took a long time for him to wake up from the anesthesia. The surgeons were concerned. He's been in and out of it since, but he is sedated," Kari explained.

"Sounds like an exciting night. I'm sure you're ready to get the hell out of here."

"You've got that right. My bed has been calling to me for the last hour."

"Anything else I need to know about our patient?"

"Overall, I'd say he's damn lucky to be alive. The guy in the other car came out relatively unscathed. It figures the one responsible gets a get out of jail free card. He was treated and released."

"Do you know what happened then?"

"Yeah, unfortunately, our patient was driving a Ferrari convertible and it collided with a big-ass pickup truck that had run straight through the stop sign."

Ella glanced through the notes on the computer screen. "No contest there," Ella said. "Any family here for Mr. Bennett?"

"He has a sister and brother listed as the emergency contacts, but the sister is presently out of the country and the brother hasn't been reached yet. Mr. Bennett's assistant was here all night, she left about an hour ago. Apparently widowed, he has a little boy, five or six years old, currently under a nanny's care. The parents live in Palm Springs and were notified. They're presumably making arrangements to get here," Kari said. "Crazy night. Three car accidents came in by squad, two required emergency surgeries. Our Mr. Bennett here being the worst of the lot."

Ella shook her head. "Glad I was off yesterday, all rested up. Which doc is on today?"

"Doctor Thompson," she said teasingly.

Ella glared. "Don't look at me like that. There is absolutely nothing going on there. You know my history with dating doctors, not going to happen again."

"I wouldn't rule him out. He's so down to earth and nice... not to mention hot as fuck!"

Ella shook her head, biting back a smile. "Don't start. Thanks for the update on our patient. Go home. You look exhausted."

"He's all yours," Kari said. "Just an FYI, this patient is a VIP, as in personal friends with the administrator. You know the Bennett wing of this hospital? His grandfather!"

Ella shrugged. "He still sits on the toilet, same as the rest of us."

Kari's lip quirked up. "Good luck, I'll leave you to it."

"Bye Kari. Get some rest."

"No worries about that as long as I can stay awake on the drive home."

Ella entered Kyle Bennett's room to check and log her patient's vitals. He was hooked up to a conglomerate of leads. The monitors beeped steadily, pulse stable, oxygen saturation good. His skin looked gray beneath his tan, dark stubble already covering his sharp jaw line. Long black lashes fanned his chiseled cheeks. *Beautiful man.*

She pulled his hospital gown aside as she slipped in the ear tips of her stethoscope. He appeared to be in great physical shape. Broad shoulders, pecs were toned and well defined beneath the soft dark hair covering his chest, and his abdomen was of the six-pack variety.

She listened to his heart, then satisfied upon hearing the strong, steady beat, moved on to his lungs,

clear. She shifted to his abdomen... taunt, muscular...
noting the sexy trail of hair continuing down from his
navel to his pubic bone. She fought to ignore the flut-
ters in her belly. *Could he be any sexier?*

The torn femoral artery had been repaired, bones
had been set, no internal bleeding, now of most
concern was staving off an infection and complications
from his head injury. He'd suffered a concussion with
swelling which they were closely monitoring.

She did a manual check of his blood pressure,
which was low but not dangerously so. Very lucky but
far from out of the woods. She pulled back the sheet to
check his lower extremities. Pulse strong at the ankles,
no swelling... *strong muscular thighs, runner?* He moved
his leg, moaning in pain. Glancing up she caught him
staring at her, his forehead wrinkled with confusion.

"You're awake," she said softly. "I'm your nurse for
today, Ella."

His brow furrowed. "Nurse? Where am I?" he asked
groggily, his eyes a deep sapphire blue.

"You're at Wayne Regional Hospital. You were in a
car accident yesterday afternoon. Can you tell me your
name?"

He looked blank, grimacing as if struggling to find
the answer.

Ella smiled reassuringly. "It's okay. Don't worry,
you've suffered a concussion, it can take time to feel
fully alert."

As she watched his expression, she saw the light
bulb go on and relief flood his features. "It's Kyle, Kyle
Bennett."

"What's the last thing you remember Mr. Bennett?"

"Leaving my office."

"You don't remember anything about your accident?"

He squinted and she saw confusion dance across his face again, followed by fear and finally a bleakness when he obviously came up blank. He squeezed his eyes shut.

"My head is exploding right now. I feel like my brains are oozing out of my ears."

"That's normal with a concussion. Stay still, let me go fetch the doc. I'll be right back."

"Wait, don't go," he said urgently. "Am I going to make it?"

"Your vitals are stable, and we've repaired the tear to your femoral artery and patched you up. Now it's up to your body to run with it. You're going to be incapacitated for a while."

"You didn't answer my question."

Seeing his distress, she touched his arm. "It will take some time for you to recover. You were in a terrible collision; your sports car was no match for the pickup truck that you plowed into. You are here now and under the best of care. The first forty-eight hours are critical, complications can arise, but that's why you're here. Dr. Thompson is on hospital rounds this morning. I would put my own life in his hands. I will be your nurse for the next twelve hours and I promise I will watch you like a hawk. I have one patient and you are it."

His gaze became distant as if trying to recall something. "Finn, my son, I need to check on my son," he said, then closed his eyes.

"I'll see what I can find out for you. My understanding is that he is under the nanny's care. Your
assistant was here all night and I'm sure she is taking
care of the important details. You need to rest. I'll go get
the doc, and check about your son. I'm sure he's being
looked after. I'll be right back. Please try not to worry."
Ella left to search for the doctor.

Spying the tall handsome man in a white labora-
tory coat at the nurses' station, Ella made a bee-line
over to greet him. "Good morning, Dr. Thompson. Our
patient in room 2016 is awake."

"Ella!" Dr. Andrew Thompson said, his eyes
lighting up with pleasure. "I'm glad you're on today. I
was just going to check on him."

"He's awake and able to converse but is somewhat
confused... not surprising. Kari said he had a rough
night, but his vitals are all stable," Ella said.

Walking side by side to check on their patient he
said, "When are you going to take me up on that dinner
invitation?"

"I must admit it is tempting," she said laughing.

"Good. I won't give up then."

"Last time I broke my own rule of keeping personal
and professional lives separate, it didn't end well
for me."

"You'll never know unless you give me a try," he
rejoined.

Ella laughed again and led the way into Mr.
Bennett's room.

Kyle Bennett appeared to be asleep, but his eyes
popped open the second he heard Ella and Dr.
Thompson discussing his case.

"Hi, I'm Dr. Thompson. Glad to see you're awake."

"Awake but I can barely form a thought. Can we cut to the chase here doc? How bad am I?"

The doctor smiled. "There is no chase, I'm afraid. You're going to be parked here for a while."

"I don't have time to be parked anywhere. Has anyone checked on my son? Where is my phone?" he demanded, voice strained from the effort.

"I was told your assistant was here earlier and she was going to take care of those details. She planned on notifying your family and any others on a need-to-know basis. As to your phone, I don't have that information but Ella, your nurse here, will find out. You are in critical condition. There will be no cell phones today," Dr. Thompson said firmly.

Kyle grimaced as he leaned back against his pillow. With his left arm in a sling and his right wrist bandaged he was pretty much incapacitated. "Can you up my pain meds? They aren't working," he asked, managing to sound commanding even in his weakened state.

"Ella will see to that after I've examined you," he said, nodding towards Ella.

Slurring slightly, he said, "Ella, my beautiful nurse."

"I think the pain pills are working better than you think," she said smiling, a heat creeping up her cheeks.

"I think he sounds quite lucid," Dr. Thompson argued, winking at her.

Ella busied herself changing one of the bags on an IV drip.

"Well, Mr. Bennett, I'll be back later to check in with you at the end of my rounds. I won't go as far as to say you're out of the woods yet, but you're stable and considering what you've been through we'll take it. We'll do our best to keep you comfortable. You're young and in good shape, you've got that going for you."

"What do you mean exactly when you say I'm not out of the woods? I could die?"

"I'll be blunt. The next thirty-six to forty-eight hours we'll be monitoring you very closely for any complications. You are still in critical condition. You sustained a terrible impact. You have swelling on the brain and your entire body was traumatized. We have repaired what we can and now you have to heal. We don't expect it, but we are always alert for any changes for the worse. Ella is assigned to your care, and she is the best. Now get some rest. That's an order."

"Thanks for not bullshitting me."

"I'll have Ella get in touch with your assistant to get information with regards to your son," he said turning to go. "Your main focus has to be on rest and healing, the more you can do that, the faster you'll be able to return to your life and take care of your son."

"Did you catch that?" Ella said.

"Which part?"

"The part about rest."

"Oh, I thought maybe you were talking about where he agreed with me, the beautiful Ella part." His lips turned up slightly, but his eyes remained closed.

Ignoring this last comment she said, "I'll increase your morphine drip to see if we can get ahead of your pain."

"Get some rest, and listen to your nurse," Dr. Thompson said as he left the room.

Kyle opened one eye to peer at Ella as she pushed buttons on the IV drip dispenser, increasing his pain medication.

"Are your eyes green or brown?" he asked drowsily.

Ella smiled, knowing that the pain meds were kicking in. "Depends on the day."

"Green with amber mixed in," he drawled.

"Enough about my eyes, on a scale of one to ten what is your pain level right now?"

"Six. Progress, down from a twelve."

"That's good then. I'll be back in a few minutes; I'm going to check on those details for you. You heard the doc, get some rest."

"Ella?"

"Yes?"

"You'll check on my son?"

"Yes."

"That's good then," he said closing his eyes.

3

*E*lla stepped into the shower and adjusted the temperature letting the hot water loosen her muscles. She thought about her unexpected and unwelcome attraction to Kyle Bennett and wished she could scrub it away as easily as she could rinse the soap from her skin. Usually, she left her work at the hospital but for some reason she'd tossed and turned the night before thinking about her blue-eyed patient.

Squeezing shampoo into her palm she massaged her scalp, picturing the way he'd looked the other day, the juxtaposition between Kyle Bennett's vulnerability and his demanding countenance. He was not an easy read that was for sure. She could normally size someone up pretty quickly.

She blew out a long breath, impatient with herself for giving so much of her mental space over to him. She rinsed her hair slowly, reluctant to leave the soothing spray of the shower. *Today I will keep my guard up no matter what. I definitely don't need the headache.* That problem solved, she hopped out of the shower and dressed for work.

~

When Ella arrived at the hospital, she talked briefly with the nurse who'd been assigned to Kyle the night before, then checked her notes before heading to his room.

"Good morning Mr. Bennett," Ella said, gently pressing her cool palm against his forehead. "You've got quite the goose egg." He'd thrown off his bedcovers and was drenched with sweat.

"I know, I finally saw it."

Her brow furrowed after swiping the thermometer across his forehead. "You have a slight fever. How are you feeling?" She tried to hide her concern. Infections were always a risk.

Kyle's eyes were glazed with pain. "Truth? I think I'm dying. The pain is unbelievable and I'm hot one minute and freezing the next."

She checked his IV drips, then pulled the sheet back further, removing the bandage from his upper thigh to check the wound. She forced herself to ignore her fluttering pulse at the sight of his sexy muscular thighs dusted with that soft dark hair. Her hands had to work dangerously close to his large bulge as she cleaned and redressed the leg. *Honestly Ella get a grip.*

"I'm going to get you some Tylenol to bring down your temperature but what else can I get for you? How about something cold to drink besides water?"

"I could use some juice or ginger-ale, or a shot of your best bourbon," he replied weakly.

She chuckled. "Ah, a bourbon man. Sorry I can't help you out with that, but we have two out of the three. Must be your lucky day, so what's it going to be?"

"Soda," he said.

"I'll be right back with that." Ella felt Kyle's eyes follow her as she left the room.

When she returned, she thought he was asleep until he said, "You smell good."

She sniffed her arm. "Must be my soap or shampoo, I never wear cologne at work."

Eyes still closed he said, "Come closer and I'll tell you."

Ignoring him she held a small plastic container with his meds and set his ginger-ale down on the table. "Here ya go."

Kyle opened his eyes and watched as she punched a straw through the plastic lid on the Styrofoam cup. She leaned over and held the drink up to his lips as they closed around the straw. He glanced up at her through his long dark lashes and their eyes locked. She dropped her gaze breaking contact, but not before a current of awareness ran between them. *It's not just me, he definitely felt it too.* "I have a couple of Tylenol for you to take."

"You sure I'm worth saving?"

"Everyone deserves a shot, even you Mr. Bennett," she teased. "Your assistant is here to see you; I'll send her in if you feel up to it."

"Yes, I need to talk to her. Thanks."

"I'll give her five minutes tops and then I'm kicking her out."

"Gotta love a dominatrix."

"I'm glad we understand each other," she said, chuckling.

4

*D*espite Kyle's pain, he watched with appreciation as she walked out the door. Even in scrubs, he could see she had a killer body. *Runner maybe?* Great ass, long legs, curvy hips, full breasts, and today her eyes were green...almost olive with flecks of amber sprinkled in. Wide toothy smile, tiny gap between her two front teeth. *Hot as fuck.*

The morphine had to be kicking in because five minutes ago he couldn't focus on anything but his pain and now he was undressing his nurse. The miracle of drugs. He could still feel where her hand had been resting on his forehead a few minutes ago. *Damn if this drug wasn't going to make him start saying things better left unsaid. I'll have to check myself.*

His longtime assistant Elenore walked in. "Wow, you look like hell," she said by way of greeting. "Could you try not scaring the shit out of us ever again?"

Voice weak but determined he said, "Hello to you too. Where's Finn?"

"Your in-laws came to get him this morning and they took him back to their house for the time being. Your sister is flying back early from Fiji she'll be home by the end of the week. Your brother is MIA. Your sister said she'll be happy to help out with Finn."

"Did the nanny say she'd stay on considering this new development?"

"She can't. She already committed to her new job which starts in three weeks. She needs at least a week to pack and put her affairs in order. She's expected in Rome, by the first."

"Damn."

"Your in-laws are happy to keep him as long as they're needed. Between them and your sister Faye, you have nothing to worry about except getting better. We'll all make sure he gets dropped off and picked up from school. As long as you find someone before school lets out for summer, we'll be in good shape. They told me to tell you to focus on yourself. They'll bring Finn for a visit soon. We all thought it best to wait until you look less, um, scary."

He'd asked the night nurse to bring him a mirror and he'd seen himself for the first time. Along with the bruising covering his body he was sporting a couple of very colorful black eyes. The lump on his forehead was about the size of a pool ball.

Shifting uncomfortably on her feet, Elenore hesitantly continued, "Your parents are flying in by the end of the week."

"God damn it! Why the hell did you call them?"

"Maybe because they're your parents?"

"Fuck me! That's all I need."

"Kyle, they had to be notified."

"Why, so my father could come here and bust my balls?"

"Maybe he'll soften when he sees your banged up body."

Kyle scowled. "Yeah, and maybe pigs can fly."

She touched his arm. "Just try not to think about it. You have a few days before they get here."

"Maybe they'll back out and stay in Palm Springs."

Her nose wrinkled. "Doubtful. Your mom was pretty freaked out."

"What a nightmare. Mother is always freaked out. So, dear ole Dad decided to allow Mom to come and visit their ne'er-do-well son."

"See maybe he *has* changed," she said smiling.

"Whatever." He grimaced as he tried to move, "How are things at the office?"

"Things are being handled. The staff are all picking up the slack and Pete will be going over your case load to make sure he stays on top of everything...in other words let it go."

"What about the class action suit?"

"Covered."

"The Encino files?"

"Assigned to April Jones."

"The affordable housing development?"

"We now have two groups opposing the development. The environmentalists and now the community abutting the land are getting in on the mix. They don't want low-income houses so close to their million-dollar homes."

"Great. My father will be thrilled to hear about this."

Elenore put her hands on her hips. "Kyle you are going to have to let go of control here for the time being. You'll be missed but things are being handled. You have a partner and a great group of lawyers to take up the slack while you're mending."

Kyle blew out his breath, leaning his head back against the pillow in defeat. He was exhausted and in pain and he knew his only course of action was to surrender... for the moment.

"You are lucky to be alive you know."

"That's what they keep telling me."

"You've got a long road to recovery. Just focus on getting stronger."

"Whatever," he said.

"How old are you? Don't be such a grump. And be cooperative with the medical staff, you need them on your side. If you behave like an entitled jerk, it will come back to haunt you."

"Go away. I hear you loud and clear," he said, eyes closed as if trying to shut out what his assistant was saying. Elenore was indispensable and she got him. She was one of the few people he'd allow to talk to him so boldly. He trusted her and knew his world would fall apart without her.

"I promise to keep you updated, on a need-to-know basis," she said.

He opened one eye and peered at her for a second.

His lip quirked when he saw that she was braced for a battle. Her eyes narrowed when he didn't respond.

"Kyle?"

"I heard you."

She tsked. "Get some rest. You need your beauty sleep."

He lifted his good arm and wiggled his fingers at her in response without bothering to open his eyes again. He heard Elenore's loud sigh as she left the room.

5

"It was absolutely the best snorkeling I've ever done!" Several days later, Faye, Kyle's sister, was regaling them with tales from her Fijian experience. "Part of the day was spent on the island of Modriki, where Tom Hanks filmed Cast Away. It was so exotic. I could live there," she said.

Ella was struck by how different she seemed from her older brother. From what she could tell, almost complete opposites. Faye was relaxed and casual, looking slightly bohemian with her delicate tattoos and colorful scarf tied like a twisted headband over her blonde hair. She was the farthest thing from cynical Ella had ever encountered in an adult. Faye seemed to have an innocence about her that was both charming and sweet.

Kyle seemed just as taken with his sister's charm as she was, and they appeared to have a strong sibling bond. Suddenly, a tall, elegant woman rushed into the room exclaiming, "My *chéri! Oh mon Dieu!* You could be dead! Look at you, you're all broken."

"Mom," Kyle said weakly.

"Kyle, my baby." She leaned down and kissed her son on his cheek, her large brown eyes misty with unshed tears.

"Ella, my mom Giselle Bennett, Mother, meet my nurse, Ella Palmer," Kyle said.

In a heavy French accent his mother said, "My pleasure, *tu es belle.*"

Ella blinked and Kyle said, "She just called you beautiful."

Giselle said, "Now, *chéri,* tell me, how is my son?"

They all turned as a male voice said, "Yes, how *is* our son?"

An older version of Kyle with graying hair stood in the doorway, not approaching the bed.

"Father so glad you could make it to my funeral," Kyle said dryly.

"Glad to see the accident didn't affect your acerbic wit," James Bennett replied to his son.

"*Mon amour,* my angel is hurting. Stop right this minute with your bickering."

"Ella, *this* is my father, James Bennett."

Ella could tell that her patient was distressed. The room so full of joy and laughter a moment before was suddenly filled with tension. "Pleased to meet you all. I will leave a message with the doctor that you're here. He can fill you in on your son's progress. Overall, he is improving daily. It's just going to take time. I do think you should limit your visit to a half-hour at a time. He needs lots of rest and no stress."

Turning toward Kyle she said, "I'm leaving for the day. Deb is next on shift. Enjoy visiting with your family." His dark expression told her how that was going to play out.

"Nice meeting you," Faye called out.

"Same. You are a wonderful storyteller," Ella said warmly. She would have loved to hang out with Faye longer. She was intriguing and someone Ella could picture as a friend.

"*A bientot,*" Giselle said.

Nodding his head stiffly, James Bennett said, "Good day."

"Working tomorrow?" Kyle asked.

"Yes, see you tomorrow."

Giselle's eyes darted between her son and Ella before pinning Ella with an intense stare. *Is it my imagination that she looks like she's sizing me up to see if I'm good enough for her son?*

"Kyle, your nurse is beautiful and kind. You need a *maman* for little Finn. Enough time has passed *chéri* it is time to settle down again," Giselle said as if Ella wasn't in the room. *Guess I wasn't imagining things.* Ella's cheeks flamed.

"Don't start *maman,*" Kyle said.

"Well, I'll be going now," Ella interjected. "Nice to meet everyone." She quickly left the room before Giselle could embarrass her any further. She overheard Giselle say, "Those tarts you bed are a waste of time. You're no better than your brother Griffin." Ella scampered away as fast as she could.

6

*K*yle watched Ella practically run from the room. "*Maman*, you embarrassed the hell out of Ella."

Giselle waved her hand dismissively. "I only speak the truth. She is stunning. And she is delightful. Now back to our conversation. You are old enough to be more discerning with who you take to bed."

"How do you know that I'm not? Have you been checking up on me *maman*?"

"Let's just say I wasn't born yesterday."

Kyle's forehead furrowed with pain as he moved to find a more comfortable position.

"Oh, my baby, you are in pain. I must call for your doctor immediately!" she exclaimed.

James Bennett interrupted his wife before she could make good on her threat. "Giselle enough! Quit coddling your son. He is a big boy and under excellent care. His nurse was just in here for God's sake!"

"But..."

"No but's. He's fine. Kyle has to live with the consequences of his actions. I'm sure he brought this on
himself. Racing around recklessly like an irresponsible
playboy."

Giselle gasped at her husband's callousness as she
placed a hand on her heart. "How could you say such a
thing? Our son could have been killed. Have you no
heart?" she said in her heavily accented voice. Kyle said
nothing but he burned with anger and humiliation.

Faye had stayed silent until now but finally jumped
in to defend her brother. "Listen, Mom, Dad, let's give
my dear brother here a break and go get a bite to eat.
He's tired and in pain. You heard Ella. No stress! Bickering will not help him one bit."

Kyle had closed his eyes attempting to shut out his
family. "Yes please, go. Father no need for you to return.
No reason to pretend you give a shit."

"Suit yourself," James huffed.

"*Mon bébé*, we shall return. Of course, your papa
loves you. You are too alike. What am I to do with you
both?"

Faye herded their parents out the door before more
damage could be done. She exchanged a sympathetic
look with Kyle as she practically pushed them out the
door. He tried to keep up his air of indifference until
they disappeared. Father had always been hardest on
him, the first born, but it never got easier.

Somehow, Faye and Griffin had managed to escape
their father's harsh criticism growing up. Kyle had tried
running interference to spare his younger sister and
brother. He thought he'd done a pretty good job of it. In

turn both looked up to him and trusted him as their confidant.

He knew Faye felt guilty about that. She had gotten away with everything. She'd admitted years ago that compounding her guilt was the relief she often felt at being spared. She was the only daughter and had rarely been denied anything. In fact, she'd managed to fly almost completely under her father's hypervigilant radar.

Faye popped her head back in the doorway and rolled her eyes. "Mama has the doctor cornered. See you in a bit."

"Take your time. And come back alone."

7

Today was the first time Finn would see his father since the accident. Kyle had been hospitalized for over a week and the insecurities arising in his son by keeping him away were becoming more harmful than any possible reaction to Kyle's appearance. The family had decided that it was time to let Finn visit and the doctor had agreed. Kyle was stronger and his bruising had faded to a colorful yellow and green so it would be a lot less scary for Finn.

"Finn this is Ella your dad's nurse. Can you say hello?" Faye asked.

Eyes downcast, Finn nodded his head shyly. "Hi." The dark smudges under his eyes tugged at Ella's heartstrings. He looked so small and lost standing in the long hospital corridor that she wanted to gather him up into her arms and protect him. All of her dormant maternal instincts suddenly kicked in.

Crouching down so she could meet him at eye level

she said, "Hi Finn. I've heard so much about you. I'm glad to finally meet you. Your dad is doing great! Even though he might look scary bad to you right now he is doing really well."

A groan came from the room and Finn's eyes grew wary. Peering into his father's room he said, "Why is he groaning then?"

"He still has some pain, but we gave him more medicine to help and he's already feeling better. Are you ready to go in and see him?"

"Yes please," he replied. His large blue eyes framed with dark lashes looked like mini versions of his dad's.

Faye held up her phone and said, "I'm going back to the waiting area. I have to call Mom and give her an update, if that's all right with you?"

"That's fine, I'll take it from here." Standing Ella held out her hand and he slipped his tiny palm into hers. "I'll be right here with you, okay? You don't have to worry about anything. It's up to me and his doc to take care of him. Just seeing you will help him feel better," Ella said.

"I'll be right back little man. Ella will take good care of you," Faye said.

Looking up at Ella as they entered Kyle's room, Finn said matter-of-factly, "My mom's in heaven."

"That means you've got an angel looking out for you."

He nodded, then said earnestly, "She must be busy cause my dad can't be with me much on account of he has to work all the time. I've got a nanny."

"You do? You are so lucky you have someone there

just for you. That means your daddy loves you very much."

"Yeah. 'Cept she's leaving."

"Aww that's too bad. I'm sure there're a gazillion nannies out there that will love taking care of you."

He shrugged.

Kyle hearing their conversation met Ella's gaze, his eyes guarded, revealing nothing. Ella observing the scene through Finn's perspective knew how fragile his father must appear to him. Tubes everywhere, a cast on one arm, bandages on his head, cuts, scrapes and fading bruises. Had to be frightening for the little guy. Despite all that, Kyle looked so much better than he had a week ago.

Finn's eyes were wide and welling with tears. "Daddy?"

"Hey buddy, come over here. I've missed you!"

Finn stood frozen to the spot. Ella had a hunch. "Finn, you won't hurt him as long as you're gentle."

"Are you sure?" His slight frame shook as he began to cry. "I don't want you to die, Daddy!"

"Finn I'm not going anywhere. Come over here," Kyle said, his voice gruff with emotion.

"It's all my fault. If I wasn't bad this wouldn't have happened."

"Buddy, what are you talking about? That's not true. It was an accident. The car that I crashed into didn't stop like they were supposed to. You had nothing to do with that. Do you understand?"

His little shoulders shook, and Ella couldn't stand it another second. She crouched down gathering Finn to her as he cried. "Oh baby, it wasn't your fault! You don't have that kind of power. Nobody does. Your daddy is going to be fine."

He quieted and wrapped his arms around Ella's neck hugging her tight. "You promise?"

"Yes, I promise. He is doing better than anyone even expected." Ella wiped his tears. "And don't you know how awesome you are? Everyone I've talked to tells me what a great kid you are. So I don't want to hear any more talk about you being bad."

"Really? Who?"

"Your grandma, your Aunt Faye, Elenore... everyone."

He sighed and knuckled his eyes. "I wish you could be my new nanny," he said.

Ella's heart ached. "Thank you, Finn, that is so sweet."

Wiping his nose with his sleeve he said, "Can you?"

"What would all of my sick patients here in the hospital do?"

Finn shrugged his shoulders.

"Ready to give your dad a gentle hug?" Although still not convinced, he nodded his head.

"Before you do, let me show you where he is hurt. Would that help?" Finn nodded again. She ruffled Finn's mop of dark curls and led him over to his father's bedside. Pulling back the covers she showed Finn the bandaged leg. "See this is the leg that's hurt. But it is going to be as good as new before you know it. Just be really careful not to bump it, okay?"

Kyle smiled at Finn. "I'll tell you if you're hurting me bud." Finn nodded solemnly.

"And this arm," she said pointing. "And see where

his ribs are wrapped, another place to be really careful with."

"Okay."

Ella lowered the bed rail so Finn could get closer. "Come here you," Kyle said. "Everything is going to be all right Finn." Finn carefully rested his head on his father's stomach and Kyle brushed his hair back from his forehead.

Finn's brow puckered as he asked, "What about Natalie? Why does she have to leave? I don't want a new nanny!"

"Worrying about that isn't your job. That's my job. You leave that stuff to the grownups," Kyle said. "Can you do that for me?"

"I'll try, but...."

"No buts."

"But I was going to say what if Ella quit her job here and came to live with us?"

"Buddy, she already has a job here at the hospital."

"But we need her," he pleaded.

Ella squeezed Finn's shoulder. "I know your dad will find the perfect nanny for you. But remember what I just told you? All the sick people need me here."

"We need you more. You could quit. My daddy is rich! He will pay you so much money. You could come live with us. Right daddy? We have a huge house!" he said, his eyes widening as he spread his arms to demonstrate how large their home was. "It's as big as a castle!"

Kyle looked embarrassed and said, "Finn. She has an important job to do at the hospital. We'll talk about this later. We've got time to find someone special, so quit worrying. The subject is closed for now. Do you understand me?"

"Yes sir," he said head bowed. Ella felt bad for him until he mischievously waved his crossed fingers at Ella, flashing a wide grin. She shook her head at him stifling a laugh.

"Well, I'll give you guys' time to visit. I'll be back in a couple of minutes," Ella said.

Finn scrunched up his face, "Do you have to go?"

"Finn, she'll be right back," Kyle said.

"But what if you get a bad pain again?"

Ella leaned down at eye level to Finn and said, "Look at me Finn."

Wide-eyed he looked at Ella intently.

"Your dad is going to be fine. In no time at all, he will be up and about, and his pain will be much less. You'll get through this together. But for right now, your dad has a button he can push if he needs me, and I will come running." Swiping her hand diagonally across her chest she said, "Cross my heart. Okay?"

When he smiled at her his face beamed with relief. Ella's heart melted at the trust she saw in his eyes. Then she left them alone to visit.

8

---

*A*fter her weekend off, Ella was in a good mood as she entered the hospital. She'd had a great time doing what she loved, volunteering for a non-profit dedicated to protecting the Loggerhead Sea turtles and their nests. They'd be monitoring now until the last hatchlings released in August.

This weekend her primary role had been to patrol the beaches at night with other volunteers to make sure the turtles could nest safely and to deter hunters. She had also assisted with some tagging and measuring of the turtles. Conservation and wildlife were close to her heart and being hands on satisfied something deep inside of her.

She'd *almost* managed to forget about Kyle Bennett but not quite. Thoughts of him had managed to insert themselves more than she would have liked. She felt bad for him and his son. Finn had brought out her mama bear instincts. They'd lost so much. Finn's visit with his dad was still fresh on her mind as she poked her head into Kyle's room.

"Good morning sunshine," she said cheerfully. "You look much better today. Very alert."

"I'm not sure alert is a good thing," he grumbled.

"Sure, it is. How do they say it? Any day we wake up is a good day... something like that."

"Ella the idealist."

Laughing Ella said, "Kyle the cynic. You're looking better but tell me how you're feeling."

He raised a brow and said, "That's the first time you've called me Kyle."

"Is it? Should I go back to Mr. Bennett?"

"No, I like it." His voice was warm and personal and felt like a caress.

"Kyle it is then," she said, her heart skipping a beat. She busied herself with his IVs to distract from the rollercoaster feeling in her belly.

"Did you take a vacation? Feels like you've been gone for weeks."

"Nope. My weekend off. I mentioned it before I left work on Friday. Pain on a scale of one to ten?" she asked.

"Four."

"I can live with that," Ella said.

"Ha, *you* can live with that?"

"You've got a point. Okay, can *you* live with that?"

"The more important question is, how can I convince you to go out with me when I break out of here... and is there any competition I have to get out of the way first?" Kyle asked.

"You are definitely feeling better. I'm not seeing anyone at the moment," she admitted.

"Does this mean I might have a chance?"

Ella tilted her head. "A chance?"

"At seducing you."

Her eyebrows shot up. "How did we go from a date to seduction so fast?"

"You feel it," he said quietly, voice like melted butter.

"Um... what?"

"This," he said, waving his hand between them. "FYI, I always go for what I want. And I generally get it."

"Good to know. Just a little friendly tip—that may get you what you want in the courtroom, but not very effective when it comes to seduction... especially with me. I've had my fill of arrogant men."

"You consider honesty arrogance then?"

She paused before answering. "I consider your presumptuousness arrogant. Getting what you want may be at odds with other parties' desires."

"So, you're saying I'm imagining the chemistry between us?"

Her eyes narrowed. "You must be very good at chess."

"How did you guess." He grinned roguishly. "What about our esteemed Dr. Thompson?"

He had lost her. "What about him?"

"It's obvious he has the hots for you."

She removed the dressing from his leg to check the wound. "I wouldn't know anything about that."

"I find that hard to believe. He practically drools

whenever you're around. Can't say I blame him. Ouch!" He grimaced as she palpated his thigh incision.

"Sorry," she said, unconvincingly. "It's strictly professional between myself and Dr. Thompson. That's all in your imagination."

"Really? Because I've been told I don't have any."

"Have any what?"

"Imagination."

Satisfied that his wound was healing and that there were no palpable clots she re-dressed his leg. "Everyone has an imagination."

"Hmm, maybe but I'm sure I'm not making up that delightful flush in your cheeks right now. The question becomes is it for me or because of our esteemed Doctor Thompson?"

She bit her lip. "I've had very bad luck dating doctors. They've been crossed off my list."

"Ah. I might have a chance then. So, what's this about you keeping a list?"

"Doesn't everyone?" She grinned. "I don't date patients either."

He frowned. "Damn list."

"Sorry."

"I won't be a patient forever."

"You're a patient right now, so the subject is closed."

"For now."

"For now," she agreed.

"Is that a promise?"

"You are tenacious, I'll give you that."

"It makes up for the imagination," he replied.

Ella put her stethoscope against his chest listening to the steady beat of his heart. She was so aware of him that she had to concentrate on her breathing to keep focused. Her fingers felt tingly where they touched his skin and she wanted to brush them across his chest. *Talk about drool.* She made the fatal mistake of meeting his gaze and got lost for a moment in the depth of his dark blue eyes. She unconsciously licked her lips and he grinned up at her.

"Ella?"

"Yes?"

"Is my heart still beating?" he chuckled warmly and she felt the heat return to her cheeks. *What is wrong with me?* She jerked the stethoscope away and straightened. He reached for her hand and placed her palm on his bare chest right over his heart.

"Feel that?"

She bit her lip and nodded.

"That's all for you. I'm not going to lie. I want you, Ella." Her body stilled as he held her hand. Fighting against herself she allowed it to rest there for a moment before tugging it from his grasp.

"Hey guys," Faye said, startling them both as she breezed into the room. "How's my big brother doing today?"

Ella took a deep slow breath as Kyle answered for her, "I think it's possible I'm going to make it. I see a glimmer of light at the end of the tunnel."

Faye's eyes darted between she and Kyle, before landing on Ella's heated cheeks. Faye graciously pretended not to notice and quickly pulled up a chair promptly regaling them with another entertaining story of travel. Ella sighed. Faye's life was so adventurous yet she was quite down to earth. Ella's life story seemed dull in comparison. She glanced over at Kyle and caught him staring.

Pulling out her smart phone Faye said, "I have a video message from Finn." She held the device so both Ella and Kyle could see the image.

"Hi Dad. I miss you so much. Guess what? I lost another tooth." He peeled his lips back with his chubby little fingers, revealing a space where his two front teeth had once been. "See? Aunt Faye had me put the tooth under my pillow for the fairy and guess what? The fairy left me candy and money! When are you coming home? Aunt Faye says maybe we can FaceTime soon. She says you're getting better. I love you, Dad. Bye."

Kyle's eyes were suspiciously glassy before rubbing his thumb across them. He cleared his throat before he spoke. "Has he had any more nightmares?"

"Last night. He ended up crawling in bed with me."

"I can't imagine how this is going to fuck him up, both parents abandoning him, Jesus. I can't believe Natalie took it upon herself to tell Finn she was leaving! She knew about his history."

"It wasn't ideal but what the heck, kids are resilient. He'll adjust. He knows you're in the hospital but unlike his mom you'll be coming home. He understands as much as a six-year-old can," Faye said. "He was four when his mom died," she explained to Ella.

Ella felt emotions she'd thought were long buried. Things she hadn't thought about for years were suddenly clamoring inside her head. "I lost both my parents in a plane crash when I was four."

Faye's eye's widened, "How terrible, I'm so sorry!"

Ella shrugged. "Thank you. I was tossed around in

foster care until I was finally adopted. I managed to somehow come out of my childhood relatively intact. Trust me, I know he'll get through this. He's got people that love him and that's the most important thing of all."

"All he could talk about after his hospital visit with his dad was you. He is your number one fan," Faye said.

Ella put her hand to her chest. "Aww, thank you for saying that. He's adorable. It's mutual." Glancing at Kyle she said, "He looks so much like you it's ridiculous."

"Unfortunately for him," Kyle said.

"I don't know... his dad is pretty hot." Laughing she said, "Did I really just say that out loud?"

"With witnesses," Faye joked.

Ella glanced at her watch. "I'll leave you two to visit. I'll be back to check in. Will you be here long Faye?"

Faye shook her head. "Nope, just a quick visit today. If I don't see you before I go thanks for taking such good care of my brother."

"You're welcome. I could listen to your stories all day."

"Bye, Ella," Faye said smiling.

"Enjoy your visit."

Kyle said nothing but nevertheless she felt his eyes burning a hole through her back as she walked out the door.

9

─────────

*T*he week had flown by and Ella, deciding to forgo cleaning her condo on her day off, headed to the beach instead. Parking, she stepped out of her jeep and heard a familiar voice.

"Well, lookie what washed up to shore," Artie called out to Ella from his usual perch at the marina. He had several poles in the water, his bait box next to him, and his catch of the day dangling in a container off the pier. Always by his side sat his loyal canine, Ralph, a big old hound dog.

"It's my only day off so I'm spending it on the water," Ella yelled back as she unloaded her board from the back of her jeep. "Come here Ralph, I've got a treat for you." Ralph lumbered over in slow motion, never in a hurry much like his human companion.

Artie and Ralph were regular fixtures at the marina where Ella often could be found on her days off. Today she had decided to bring her paddle board instead of her kayak.

"Maybe I'll get lucky today and commune with some dolphins," she said, emptying her pocket of the remaining treats as Ralph's tail wagged leisurely from side to side. "Even your tail is slow buddy," she joked, scratching him behind his ears.

"When ya going to trade that relic in on a new one?" Artie asked, nodding at her jeep.

"You know that will never happen. They don't make them like this anymore. Annabelle's a classic. I'll drive her until she has nothing left to give."

"What year is she?"

"Nineteen seventy-eight."

He guffawed. "Classic? More like a rattletrap if you ask me."

"Don't listen to him Annabelle," she said to her classic Jeep CJ7. "I'll have you know, Artie, she is a special limited edition! Have you ever heard of *The Dukes of Hazard*? This, my friend, is the same model that Daisy Duke drove." She had paid big bucks to have it completely restored after a patient had gifted her with it. It had been sitting abandoned in his barn for years and when he found out she was a classic Jeep enthusiast he was happy it would find life again. She babied it like it was priceless because to her it was.

"How did the turtle watch go?"

"It was fun and as always it was good to help out," she replied, while adding extra sunscreen to her face. She hauled her board to the water's edge, tethering the leash attached to the board to her ankle. She waded in until she was standing knee deep. Kneeling at the center of the board, carefully placing her feet where her knees had been, she slowly stood up, keeping knees bent until she knew she was balanced. Planting the paddle in the water, she alternated strokes from the right side to the left to push away from shore.

Not only was paddle boarding a great workout, it was hard to beat as a way to explore nature. She had seen some incredible things while out on her board. She always came away refreshed and energized. Listening to the waves lap against the board was soothing. The salty sea air and the sun had the effect of slowing her mind and had become a meditation practice of sorts. She often ran into others either on their boards or in kayaks, but today she seemed to have the bay to herself.

She wore a pair of board shorts over her swimsuit and a floppy waterproof hat for sun protection. She also carried a safety whistle to warn other boaters... just in case. She'd have no chance in a run-in with a boat, much like her patient Mr. Bennett's Ferrari and the Hemi truck.

Dang it! There I go again. Her thoughts inevitably kept drifting back to Kyle Bennett. Of course, he was drop dead gorgeous but he wasn't the first good looking patient she'd taken care of. And yes... that raw power he exuded despite his critical injuries was seriously attractive. And the fact that he seemed to be such a great dad had really gotten to her. *Gorgeous, sexy, all of that, and damn those dark blue eyes, almost navy, sparkling like sapphires even through his pain.*

Her professionalism warred with her attraction. When she touched him, her skin felt seared. She felt things she hadn't for a long time. Heat and excitement, long-dormant, were waking up and licking like fire through her veins.

She chewed on her bottom lip picturing his ripped muscular body, *perfection. Okay...that's my cue...time to change channels,* yet it wasn't quite that easy to switch off the electricity she was feeling. Familiar, yet it had been a long time since she had felt this alive.

A loggerhead turtle poked his head up to the surface grabbing her attention so Ella stopped paddling. She smiled. "Hey buddy. I was just helping your comrades stay safe last week." The turtle eyed her for a moment before ducking under and disappearing back into the water's depths.

Encounters with North Carolina's native wildlife never got old and always filled her with awe. The breeze and sun along with the exertion had tired her out and she decided to head back. No dolphins today... maybe next time.

She was looking forward to work tomorrow and wasn't oblivious to the fact that work had become a little brighter since Kyle had landed on her radar. Oh yeah, she had the itch for sure. *Dang it!*

⌇

*T*he local pizza joint was on speed dial and she decided to call ahead for pickup on her way home. Cooking was the last thing she wanted to do tonight. She'd already decided to start that new mystery she'd picked up from the library earlier today. It had taken two years for her favorite British author to release another book and now it was sitting at home just waiting for her to begin.

"Want a couple of fish for your dinner tonight?" Artie asked. He walked over to his own car which was parked next to hers.

Wrinkling her nose, she said, "No thanks, it's pizza for me, I can't deal with cleaning fish, or cooking them for that matter."

"Don't say I never offered."

"I think you already knew my answer. I should have been less predictable and said yes, this time."

"One of these days I'll teach you how to clean them."

"Don't hold your breath."

"Enjoy your pizza while I dine on flounder tonight."

"Quit rubbing it in, see ya Artie."

"Bye Ella."

Humming under her breath, Ella stowed her board in the back end of the Jeep. Any chance she got she had the soft top off. Driving with the warm breeze blowing and her radio cranked up was the best. It was spring in the Carolinas. Didn't get any better than this!

She drove to the pizzeria and picked up the pie then set it on the passenger seat beside her. The smell of pizza assaulted her senses and she had to grab a slice and eat it on the way home. That of course meant wearing it, as a blob of sauce and cheese landed on her breasts. She took a big bite *Hot hot hot!* It was worth the burnt tongue and soiled shirt. Best pizza in North Carolina she was convinced.

"Kee-kee did you miss me?" Ella said as she walked inside.

Daisy wrapped around her legs, weaving in and out as Ella tried not to trip or step on her. "I guess you're telling me you're hungry too?"

"M-e-o-w."

"Okay, I'll feed you first."

She set the pizza on the kitchen island counter then retrieved a can of cat food. She spooned out some wet food on a plate then stuck the rest in the refrigerator. She filled the *Garfield* ceramic bowl to overflowing with dry kibble, because Daisy went into panic mode if it went below the halfway mark. The feline lapped up the tuna, purring loudly.

Ella opened a bottle of Merlot and poured herself a glass. Kicking off her flip-flops she perched on a stool at the counter.

"Alexa play Brett Young." Alexa complied and like magic music was streaming through the airwaves of her kitchen. His voice and lyrics always touched her soul. Despite having grown up being tossed around in foster care most of her childhood, she was still cautiously romantic at heart. She didn't know if that made her stupid or resilient but there it was. She did want her happily ever after. *Why am I thinking about this now?*

Irritated, she said, "Alexa play Bruno Mars." The minute the upbeat soundtrack began, her mood went from sentimental to cheerful in an instant. *Now that's more like it.*

10

---

*E*lla would be lying to herself if she said she didn't take a little extra care with her hair and makeup preparing for work. Even as she applied lip gloss, she admonished herself for it. Two weeks into caring for Mr. Bennett had added a little lift to her daily grind. She refused to overanalyze. She would just enjoy the sexy distraction while she had it.

A half hour later she arrived at the hospital coffee in hand. She listened to the update on Kyle; he was progressing, but he had a long way to go. Apparently, he had been quite restless during the night.

Kari rolled her eyes saying, "Quite the pain in the ass frankly."

Stowing her purse in a cabinet behind the nurses' station, Ella grabbed a stethoscope and hung it around her neck. "Are you surprised?"

"Not really. Rich, arrogant and entitled. Hey, that could be the title for your relationship memoirs," she joked. "After dating our resident god Dr. Shelby, Mr. Bennett must seem like a walk in the park."

"Very funny Kari. Actually, he's not so bad."

Kari rolled her eyes. "For you maybe."

Ella lifted one shoulder and grinned. "I lead a charmed life. What can I say. Thanks, I'll take it from here."

Kari smirked and said, "Have fun."

"Knock knock," she said as she quietly entered Kyle's room. He was sitting up in bed trying to feed himself. "Need some help? Pretty challenging with one broken arm and a sprained wrist."

Kyle did a double take then his gaze slowly drifted down her body. "You're here. Thank God, that other nurse is a real tyrant."

"Why do you say that? Is it because she makes you comply with the doctor's orders?"

"Because she's a bully and gets far too much satisfaction from bossing me around. Dammit!" he snapped, as a blob of chocolate pudding fell off his spoon and onto the front of his hospital gown.

"If you don't comply you won't get better. Now let me help you with that pudding." Taking the spoon from his bandaged wrist she said, "Open wide."

His eyes gleamed with fire, but he complied. She couldn't help but tease him a little by taking her time approaching his mouth while he held it open. He grabbed her hand and squeezed even as he winced in pain from the effort. It was like an electric jolt going up her arm. Her eyes locked with his.

Kyle's gaze dipped to her lips as he guided her hand toward his mouth. He intentionally brushed his finger-tips up her forearm while she held the full spoon of pudding. She couldn't tear her gaze away as he opened his mouth for the bite and closed his lips around the spoon. The corners of his eyes crinkled knowingly when he glanced up and busted her gawking. She gulped.

"More," he demanded.

She glared. "Excuse me?"

His eyes sparkled devilishly. "Please. Another bite please."

"You're feeling frisky today."

"Yes, and it has to do with the present company."

Ella tried not to give away how his words affected her. *It's downright embarrassing how much I want him!* Her eyes unintentionally dropped down to his lap and she sucked in her breath.

He laughed, a warm resonant sound that filled the room. "Now you can't tell me this hasn't happened to you with the majority of your male patients."

Flustered she said, "Um... no, not really. Most of my patients have some impulse control."

He laughed. "I'll blame it on the drugs."

"And I'll give you the benefit of the doubt, Mr. Bennett," she said sounding prim and proper... completely unlike herself.

"I've been demoted to Mr. Bennett again?" he joked. "I like Kyle better. Remember?"

"I remember."

"You feel it, too."

"What I feel is irrelevant right now. Quit flirting with me. It throws me off."

"I'm not flirting... I'm using my seductive charm on you. No one can resist. Its proven. And if I'm not mistaken, you like it."

"There's that hubris again. Not to mention that misplaced imagination we've talked about," she said.

"Whatever you say Nurse Palmer."

"I'm inclined to think you don't need my help with this pudding, you seemed pretty strong when you gripped my hand."

"Yeah, but it hurt like hell. Plus, I have no coordination in my non-dominant hand which is why I'm wearing my pudding. Just one more bite." His eyes gleamed wickedly.

She jabbed the spoon into the plastic container and practically shoved it toward his mouth.

"Whoa, Nurse Ratchet, go easy!"

She wanted to smack him with the spoon but resisted the urge. "I think I liked you better when you were a ball of pain," she said.

"And *you* were a much nicer person back then. You might want to think about that. I'm totally at your mercy and you practically lodged that spoon down my throat."

She couldn't help it, she laughed out loud. She would have rather stayed irritated with him, it seemed a safer bet, but she never had been good with the odds.

"I never!" She exclaimed.

"Some kind of nurse you turned out to be."

"Just wait until I have a fork in my hand," she warned.

He leaned back against the raised bed and smiled at her, his eyes oozing warmth. Ella felt it all the way to her toes.

"I'm glad you're back. Please no more days off. Nobody compares to you. I'd be dead now if it were up to the others, seriously," he said.

"Ha! Not true," she said. "I know for a fact that every nurse that has been assigned to your care is highly competent. Haven't you heard the old saying that you catch more bees with honey than vinegar?"

"Takes too much energy. Everyone keeps telling me I have to focus on myself. How am I supposed to get better if I have to waste time being nice to everyone?"

"It takes just as much energy... maybe even more, to be negative as it does to be positive. You get what you put out in the world."

"So, Ella the philosopher, what do you put out?"

"Your lights if you don't watch it." His laugh was low and warm making her belly flutter.

Kyle watched her as she changed the bag on the IV drip and his attention made her edgy. "Quit staring at me, you're making me nervous."

"You are stunning," he said, voice husky.

Her hands stilled. She felt like a parade of butterflies were fluttering in her belly. Ella took a steadying breath before replying, "Thanks, I'm sure after being cooped up in here, most anyone would look like eye candy."

"We've been over this before. You aren't most anyone to me, Ella. Have you thought anymore about us dating? What's going to happen once I'm no longer your patient?"

Flustered she said, "Right now I'm still your nurse and I'm on the clock. I told you I keep my personal and professional lives separate Mr. Bennett."

"Kyle."

"Whatever."

"Don't get all prickly. You could look at it as throwing your patient a bone. A guy needs some hope...a reason to get better. Mental health should certainly count as patient care."

"If only you needed an injection, it would give me infinite pleasure to jab you with a needle right about now," she responded.

"Hot damn! I never expected *you* to be into BDSM." he said with a wicked grin.

"You are a mess," she said, giving in to a smile.

"In all seriousness, what do you do for fun? You look healthy and kind of outdoorsy," he said.

"I love the water, sailing, paddle-boarding, kayaking, swimming, you name it, if it's water I'm in. I also run a few days a week. Only about four miles at a time, but it keeps the brain and bod happy."

"I'm impressed but not surprised. You're graceful, I kind of figured you to be an athlete. Not to mention your killer body."

Ignoring the compliment she asked, "How about you? No, let me guess, gym four to five days a week, dictating while you run on your treadmill."

"Um, busted. I'm lucky to squeeze four runs in a week. I have two pools one indoors and one out. I do laps most evenings. And yes, I have a gym at home which comes in handy. I manage to get in a few work-outs during the week. On the rare occasions that I take a day off, I take my boat out on the water or sometimes it's my plane."

"You poor dear. I'm sorry I asked. But the pool really is going to come in handy for your rehab, once the cast comes off. For that matter so will the gym. You're fortunate to have them."

"I've been thinking about that, I can't wait to be home floating around. If I wrap my arm in a plastic bag, I should be able to get in the pool, right?"

"Yes. You don't strike me as the 'floating around' type but I'm happy to hear you say that. You're going to have to take it easy for the next month or so to give your body time to heal."

"Yes ma'am, so I've been told ad nauseam," Kyle replied.

"Is there anything else I can get for you?"

"I'm good, for now" he said, winking.

"I'll be back in to check on you, I'm glad you're doing so well. Just press your button if you need anything."

"I'll rest a lot easier now that you're here."

Ella was trying to temper her attraction, but it was increasingly difficult. He would soon be stepping down from the intensive care unit, and she felt a wave of loss at that thought. She couldn't remember the last time she had been this attracted to a man, maybe never.

11

Kyle took off his reading glasses and tossed *The New York Times* aside just as Elenore walked through the door.

"Hello Boss, you're actually sitting up and reading!"

"And bored out of my mind."

"You must be feeling better." She pulled up a chair beside his bed. "I hate to bring this to your attention while you're laid up, but I think you need to know," Elenore said.

"Spill it."

"We had to call nine-one-one yesterday because Gillian noticed something suspicious about a package delivered to the firm. No return address, dirty, too much postage, and excessive tape. It just didn't look right, and it smelled funny."

"Did you have to evacuate?"

Elenore nodded. "Yes, they advised it when we called. We were instructed to call the fire department as well. They sent the HAZMAT unit. It was chaotic to say the least. Gillian was freaked out because she is the one who handled it."

"Who wouldn't be?"

"The police questioned everyone at the office. Wanting to know about any threats from clients or adversaries. I told them about the sabotage to your father's equipment at the building site. Other than that, there hasn't been anything else to my knowledge. Pete was out for the day, so I filled him in this morning. I'm sure they'll be asking you questions. I'm surprised they haven't shown up already."

He pinched the bridge of his nose. "Damn, not good. Of all times, when I'm stuck here and useless really. It's so fucking frustrating. Where the hell was Pete all day?" he asked, referring to his partner and best friend from law school.

"He has been MIA all week. I did relay everything to him when he finally returned my phone calls."

"I haven't heard from him since I was first admitted."

She frowned and shook her head. "I don't know what's going on with him. Anyway, the test results from the powder came back already and were negative for any harmful substances, but it's still disconcerting," Elenore said.

"Was it delivered with the regular mail or just left at the door? We need to check out security camera footage."

"Dropped off with the mail, but it might still be worth reviewing to see if there is anyone suspicious lurking around after hours. I'll have someone get going on that when I get back to the office."

"I could probably manage that much if someone could bring me my laptop," Kyle said.

"That would be a no," Ella said catching the tail end of their conversation.

Kyle's body went on full alert. She looked sexy as hell with her thick dark hair and sparkling eyes.

"You aren't my boss," Kyle grumbled. "I'm tired of feeling like a feeble invalid. Viewing my laptop hardly qualifies as strenuous activity."

"If we let you open that can of worms, you'll be working full time within hours. Do we look stupid?" She and Elenore exchanged knowing looks.

Elenore stood up to leave. "Listen to your nurse. She seems to be familiar with your Type A personality traits. I'll keep you posted if there is anything that needs your attention. I'd expect a visit from the police."

"Technically she's not my nurse anymore since I'm no longer in ICU."

"Maybe not, but she still knows what's good for you," Elenore said.

His mouth twisted. "She and everyone else it would seem. Thanks for holding down the fort Elenore. Can't say you made my day, but I needed to know."

"I'll walk out with you," Ella said. "I just popped in on my way out to pick up carryout lunch for some of the staff. Kyle, I'm going to Panera; can I get you some real food?"

"Yes! Please, I'll have soup and a sandwich." He frowned and said, "I just realized that I don't have any money on me, I guess I'll have to pass."

"I'm sure I can spring for it this time," Ella said smiling at the irony of a penniless billionaire. "I'll be back."

"Real food. Thank you." He watched Ella leave then turned his attention back to his assistant.

"You like her," she said eyes gleaming.

"No comment. Weren't you leaving? Please tell my asshole partner to swing by as soon as possible."

"She is pretty amazing. I'll talk to Pete," she said over her shoulder. "Bye now."

12

When Ella returned with their lunches, Kyle had a visitor. A blonde blue-eyed beauty who was currently sizing Ella up.

"Ella, come on in, you aren't interrupting anything," Kyle said.

"Excuse me?" the blonde said obviously miffed.

Ella smiled at the woman then looked at Kyle. "I just ran into your doctor and he told me you'll be going home soon," Ella said. It had been over three weeks since Kyle had been admitted. She was off for the next several days and wanted to say goodbye in case he was discharged before she worked again. He'd been moved from ICU a few days prior and she knew Kyle was anxious to get home.

"That's what they say, I sure as hell hope so. But I will still have to have a home health care nurse for some time. Know anyone?" he asked, cocking an eyebrow.

"I'm sure the hospital will make recommendations."

"What about you?"

Her eyes narrowed. "Me? We've been over that."

"Yes, you. I'm serious. I know what you said before but I'll pay you double what you're making... triple even. You can take a temporary leave, a month to six weeks is what they're telling me. Why not?"

"Kyle, my love, she already has a job," the blonde interjected clearly trying to derail this discussion.

"Yes, and she still will after her temporary leave."

"I don't think my supervisor Deloris would take too kindly being one nurse down. They depend on me. I can't take a leave of absence just because I feel like it."

"You don't know until you ask."

"Trust me on that. You don't know the head nurse. She makes Cruella de Vil look like Mary Poppins."

"I find it hard to believe you'd be intimidated by anyone. Come on just think about it. Everyone can use a change, think of this as an adventure. Aren't you even curious? Two pools, a gym, your own suite, wake up and already be at your job, anything and everything you crave at your fingertips. Not even the least bit interested?"

"Not really."

"What could I throw in to entice you?"

Kyle's guest frowned at him before pinning Ella with a haughty stare. "I'm Charlene by the way. Kyle quit pressuring her. She said no. You can't buy everything or everyone. I can certainly come around more and help out."

"I'm sure your money marketing skills would be

invaluable as a home health care nurse. Forget it Charlene," he said sharply.

"No need to be rude about it," she said huffily.

Ella jumped in before the conversation could become more heated. "I'm flattered. Honestly. The answer, which I'm sure you aren't accustomed to hearing, is still no."

Kyle's lips tightened with displeasure. His scowl might be intimidating to some and most likely useful in court, but in Ella's opinion, it only made his entitlement more glaring and brought out her own stubbornness.

Fists balled up she took a deep calming breath before speaking. "I wish you luck and continued healing. I'm glad you have that level of confidence in me and that you think so highly of the care you received here, I really mean that."

Scowling he said, "I'm sorry if you find the idea of working for me so distasteful."

"No, I'm not saying that."

Behind the scowl she could see his hurt and frustration and she had a moment of doubt. *Should I be considering his offer?*

As if sensing her hesitation, he leaned forward looking more determined. "Look Ella, you're by far the most competent nurse in this unit. I really need you and Finn already trusts you. I wish you'd at least agree to think about it, would you do that for me?" he said, his voice low and persuasive.

"I just can't right now. Please don't take this personally. I'm sure you'll find someone you're just as comfortable with," she said firmly.

Kyle was obviously upset that she wouldn't even

consider his offer. She was sure most people would jump at the chance for the freedom this job would afford, not to mention flexible hours and luxurious accommodations. Money was no object for him, and he was used to the power it afforded him. But it was still a firm no. Too risky. He was dangerous... almost like a drug for her.

"Listen I'm going to take my lunch to the lounge area and eat with the staff. If I don't see you before you go, take care. It's been great getting to know you and please give my best to Faye and Finn. They're great."

"You'd get to hang out with them more if you'd take me up on my offer...just saying."

Charlene jumped up from her chair as if trying to push Ella's exit along.

"Goodbye Ella, thanks for taking such good care of my man."

Kyle rolled his eyes behind her back and Ella had to stifle a grin.

"See you. You take care of yourself and go easy," Ella said

Kyle's smoldering gaze brought heat to her cheeks. "Bye Ella."

13

---

*T*hank God her bestie Deb was coming over for dinner tonight. She felt desperate for someone to talk to about her attraction to Kyle and her decision to refuse the job offer. Since Deb was also a nurse, she'd get the conflict of interest more than most. Ella had already decided on the menu and selected a wine to compliment the meal. She enjoyed cooking when she had the time as long as it wasn't cooking for one. This was a welcome distraction. Tonight, couldn't get here quick enough.

~

*E*lla's eyes were watering from chopping onions when she heard Deb's knock at the door. She called, "Come on in its open."

Deb smiled brightly as she pushed through the door with her arms full. "I brought dessert and a bottle of wine. Chocolate filled tarts from Clarion Bakery. Is there anything I can do to help?" Deb asked, as she placed the pastries on the counter.

"Open the wine and pour us a glass, I've got a bottle chilling in the fridge," Ella said. "Then you can pull up a stool and talk to me while I chop garlic."

"Sounds like a plan. I'll put the bottle I brought in the fridge to chill." Deb stood on her tip toes to reach for two wine goblets then twisted off the cap of the amber liquid, pouring generous portions into each glass. Taking her first sip she sighed, rolling her eyes heavenward. "Bliss."

"Totally. Here's to bliss," Ella said raising her glass for a toast.

"What was so urgent and secretive that you couldn't tell me at work?" Deb asked.

"Well... it's about Kyle Bennett, he propositioned me today."

"*What?*" Deb had just taken another sip and practically choked on her wine.

"Not like that, propositioned as in a job proposition." Ella clarified.

"What kind of job?"

"He needs a home healthcare nurse."

Deb took another sip of wine. "Sounds intriguing."

"He offered me triple my salary. I must admit I was tempted. He has a pool, a gym... I'd have my own suite. I'd have flexibility, get out of that gray dreary hospital for a month." Ella bit her lip. "I doubt our boss from hell would even consider letting me take the time off anyway."

"I'm not so sure... she might. I mean look at his family connections," Deb said.

"Yeah, but don't forget who we're talking about."

Deb wrinkled her nose. "True but not everyone has a granddaddy with a hospital wing named after them... that would give him plenty of leverage."

"I'm not interested. I may be a little tempted but it would be a disaster."

Deb's eyes twinkled mischievously. "Maybe I should apply for the job. Just kidding... but if you're even the slightest bit interested you should at least try asking."

Ella's brows knitted. "It's complicated."

"How so? Are you developing feelings for him?"

Ella's chopping took on a ruthlessness as her knife pulverized the garlic. "Yes... no... Maybe? Our chemistry is wicked."

"I'm not surprised. I could see that one coming from a mile away. All the more reason to say yes in my humble opinion," Deb said. "Why are you holding back, are you scared?"

"Honestly? Yes, terrified. I'm attracted to him but I doubt if he is the relationship type. He's rich and he's gorgeous and can have anyone he wants."

"So? Why can't that be you?"

Ella shrugged. "Because, he's out of my league. I'm just a foster girl from the hood," she said the joke falling flat.

"I'm shocked to hear you talk like that. And I know who's to blame. Dr. Fuckhead! He did a number on you Ella. You're an incredibly beautiful woman with the passion and brains to go with it."

Ella threw the garlic with the other ingredients into

a bowl and mixed them together. "Besides that, you know me, I like to keep work and play separate. And he's used to everyone jumping at his slightest whim and I refuse to be another notch in his bedpost."

"So, you're telling me that you'd let a great opportunity go by just because you're chicken?"

"Maybe."

"That's crazy."

"Really? And how do you see this playing out?"

Deb stood up and twirled around theatrically, putting her hands over her heart, then said, "Nurse Cinderella meets billionaire patient, Prince Charming; he whisks her away to Neverland and they live happily ever after. The end." Bowing, she grinned at her friend.

"You're mixing your fairy tales."

"You get the drift."

Laughing, Ella put the finishing touches to the casserole and stuck it in the oven. "Alexa, set timer for forty minutes."

"Timer set, forty minutes starting now," the Alexa app responded.

"I need one of those, hint hint, my birthday's just around the corner," Deb said.

"I'll keep that in mind. I love Alexa. She keeps me on track. I use her for reminders for everything. I swear she's half of my brain."

"Exactly what I need."

"Let's go sit in the living room until Alexa calls us," Ella said, while re-filling their wine glasses.

"Okay, so let's talk about what would happen if you changed your mind and said yes?"

Ella sat down on the couch tucking her hair behind

her ears. Her eyes lost focus as she considered the question. "First of all... it's *not* going to happen... but if it did... my new boss would have dreamy blue eyes, thick dark hair, gorgeous body, lean and muscular, stunning smile, the straightest, whitest teeth *ever*, he must have had braces, eyes that crinkle when he smiles, long black lashes." She sighed.

"Girl, I feel ya. You've got it bad."

Ella rolled her eyes. "Ya think? That's the main reason I can't take the job."

"Okay... If you *really* don't want the job, I could totally take it. You'll vouch for me with Mr. Bennett, won't you?"

Ella laughed out loud. "That would be conspiracy to commit murder. You wouldn't be able to put up with him for a day."

"That's not fair. I'll have you know I'm meditating now and I'm a much more patient person."

"I give your new program a month, tops."

Deb stuck out her tongue. "Now you're just being mean."

"I'd stick with the hospital if I were you."

She sighed dramatically. "Yes, I suppose, he wants you anyway."

"Plus, you aren't on Deloris' most hated list, she likes you. It's a lot better atmosphere for you at the hospital than it is for me."

"True but a girl can dream. It sounds like the perfect setup. Plus, who knows, maybe he and I would fall in love and live happily ever after."

Ella snickered. "Someday Mr. Wonderful is going to sweep you off your feet."

"Same goes for you but you have to be open enough to let it happen. Get out of your self-imposed man exile. It's been two years, plenty of time for you to lick your wounds and move on."

"I have moved on. You know that feeling, kind of tingly inside like you're waking up after a long hibernation...it's happening. Scares me to death!"

"And your gorgeous patient is responsible. All I can say is that it's about time, and I think you should take a leap and go for it," Deb said.

"I can't think about it anymore tonight. Let's change the subject. Any new gossip you haven't filled me in on?" Ella said.

"Same ole, except I just booked a fall vacation. My cousin and I are going to wine country, Napa Valley!"

"That's fantastic. With a tour group?"

"Yes."

"Maybe you'll meet a guy on your trip."

The loud alert from Alexa with her reminder sounded; dinner was ready. "You can tell me all about your itinerary while we eat. I'm jealous. That's one trip I'd love to be on."

The table was already set, and the long-tapered candles flickered softly. Deb poured the last of the bottle into their glasses while Ella pulled out the casserole. "Let's eat. I don't know about you but I'm starving."

"Me too. Looks delicious."

"Dig in and don't be shy."

"Never been accused of that." Deb took a huge bite of the creamy chicken casserole. "Mmm."

"You like?"

Deb nodded her head rolling her eyes back with pleasure. "I love Fontina cheese. Is there Swiss as well?"

"Yep. Really cheesy. Now about that trip you're planning..."

~

Three hours later Ella closed the door behind her friend, feeling grateful and content. Nothing like girl time to get your head on straight. She still knew she had made the right decision to turn the job down, but she felt lighter after confiding about her growing attraction to Kyle. Who knew what the future might hold? After he was stronger, if he did reach out, she would consider going out with him. What did she have to lose?

14

*E*lla's phone rang at eight the following morning. It was a call from the hospital; she frowned. "Hello," she said groggily.

"Ella this is Deloris. I need you to come into my office sometime this morning. As soon as possible."

"Of course. What's this about?"

"We'll talk when you arrive," the head nurse said, and abruptly hung up.

Oh my God! What did I do? Ella racked her brain trying to think of every move she'd made the last day she'd worked. This had to be big. Deloris Henry never called on the weekends. Actually, she had never called her after hours ever... *I must have really fucked up.* She jumped out of bed, startling her cat out of a deep sleep. Daisy glared at her through squinted eyes.

"Sorry chica. I'm not happy about this either. There goes my morning run." Adrenaline surging, Ella scurried to the bathroom to brush her teeth and run a comb through her hair. She threw on her jeans, a tee shirt, and her Converse and flew down the stairs. She decided to get a coffee at the drive-thru on her way.

~

"Close the door behind you," the head nurse said sternly.

With shaky hands, Ella quietly closed the door effectively trapping herself inside with the giant hornet.

Ms. Henry waved her hand towards the chair across the desk facing her. "Have a seat."

Deloris Henry had a pointed nose, sharp features, her grey hair pulled up into a bun so tight it looked painful. Her eyes glared at Ella behind dark round glasses. She had an intimidating manner in the best of times; now, sitting across from her on the receiving end of her formidable stare, Ella was fighting not to squirm like a child. She stuck her hands between her thighs to keep them still. After what felt like minutes, Ella lost the stare contest and broke the silence.

"Have I done something wrong?"

"Do you have something you'd like to confess to?"

Ella clenched her fists. "Well, calling me in on a Saturday, my day off, is highly unusual to say the least. I can only assume it's about something important."

Steepling her fingers, Deloris continued to burn holes through Ella; paired with her disapproving scowl, it literally felt like torture.

"So please do tell me about your relationship with our patient Kyle Bennett."

Ella felt her cheeks grow warm, *damn it*, and tried

valiantly not to look guilty. Thrown completely off balance her hands went clammy with nervousness. "My relationship? With Mr. Bennett?"

"Yes, your *relationship* with Mr. Bennett."

Deloris Henry had the uncanny ability to use silence as a powerful weapon. It was most effective. It was almost impossible to hold the tension and not begin babbling.

"Well, as you're fully aware I was his primary nurse while he was in ICU. He was admitted almost four weeks ago and has made beautiful progress. Dr. Thompson said he will be released in the next couple of days."

"Your *friend* Dr. Thompson. And how does he feel about your dalliance with a patient here at Wayne Regional?"

Ella was quickly getting over her fear as anger pushed it aside. She straightened, her hackles up.

"Dalliance? What are you implying Ms. Henry?"

"I had a little visit from the hospital administrator this morning."

Ella stiffened wondering where this was leading.

"Apparently Mr. Bennett has taken a shine to you and wants to make use of your *skills*. He has requested that you be allowed to take an extended leave of absence to be his personal home healthcare nurse."

Ella let out a breath in relief. "Oh that." She smiled and waved her hand. "Yes, he asked me the other day and I told him no, in no uncertain terms."

"Did you now?" she replied, looking smug.

"Is that what this is about? I would never leave you

in the lurch like that. I told him the hospital would make recommendations but that I was needed here."

"*If* you're telling the truth, he didn't take no for an answer and unfortunately I now have no choice but to work with one staff member down."

Ella sputtered. "But why? I said no!"

"As you are probably aware, the Bennetts are very generous donors to this hospital. It's important that we keep benefactors happy... I'm sure you understand what I'm saying."

"No, I don't! I certainly have a say in this."

"About as much as I do," she replied scowling. "I don't know why you're complaining. You'll be paid well; you'll get points for helping out one of our biggest contributors and you'll have landed the big fish you've always been hoping to catch."

Ella stood abruptly, facing her boss. "I am insulted by your insinuation that I have been anything but professional."

"You're young and beautiful. I've had my eye on you and have seen your flirtatiousness with the doctors on staff. We both know about your affair with Dr. Shelby. You blatantly pursued him and look where that got you."

Ella recoiled like she'd been slapped. She could feel the blood drain from her face. Her voice shook as she said, "Ms. Henry that was uncalled for and ugly! You have no right to assume you know anything about me or my intentions. For the record you have that one completely wrong. It appears, we are both stuck between a rock and a hard place. Given that you're issuing an order, I will do *you* the favor of deciding on whether I will submit to Mr. Bennett's demands."

"Ha! A favor for me? Now *that's* priceless," Delores said derisively.

Ella held up her hand. "If I were you, I'd quit while you're ahead. *If* I decide to do the hospital this favor, just remember you now owe me. And if you ever try to sully my reputation again, I will go to the administrator and place a formal complaint. Do we understand each other?"

"You'd better watch your step Ms. Palmer. I'm not easily intimidated. I run a tight ship here and no one is indispensable. Do *we* understand each other?'

Ella's face was on fire with a rage she was fighting to keep under control. "Yes, completely," she said through gritted teeth. Without another word she stormed out of the office and headed straight for Kyle Bennett's room.

15

$\mathcal{E}$lla felt like steam was coming out of her ears just like in the cartoons, she was so infuriated. Her energy practically crackled as she burst into Kyle Bennett's room.

"How dare you!" Ella said with quiet fury.

Kyle sitting up in a chair, looked at her innocently, completely unimpressed with her obvious distress. "Hello to you too," he said.

Ella turned and closed the door behind her marching over to him. "What gives you the right to force someone to work for you against their will? Does it make you feel all macho and powerful?"

"Calm down. It's not that dramatic."

"Dramatic?" she sputtered. "Really? Who do you think you are? You barely know me. I'm a professional yet somehow you act like you're entitled to my services. If you say jump, I'm supposed to ask how high? You've got the wrong girl."

"I don't know why you're so pissed off. You'll be paid more than you make here in four months, you'll have a change of scenery, and you'll get to return to your job when it's all said and done."

"I just had to sit through an ugly meeting with my head nurse who implied that I had led you on with the intention of snagging you as my prize! I was completely humiliated. Do you even care?"

"What she assumed was beyond my control," he said coolly. "What would you like me to do about it? Should I have Joe talk with her?" he asked referring to the administrator.

"No! Don't you get it? You can't manipulate and get your way with everything. I can handle Ms. Henry all by myself. I simply want to point out that your high-handedness was out of line and put me in an incredibly awkward position. If you talk to Joe, God only knows what the fallout from that would be."

Eyes narrowed he nodded slowly. "So, I guess you just need to vent. I'm all ears," he said his tone mollifying.

His demeanor only stoked her fire. Eyes blazing, with steel in her voice she replied, "Vent? This isn't venting, this is *Ella furious*! Your arrogance and entitlement are beyond the pale. You think your money can buy anything or anyone."

"Are you done? Listen I thought I was doing you a favor and helping myself at the same time. I'm sorry if your boss has the wrong idea. I'll be happy to correct that with her. Other than that, what would you like me to do?"

"You mean besides you fucking yourself? The

damage is done. Thanks to you my reputation is screwed... again, my career could be in jeopardy, and I'm now your 'personal' nurse. If, and I mean *if,* I decide to work for you and not just give my notice... we are going to have a long discussion about the ground rules."

"Yes, dear," he said, obviously suppressing a grin, almost sending her into the stratosphere.

"You think this is funny? Oh my God, you are unbelievable!" With angry tears in her eyes, she turned and stomped to the door needing to get out of there before they spilled over.

"Hold on a sec Elle. I'm just a guy trying to heal from an injury. I'm weak and tired and I need someone I trust to help me recover. I trust you. In my world trustworthy people are far and few between. If that makes me an asshole, so be it."

Taking a deep steadying breath, she turned back around to face him. She made an effort to calm down before answering. Voice shaky she replied, "It is beyond belief that you assume I'll do your bidding and be thrilled about it just because you say so."

Sizing Ella up he peered at her through narrowed eyes saying, "What would it take? Name your price."

"Are you really that dense? Haven't you listened to a word I've said? Let me spell it out for you. I am not for sale! There isn't enough money in the world. You are a rich, entitled asshole. Does that get through that thick skull of yours?"

His eyes flashed briefly with anger, before he checked it. "I won't apologize for requesting this favor from my friend. In my mind I was helping you and myself at the same time. You're twisting this into some kind of power-play that it most definitely is not. I need a nurse. You're a nurse. The best I've encountered. I am offering you any amount of money it will take. Name your price."

Hands on her hips, Ella stood there incredulous. "I just can't with you. End of conversation. Goodbye Mr. Bennett."

"Wait! Ella!"

She was already halfway down the corridor fueled by fury. She was practically hyperventilating she was so enraged. *Damn that man!* She wished she'd never met him. Her position was untenable. She either had to hand in her resignation or work for the most conceited, self-important, patronizing, condescending, asshole she had ever met. *And the sexiest... don't forget that one Ella. Shut-up!*

16

*K*yle had too much time to think. When he closed his eyes, all he could see was Ella's look of disgust and disappointment. The anger he could take, it was her revulsion that had been like a punch in the gut. He knew he'd been playing with fire to go over her head but that hadn't stopped him. If he wanted something, he went for it, damn the consequences.

In his own defense, he had made a very generous offer. One that most would jump at. But Ella was not most people. It seemed as if money had no leverage with her. She was stubborn. And right now, she was being ridiculously so. *Damn it!* He vacillated between admiration and frustration. He wasn't accustomed to the word no. He didn't like it. She should be thanking him for the opportunity instead of making him feel like a loathsome excuse of a human. But his excuses fell flat even to himself.

He'd never admit it but underneath his irritation he felt a small thrill. It was new and slightly refreshing to find someone who couldn't be influenced by his fortune. She wasn't the least bit afraid to go up against him. He was accustomed to people bending over backwards to accommodate him and he couldn't help but admire Ella's chutzpah.

He was shocked to realize he was feeling as smitten as a school boy. *Not good.* Ella had gotten under his skin in a big way. He hadn't missed the tears in her eyes and had been surprised to discover that he still had a conscience. Until now he'd been convinced his cynicism reflected reality and had dulled his ability to feel much of anything. He truly believed most people were opportunists and greedy, but maybe there *were* some exceptions.

Do I actually feel guilty? Ridiculous! What do I have to feel bad about? I'm offering her the world on a platter. He wasn't comfortable with this sudden self-reflection and Ella was bringing unwelcome and long-buried emotions to the surface. *Is there any way for me to pacify her and still get what I want?*

17

"Slow down and start from the beginning," Deb said. They were sitting on the beach, the sand warm and soft between their toes. It was high tide and the crashing waves matched Ella's current emotional state. Deb had responded immediately to her urgent voicemail. Ella wasn't prone to being overly dramatic.

Ella sat with her knees propped up sifting sand through her fingertips as the ocean breeze loosened tendrils of her long, dark hair from its clasp. She stared at the horizon in deep thought before she began talking again and once unleashed, left nothing out.

Deb listened to her friend vent. "He wasn't even apologetic?"

"No! He didn't think he'd done anything wrong. He was doing us both a favor, he said. The fucking nerve of that man."

"What are you going to do?"

"The way I see it, I have two choices, quit or go work for an autocrat."

"Let's frame this a little differently. What if you were to go work for him, take advantage of what he's offering. Tell him you'll say yes, but only if he quadruples the amount. Then make him pay. You take the upper hand. You decide the conditions."

"Keep talking," Ella said warming up to the idea.

"Your terms, your rules, you win."

"How will I be able to tolerate working for him?"

"Just be your professional self. You liked him just fine before he played God with your career."

"Did I? I forgot," she said scowling. "Anyway, that's history now."

"Look at it this way, you'll make tons of money, you'll get out of that dreary hospital, and you'll get a break from Deloris."

"Maybe you're right."

"Of course, I'm right. Mr. Bennett may have just met his match. He has no idea who he's messing with. I'd place my bet on you that he is about to get more than he ever bargained for."

Her eyes gleaming, Ella said, "I like the way you think my friend."

18

*E*lla, taking Deb's advice, had decided to turn the tables on Kyle Bennett and agree to work for him on her own terms. She kept going over the conversation she'd had when she'd laid out her demand that he quadruple her salary. He'd looked shocked before his eyes had hardened into flinty chips, his lips twisting with cynicism. But he'd agreed to her terms.

She might want to believe that she had the upper hand but the truth was she was embarrassed by how much she still desired him. She had felt like a gold digger seeing his contempt, but quickly squelched that notion considering he had been the one who had put her in this position in the first place.

Now three days later, she was about to enter the lion's den. Her pulse raced as she approached the arched wrought iron security gate mounted to imposing stone columns. The gates began to swing open automatically as she pulled up. She drove through without having to get out of her jeep. She followed the long curving drive through a tree-lined lawn, perfectly manicured and lavishly landscaped. There were several workers trimming the shrubs and weeding the colorful perennial beds loaded with ornamental and fountain grasses.

She almost gasped when the house, a mansion more like, came into view. She was going to have to reconsider her initial judgement, scratching wealthy attorney...substituting it with filthy rich trust fund heir which was more on point. *Oh, my my, so this is how the one percent actually live.* She had never stepped foot... not even close to anything this opulent in her entire thirty years on the planet.

Rather than making her feel inferior, it actually had the opposite effect. Instead, she felt prickly and annoyed that there was such disparity between the rich and the poor. She was practically righteous in her contempt. Hell, she herself made a decent salary, but this was ridiculous. Nothing anyone did could be this valuable. She wound around the circular drive and parked in front of the entrance.

She could hear the chimes echoing through the screens of the double French doors as she pressed the doorbell.

A man approached from the interior of the grand foyer. "You must be Mr. Bennett's nurse, Ms. Palmer as I recall? Mr. Bennett is expecting you." He stepped back from the door motioning with a sweep of his arm for Ella to enter. She picked up her cat carrier with Daisy inside and entered.

"Thank you. You can call me Ella," she said smiling and extending her hand for a shake.

He returned her smile bowing slightly before taking her hand in his for a brief clasp.

"I'm the house manager, Richard Drake, or in old school terms, the butler. A pleasure to meet you. Come this way," he said motioning for her to follow. "I'll have someone on staff bring in your luggage. After I take you to see Mr. Bennett, I will show you to your quarters so you can settle in. Just leave the cat there for now. We'll deliver her to your room." He leaned down to stick his finger up to the mesh front panel and let Daisy sniff him.

"And who do we have here?"

"This is Daisy."

"She is a beauty."

"Thank you." Peering into the carrier she said, "I'll see you soon." A frightened pair of green eyes stared back at her. "Don't worry, mama will get you out of there."

After hiking up the marble spiral staircase to the second level, they walked down a wide corridor, looking more like an art gallery than someone's home. It was lined with oil paintings, the occasional settee, wing chairs and antique credenzas. They continued until they reached the end of the wing.

Kyle was on the phone listening to someone when Ella entered his bedroom. He watched her approach, eyeing her like she was his next meal. There was an intensity to his gaze that made Ella feel like he had stripped off her clothing and laid her bare.

"I've got to go, my nurse just arrived," he said, then hung up abruptly.

"Hello again," Ella said coolly.

He glanced pointedly at his watch. "You've finally made it?"

Ella bristled. *Geesh what is it about this man?* "What time were you expecting me?"

"I *assumed* you'd be here to help me settle in when I got home from the hospital. Wasn't that our agreement?"

"I must have missed that memo. I had no idea I was expected to be here prior to your arrival."

"I don't think it was presumptuous of me to assume the person I'd hired to take care of me, one whom I'm paying out the ass for, be here when I arrived home. You're here now so we can move on. Rich will get you settled in and set you up with a two-way radio. That way I'll be able to get your attention whenever I need it."

"This just keeps getting better," she mumbled under her breath.

"Pardon me?"

"Nothing. But wouldn't a text be just as effective?"

"Ella I'm in pain. I needed my meds an hour ago! If you prefer texting that's fine with me."

"Right. I picked up your prescriptions on my way in." She held up a white pharmacy bag. "I'll give you your meds then go get settled in my room."

"I'll have to admit I'm still surprised you accepted the position. Who'd have thought that even the principled Ella Palmer could be swayed. I guess money does talk."

Stinging from his rebuke, she said, "I guess so and I'm not cheap." She took a deep breath exhaling slowly. *How dare he twist it like that! He is the one in the wrong here not me!*

"Apparently not. I'll have to make sure I get my money's worth."

"I'm sure you will." She held out a tiny cup with his pills in it and shook it into his open palm.

"We'll see," he said. He grabbed a glass of water from the bedside table and swallowed his medication. "At last. Thanks."

"Just doing my job," she said through gritted teeth.

"You're free to go get settled in. I think you'll be very comfortable in the guest suite. It's at the other end, right down the hall. My son's room is right next to mine. He won't be joining us until the end of the week. We thought it best to give me a few days to gain some strength."

"I think that's wise," Ella said. "Nice place you have here," she deadpanned.

His eyes jerked up to meet hers. "Not up to your expectations?" His voice dripped with sarcasm.

"Don't be ridiculous. Your place is off the charts. I've never seen anything like it."

He gave a half shrug. "I suppose it is."

Ella shook her head in wonderment that anyone could take this opulence for granted. Most homes she had lived in growing up were about the size of his bedroom.

Mr. Drake stepped in and said, "I'll show Ms.

Palmer to her quarters. She needs to get her cat acquainted with the new surroundings."

"After I get Daisy settled in, I'll come back and do my assessment."

"I'll be here no doubt," he said, the dark circles under his eyes were the tell that he was exhausted from the trek home from the hospital. Sometimes a patient didn't realize how impaired they really were until their reentry into their old life. Then it could be quite shocking to realize their limitations.

He raked his hand through his dark, almost black hair. "Make yourself at home. All the amenities are available to you. Rich will give you the grand tour. No formalities, no dress-code. I want you to feel like you're at home. The fridge is fully stocked. I have a chef that will prepare our evening meals but we're on our own for breakfast and lunch...unless that's a problem? Rich is here Monday through Friday nine to five and has his own private cottage on the grounds. He is basically always on call, right Rich?" he said, smiling sheepishly.

"It is one of my great fortunes to be working for you, Mr. Bennett."

"Stop. I'm sure Ella thinks I paid you to say that. Her opinion of me is only slightly higher than a pile of cow dung."

"You flatter yourself," she replied.

He chuckled as she haughtily marched out of the room behind Richard.

19

"Here you are," Mr. Drake said, opening the door to her temporary residence.

"Holy shit!" slipped out before she could stop it. Embarrassed she quickly covered her mouth with her hand. "I'm so sorry, please excuse me."

Mr. Drake smiled. "I understand Ms. Palmer. It is grand indeed by anyone's standards."

"You can say that again." She sucked in her breath as she took in her surroundings. There were vases of beautiful cut flowers filling the room. A large gift box wrapped in gold foil with a bow sat on her bed.

"I'll leave you alone. I thought perhaps the litter box could be placed in the entry to the walk-in closet over there," he said pointing to the west corner of the room. "It's tiled so there's no need to worry about the floors and you can keep the door closed off from your clothing."

"Thank you, Mr. Drake."

"My pleasure. Feel free to make use of the pool and spa while you're here. There is a sauna and steam room off the gym. I'll give you a tour after you get unpacked."

"That would be great."

"Please call me Richard or Rich," he said smiling kindly.

"Okay. Let's start with Richard. How long have you worked for Kyle?"

"I've been working for the Bennett family for over thirty-five years. Since before Kyle was born."

"Wow!"

"Yes, you can say that again. I'm not at all sure where that time has gone." He arched a brow. "Shall I return, say in twenty minutes, for the tour?"

"Make it thirty," she said smiling. "Thank you."

"Consider it done." He bowed slightly at the waist and backed out of the doorway leaving her and Daisy alone in the massive apartment-sized guest quarters. She unzipped the crate and Daisy strolled out curious about her new surroundings.

"Look at this Daisy. There is even a small kitchenette... it's got a coffee maker and mini fridge for God's sake!" She walked to the double French doors and looked out, admiring the view of the pool. It was massive.

She spied another vase filled with the most exquisite roses she had ever seen. Walking over to investigate she bent down to sniff, taking delight at the light rose fragrance. The outer petals of the rosettes were a soft peach blending to an apricot center. She pulled out the card and opened it. *Ella, My heartfelt gratitude. Your help in my time of need is appreciated. K.B.*

Oh really? How convenient. Practically calls me a mercenary, completely disrupts my life, puts a serious dent in my already tarnished reputation, then thinks a couple dozen roses are going to make it okay. It was going to take a whole lot more *mea culpa* from him, for her to even consider letting him off the hook from which he was currently dangling.

She reached for the fancy box and lifted the lid. Her hands automatically stroked the fine silk lingerie in a pale shade of aquamarine. She pulled out a matching lightweight dressing gown and rubbed it against her cheek. *Sumptuous.*

Whoever had brought Daisy and her luggage had also deposited the newly purchased litter box and litter in the entryway to the closet. She took the time to set that up and made sure Daisy knew where it was. She put out the cat dish in the galley kitchen and heaped Daisy's favorite dried food in one side and water in the other.

She picked Daisy up and nuzzled her soft fur sitting down on the edge of the bed. "I know you're freaked out now but in a few days we'll both be adjusted. I promise." She looked incredulously around the room that was going to be her home for the next month. "Some digs huh? We better not get too used to this but we can enjoy it while we have it."

Setting Daisy on the bed beside her she stood up. Deciding to take Kyle at his word and make herself at home she changed into a pair of shorts and a tank top.

She opened her French doors and stepped out onto the balcony. A gentle breeze stirred her hair. Inhaling the floral scent in the air, she spied magnificent magnolias in full bloom dotting the landscape. There were white and pink dogwoods as well. The poolside was ablaze with color from the perennial beds surrounding the area and the potted urns filled with bright annuals. An arbor next to the pool house had twisted vines climbing and weaving around the cedar beams, the purple blooms of wisteria dangling like clusters of grapes. *Wow! Is this really happening?*

20

*A*n hour later, Ella's head was spinning after the grand tour. *Geesh!* A game room, a home theater, a library for God's sake! Family kitchen, formal dining room, butler pantry, wine cellar, a study, personal gym, sauna, steam room, whirlpool, indoor and outdoor pools, sunroom, grand room, and even a music room with the requisite baby grand piano...it blew her away.

Ending her tour, Richard deposited her back at Kyle's bedroom door after she'd picked up her medical bag. He was asleep so she allowed herself a few moments to just stare.

"Like what you see?" Kyle said lazily.

She startled then quickly excused her ogling. *Oops.* "I was just looking for any signs of your bruises. You'd never even know that they had been there. You're healing fast." *Sounds plausible. Fake it till you make it.*

He looked like he was biting back a smile as he

returned the favor, his eyes slowly raking over her body from her head all the way to her sandaled feet then back up again. He obviously liked what he saw because his eyes smoldered with heat. "Glad to get your professional analysis," he said. "You in those shorts? Damn! Those thighs are about to give me a heart attack."

Flustered she said, "Um... well I thought you said casual and I... um... this is what I'd wear at home and..."

He cut her off mid-sentence. "Lighten up Ella. It was a compliment."

"Of course. Um, I guess you're feeling better, more rested?"

"I wouldn't say certain parts feel rested at the moment." When she glared, he grinned arching a brow. "My heart for instance. Get your mind out of the gutter Ms. Palmer. What did you think I meant?"

"Spare me your verbal gymnastics. Maybe now is as good a time as any to have that discussion about the rules."

"Rules, what rules?"

"The one's I alluded to when I agreed to accept this job."

"I'm all ears, but can I have a drink first?"

"Of course." She sat her satchel with her medical paraphernalia on the floor next to his bed then walked over to a side table to get the small pitcher of ice water someone had left there. She was hyperaware of his eyes following her every move.

After refilling his cup, Ella pulled up a chair and sat facing Kyle, who continued to stare at her with impenetrable eyes.

She cleared her throat. "First, this is to remain strictly professional." When he stayed silent, she continued, "I'm your nurse and nothing more. No more comments about my legs or any other parts of my anatomy."

His eyes glittered, but he held his tongue.

"Well? Aren't you going to respond?"

"I'm listening, please go on, this is most intriguing."

She clasped her hands in her lap to keep from wringing them. "Yes, I do work for you but that doesn't mean you get to order me around. You will treat me with respect, or I walk. Do we understand one another Mr. Bennett?"

"One hundred percent Ms. Palmer. Shouldn't be a problem. You're certainly beautiful and all that but opportunists bore me. I've had enough to last several lifetimes. So, rule numero uno... no flirting. Do I have that right? Anything else?"

Ella blushed beet red at the insult but kept her cool. "Let's do that assessment now."

He winked. "I'm all yours. Oh, sorry is that considered flirting?"

"You're impossible," she huffed.

"Feelings are mutual," he replied.

This is going to be a long month.

21

As Kyle watched her wrap the blood pressure cuff around his arm, he felt a pang of remorse for acting like such a dick. *She'd brought it on herself by taking advantage of his wealth and then by acting all high and mighty about it.*

He prided himself on his ability to read a person, so he'd been stunned by Ella's ultimatum and reversal. When she'd demanded two times his original proposal, which was overly generous to begin with, he had told himself it was better to know now who he was dealing with. Pushing aside his disappointment he knew it was better to be blindsided now rather than further down the line. He'd determinedly squelched any barely acknowledged hope that Ella could be something more than a casual fling. *Ah, but I do still want her.*

Kyle relaxed his shoulders, deciding to enjoy the view of her fine as fuck ass. Rules be damned. He wanted to enjoy this mini-victory and get his damn money's worth. Hey, as things were now, he'd be *happy* to have a casual fling with Ella. He didn't mind making a little effort to get her into his bed. He'd moved past his romantic delusions and no longer trusted her intentions anyway. Even if he *had* twisted her arm by going over her head, she didn't have to raise the stakes and exploit his wealth and need. It pissed him off that he still had this intense craving for Ella but there it was.

She grabbed his wrist checking his heart rate while the cuff squeezed his other arm. Her touch pulsed through him and he watched her graceful movements as she noted the blood pressure results in a log, then ran a thermometer across his forehead. "How is your pain level today from one to ten?"

"Four after the meds...was a nine before you got here."

She placed her stethoscope against his bare chest and said, "Take a couple of deep breaths for me." Kyle liked her attention and the warmth of her hand against his skin and felt an immediate response.

"Lean forward so I can reach your back... now a couple deep breaths," she said. "Sounds good, lungs are clear, blood pressure and temperature normal. Now I'll check your surgical site and change the dressing."

She used the sheet to drape him like a pro, then pulled his boxers down over his hips to gain access. He could feel his dick twitch and tried valiantly to suppress it. He tried thinking of anything that might distract him from her gentle hands right next to his cock...epic fail.

He saw her cheeks turn pink when she noticed his response and suppressed a smile. Ignoring it she removed the bandages and examined the wound.

"Healing nicely. I'll clean it then change the bandage. You'll be good to go."

"You haven't lost your touch," he said needling her.

Kyle could tell she was doing her best to ignore him as she finished cleaning his surgical site and rebandaged it. However, he could also tell by her quickened breath and flushed cheeks that Ella was more than aware of the heat between them. She was like a drug... intoxicating and dangerous, and he knew he had to be careful to remember that even Ella Palmer was susceptible to the allure of his money.

"Are your accommodations acceptable?" he asked.

"Yes, more than that, luxurious by anyone's standards. Thank you for asking," she replied coolly.

He wanted to rewind, go back before she had shown him her true colors. One would think he'd be used to it by now, but this one hurt. He hadn't realized how much he'd been seeing a potential future with Ella until it all came crashing down. Yes, he had what he wanted... she was working for him as his own private nurse but now he questioned if the connection they had was real or was she like everyone else and only attracted to his money? *Fuck it. She'd get paid and paid well.*

He didn't doubt that she desired him but like every relationship in his past it was always messy... could she see him, the man beneath the power and money? He'd thought so before.

Like most things, life wasn't black and white... even he would be hard put to separate himself from his lifestyle. It was as much a part of him as his limbs. He'd been born into his fortune and he'd never known any different. *Does that make me a bad person?*

Tired and irritated he didn't want to think about it anymore. He'd bide his time and see what happened. When she changed her mind about becoming his lover, which he knew was just a matter of time, he would be more than happy for her to warm his bed.

22

*E*lla was stretched out on a poolside lounger next to her sleeping patient. It was day three and she had to admit she could get used to this. Lazing around a pool, getting a tan, and being able to take advantage of the lap pool and gym was sinfully luxe. She never had to leave the house and could still stay in shape. Last evening, they had watched the latest Chris Hemsworth release in his home theater. Wine, privacy and plush reclining chairs, may as well enjoy it while it lasted.

The sun was warming up and Ella decided to take another dip before going inside to get Kyle's medications. She stood and stretched her arms overhead. She glanced down at Kyle, sound asleep, watching his muscular chest rise and fall with each breath.

His shoulders were broad and strong, his skin a gorgeous Mediterranean tan. He was unshaven, some referred to it as designer stubble... and *that* description fit him to a tee. He was always well put together even when he was only in his underwear...*Derek Rose* pure silk boxers. Curious, she'd googled them and was shocked at the $165 price tag! Even his underwear was lavish.

She dove into the refreshingly cool water and touched the bottom. Kicking hard she swam the length of the pool without coming up for air until she reached the end. She surfaced and blew out her breath, slicking back dripping hair from her face. She heard clapping and looked over to see Kyle watching as he applauded.

"Are you a dolphin or what? I thought I was going to have to jump in to save you," he said.

She laughed. "I may be part dolphin," she admitted. His warm chuckle traveled across the water and went straight to her belly. She dove back under and made several laps before hoisting herself up onto the side of the pool. Her legs dangled in the water as she let the sun dry her. Leaning back on her hands she tilted her face towards the rays, basking while the gentle breeze offset the heat.

She sensed him before she heard his cane thwacking the concrete beside her. When she glanced up, he was towering over her. "Do you want to dangle your feet in the water?" she asked.

"I'll go down to the shallow end and use the railing. Join me?"

"Sure," she said hopping up. She held his free arm loosely as they made their way to the shallow end of the pool. He grabbed the hand rail leading down the steps into the water then lowered himself onto the pool's edge, submerging his feet into the cool water. Ella sat beside him.

"Are you settling in okay?"

"Yes, thank you. I feel a little guilty actually. Don't you have servants' quarters I can live in?" she said only half joking.

His lips twitched. "I'm glad you're comfortable."

"We're making ourselves at home."

He arched a brow. "You and the cat?"

She smiled. "Yes, me and the kitty."

"Does kitty have a name?"

"Daisy."

"You know Finn is going to be ecstatic. He's been bugging me to let him have a cat or a dog for what feels like forever."

"You and Finn are welcome to come meet her anytime. She's very uncat like. She loves people. I think she thinks she's a dog."

"Finn will be home tomorrow."

Ella looked at him from the corner of her eye. "I know. Are you ready?"

"Yeah, I miss him."

"I'm sure he'll be glad to be home with his dad. He seems like a great kid. I look forward to getting to know him."

"You won't be able to get away from him," Kyle said smiling.

"It will be nice to have kid energy around."

"The house is pretty big with only us and the staff clanging around."

Ella stretched her arms overhead. "Ready to go in?"

"Yes. I'm hungry. How about you?"

"Yes. Starving."

Kyle grabbed the rail and pulled himself up struggling to keep his full weight off his injured leg. Ella grabbed his cane handing it to him once he was steady.

"Thanks," he said.

"Welcome." She stuck out her elbow and he slipped his hand through the crook and they headed indoors.

23

---

*A*fter a quick snack they returned to the pool setting up under the poolside arbor to relax. Kyle let Ella think he was still asleep so he could watch her watching him, under the cover of his dark shades. She appeared to like what she saw judging by her thorough perusal. He was enjoying his view just as much. She was stunning, her dark wavy hair tumbling in wild disarray around her shoulders. Her movements graceful, like a dancer.

He didn't think he could ever tire of looking at her. Her smooth satin skin was tanned and flawless, except for that tiny mole on her right breast which was driving him crazy with desire. She filled out her bikini top, dangerously close to spilling out. He wouldn't complain. *Bring it on!*

A guy could dream. She walked to the edge of the pool, long legs, an ass to die for...which was currently on full display since her bikini bottoms had wedged between her cheeks. He felt himself growing hard. He had never wanted a woman as much as he did Ella. He had thought she was the whole package which made her sellout even more disappointing. It reminded him of his own character flaws, and he felt a pang of remorse remembering how empty his marriage had become before Jemma had gotten sick.

Jemma. They had loved each other in the beginning, but the flames had quickly burnt out. Too young, too naïve, too little in common. He carried the guilt knowing his ambitions had taken top priority and his endless hours at work had left his wife alone too many nights. He had given her everything money could buy, exotic trips, expensive cars, diamonds and gold, and at first that had been enough for her.

When she had an affair in their third year of marriage, he shouldered the responsibility for that. She had been lonely, and he hadn't been there for her.

Unfortunately, by this time they had another life to think about besides their own, Finn.

They entered marriage counseling and had been working on their relationship when she was diagnosed with metastatic brain cancer. Devastating news. He had to live with himself knowing he had failed Jemma and their wedding vows. Since her death, he had bedded women, but none had scratched more than the surface. Until now. *Ella.*

And...she despised him.

They had established a routine over the last several days. Ella's bedside manner was professional, guarded and cool, but today he had felt the temperature rise a notch to just above freezing. He felt like she was beginning to thaw. Still somewhat aloof, she was no longer acting like an ice maiden. Progress.

Tomorrow Finn would be coming home. He had always felt overwhelmed by the daunting task of parenting—that had been true even when Jemma was alive. He had never felt competent as a father. Hell, at this point he would gladly settle for adequate. Considering his own childhood, it wasn't surprising he lacked any skills. Multiple nannies, a smothering beauty queen for a mother and a critical and distant father had left him with zero examples on good parenting.

In their marriage, the parenting had been planted squarely on Jemma's shoulders. Gentle, loving and kind... she had been a natural. Kyle's role was to provide, and at that, he was exceptional. But now, left with no choice, he was forced to face his inadequacies. Without his career to hide behind he was terrified. He feared being exposed for the failure he knew he was.

Ella had confessed how much she loved the water and he knew it was true as she jumped back into the pool for more. After she finished a few laps, she pulled her dripping body gracefully out of the pool. He watched as she sauntered leisurely back to the lounger to grab a beach towel. Squeezing off the excess water she briskly towel-dried her hair then bent over to dry off her legs.

"Need some help?" Kyle asked, voice husky.

Looking up, she rolled her eyes and said, "From the one-armed bandit? No thanks, I'm going to let the sunshine and breeze do the rest."

"If you're sure."

"I'm positive."

"I've asked the chef to prepare something special for our dinner tonight. I need to feel human again. I want to actually get dressed and out of my boxers."

She shrugged. "Okay."

"You'll join me then... for dinner?"

He felt slightly unsure of himself which was totally at odds from his usual self-confidence.

"I suppose," she said slowly.

"Good. Thank you."

"Yep."

"You'll have to help me get dressed. Rich will be off for the day."

Her eyes narrowed as she considered his statement. "Okay...I am your nurse, it's not my first rodeo. I think I can manage."

"Just sayin," he replied, giving her a lopsided grin. "After the other day, our conversation, I thought it might be against your rules."

Haughtily she said, "As you so eloquently put it, you're paying me the big bucks and we both have to eat. Why would this evening be any different than the last three?"

"Ella, listen," he began only to be interrupted.

"Dinner between nurse and patient, not to be confused with a date. Got that?"

"Loud and clear. How much longer are you going to punish me?" Kyle said quietly.

"Oh, trust me, I'm not punishing you, this is the new normal."

"I don't believe you."

She shrugged. "Suit yourself, believe what you want to believe. I don't care."

"I think you do."

She scoffed. "Get over yourself."

"What if I beg for your forgiveness?"

"Forgive what? According to you there is nothing to forgive. I should be grateful."

"Ella, come on, we were both heated, I've had time to think about it..."

Ella raised her eyebrows. "And?"

"I didn't mean anything by it. I was trying to do us both a favor."

"Really Kyle? That's what you've "thought about" and that's the best you could come up with?"

"What is that supposed to mean?"

"If I have to spell it out for you, it doesn't amount to much."

"Ella, I'm trying to apologize."

"You're failing miserably."

"You're being unreasonable. Why am I not surprised?" Kyle said unable to maintain his cool.

"Good talk. Now can we move on? I'm bored."

"Ouch!"

24

———————

She glared at him before marching back into the house to get his meds. Maybe she could round up a little laxative to slip into his drink. She smiled wickedly to herself. A girl could fantasize.

When she returned, she slipped a tee shirt over her bikini before giving him his meds. As she bent over to grab his water, she caught him staring the heat of his gaze making her feel hot all over. She was infuriated with herself for becoming aroused. She decidedly ignored his scorching look and the tingling between her legs.

Ella said, "I'm going to shower and get dressed. Are you alright sitting out here until I return?"

"Scared?" he drawled.

She scoffed. "Of what?"

"Of yourself," he replied.

Well damn. "I'll be back. Maybe you can nap."

He held up his book. "I'll read."

Ella strode away knocked off balance once again. Other than her conflicting emotions, this job was so easy she almost felt guilty. Almost...except as she repeatedly reminded herself the reason she was here was because a powerful billionaire used his power and money to coerce her to work for him. *I will happily take full advantage of this situation, thank you very much.*

～

*D*ressing for dinner she looked ruefully at the large pile of discarded clothing laying on her bed. She'd finally settled on a short-flowered sundress with spaghetti straps, belted at the waist with a loose flirty skirt. The soft silky material was sexy and flattering. Her legs were bare, and she wore a pair of slip-on black patent-leather flat-heeled sandals. She had even painted her toenails a bright fire engine red. As she was applying matching red lipstick there was a knock at the door.

"Come in."

Richard stood at the door holding a small brightly wrapped gift box.

Her eyes went round. "For me?"

"Yes. Kyle wanted me to deliver this to you before dinner."

"What for?" she wondered aloud.

"Mr. Bennett doesn't need any reason."

"Thank you for the delivery."

"You are most welcome. I'm leaving for the night. Enjoy your meal."

"I'm sure I will. Night."

Ella quickly ripped the paper from around the fancy box. The lid had gilded lettering *Clive Christian Imperial No. 1 Majesty*. Opening the lid of the walnut box, she saw a small bottle nestled in red velvet, that looked like a mini decanter of the finest crystal. She knew she wasn't looking at your run-of-the-mill department store perfume. She would google it later. On second thought, maybe she didn't want to know.

She sniffed first then dabbed the perfume behind each ear. She could smell sandalwood and musk with hints of bergamot and a nuance of something sweet and citrusy. She couldn't deny that she had never smelled a perfume this divine.

Curiosity aroused, she decided to google it after all. She stared at her phone in disbelief and sank down onto the chair in front of the vanity table, thunderstruck. Twelve thousand seven hundred twenty-one dollars and eighty-nine cents an ounce! She felt like gagging. That was over two months of her wages. She marched out the door, fuming.

She knocked, then entered Kyles room. He sat on a chair waiting for her to help him finish getting dressed. His eyes flashed when he saw her.

"Ella."

Heart thundering, she thrust the wooden box toward him and said, "What the hell is this?"

"An apology gift?" he said tentatively.

"I don't need a twelve-thousand-dollar bottle of perfume! That's almost enough to pay off my student loans! What's wrong with you?"

"I thought you would like it."

"Of course I 'like' it. That's not the point."

"What *is* the point?" he asked, seeming genuinely confused.

"The point is you are trying to buy your way out of your back-stabbing betrayal! You ruined my reputation at work, jeopardized my career, strong-armed me into complying with your wishes even though I had clearly said *no*, and now you are trying to fix it with a twelve-thousand-dollar band-aid."

Kyle held out his hand for the perfume and she snatched it back. "Oh no you don't, I'm keeping it!"

His mouth hung open, now utterly lost. "You're keeping it?"

"Yes, it's been opened. You can't return it now."

"And you *like* it," he said slowly, trying to contain a grin.

"Yes, and you deserve to be out the twelve-grand on principle."

"Can I put some pants on now? I'm feeling pretty vulnerable."

She bit her lip on a smile. "Sure. Where are they?"

"On the hanger over by the closet."

Kneeling down in front of him, she held the waist band so he could slip his legs into the dark navy dress slacks. "Stand up, let me button you up." When her knuckles brushed against his taut abdomen he sucked in a breath. She looked up at him through her lashes.

"Here you hold the top while I tug on the zipper."

He touched her silver hooped earring before brushing his fingers through her hair, "I'm glad you wore your hair down."

"Um okay, there you go. Now where's your shirt?" He nodded toward the closet door.

"That would be the white linen dress shirt with a thousand buttons? Buttons? Are you serious?"

"Yes, I wanted to look good for you. Plus, I need to feel a sense of normalcy. Humor me."

She held out the short-sleeved linen dress shirt so he could slip his injured arm through first. Her fingers fumbled on the top button as she brushed against his chest hair. Soft and sexy as hell, the heat under her hands as she looped the buttons branded her.

He leaned down to sniff at her hair. "It was worth every cent."

"Don't push your luck," she said through gritted teeth, finishing with the last button.

"We don't want to keep the chef waiting. He can be quite the diva."

"Ready when you are."

He sat back down on the edge of the bed to slip on his brown Italian leather loafers.

"Here let me help you with your sling," she said, wrapping it around his neck and sliding his arm through. She grabbed the cane propped against his bed and handed it to him. He grimaced slightly as he took the first step. He moved cautiously and very slowly, reminding her of how far he still had to go. Ella walked closely beside him as they made their way to the formal dining room.

25

The polished mahogany table with centerpieces of small potted greenery seemed to glow from the long-tapered candles. A fire blazed in the two-way fireplace at the far end of the room, creating a cozy elegance. The crystal chandelier hung centered over the table which was set for two but could probably seat twelve. Soft instrumental jazz streamed through the sound system.

A waiter in a black and white uniform stood next to the table awaiting their arrival. He pulled out a white cloth chair for Ella, while Kyle seated himself next to her at the head of the table.

"Wine, sir?"

"Yes." Raising his eyebrows at Ella he said, "If my nurse says it's all right for me to imbibe."

"One glass shouldn't kill you."

"One glass it is. Have the chef select whatever compliments the meal."

"I'll be right back with that Mr. Bennett."

Ella looked around. "This is so beautiful. Breathtakingly so. I honestly feel like I'm in a fairy tale."

"Can I be your prince?"

The corner of her mouth quirked up. "More like Lord Voldemort."

He flinched. "Thanks a lot."

Suppressing a smile, she said, "You're welcome."

The waiter appeared with the wine and poured them each a glass of the amber liquid. "Sauvignon Blanc to go with your snapper entree tonight, sir."

"Beautiful," he said approving of the selection.

"Your appetizers will be out shortly. I'll bring the bread and dipping oil."

"Thank you."

"Mm delicious, it has a hint of lime zest that balances well with the fruitiness," Ella said appreciatively.

"I agree, I see you have a discerning palate."

"A nice way of saying I'm a certified wino."

He chuckled. "Help yourself. I have a whole wine cellar at your disposal."

"Don't tell me that I'll be sipping poolside every day. I'll admit I'm feeling a bit overwhelmed by all this." She swept her hand gesturing at their opulent surroundings. "I just can't wrap my mind around living like this. I'm sorry to go on like this... I know you grew up this way so its normal for you."

"Yes, but it means nothing."

"Easy to say when you have it all."

"I suppose you're right. I can't help where I came from. I hardly got to choose my parents."

"Luck of the draw."

"Some might call it luck, and some might call it a curse."

"How so?" Ella had glimpsed a haunted look cross his face before it was quickly veiled, leaving her to wonder if she'd imagined it.

"It can be lonely. For instance, does one like me for who I am or for what I can do for them? Can they see beyond my wealth? Because power is an illusion anyway and money is really paper and commodities. It's strange because it really doesn't exist except in our social construct."

"And yet here we are, drinking fine wine and about to consume a meal prepared by your personal chef."

"I'm not going to apologize for my good fortune."

Without thinking, Ella reached for his hand and clasped it. "I don't expect you to, I didn't mean that to sound the way it came off, all judgy. I know you come from a long line of philanthropists."

"Don't get me wrong, I like my toys and I enjoy the finer things in life, but to me they have no meaning beyond their creature comforts. As the saying goes, you can't buy love or happiness and I'm certainly proof of that."

"You can't buy happiness, but it sure helps."

"And you? Are you able to see beyond the billionaire trappings?"

"You know you can't have it both ways. Buying expensive flowers, perfume, trying to buy *me*, then complaining that people only want what they can get from you."

"Touché. But was I wrong about you?"

"In what way?"

"I thought you were different. I didn't take you for being materialistic."

"I'm not."

"How can you say that when you demanded such a high price for your services? I must admit that I was disappointed. I'm usually a pretty good judge of character."

"Excuse me, but what did you expect me to do? You manipulated and coerced me into accepting a job I didn't want. Of course, you're going to pay." She was a little taken aback by the hurt in his eyes.

The wine, along with the atmosphere and his vulnerability were softening her edges... *careful Ella.*

"Maybe I'm being obtuse, but I still don't understand why you're so upset. I'm paying you a very generous salary and you get to go back to your old job."

"Just when I was softening you have to open your mouth and say something idiotic," she said. "Perhaps we should change the subject."

"Fine."

The silence was deafening, neither wanting to be the first to give in. Finally, Kyle caved. "Tell me about your life outside of the hospital," he said.

"It's pretty simple, for someone like you probably boring."

"I doubt that." He stared at her intently, his eyes felt like they were seeing into her soul.

"Really, it's true... work, water sports, occasional dinner with friends."

"You said your parents were both gone?"

"Yes, my biological and my adopted parents have all passed."

"I'm sorry. I do remember you telling me that. I apologize if I ask you to repeat anything. I was pretty out of it for a while."

The waiter surreptitiously appeared, placing a small dish with a variety of olives next to the bread-basket with a warm baguette nestled inside the cloth. He poured a generous portion of olive oil onto a small plate and added ground pepper and freshly grated parmesan cheese for dipping. "I'll be back with your first course and salads."

"Thank you."

They both reached for the bread at the same time, their hands brushing. Kyle's eyes burned with intensity, "You do realize that you are an exquisite creature, don't you? How could you not?"

"I don't know how to answer that."

Kyle devoured her with his eyes. As if hypnotized, she couldn't look away. Ella couldn't decide what made him sexier, his chiseled features, his dark designer stubble, or was it his sinfully blue eyes and thick dark lashes? She was caught in his web, *mesmerized*. He was the sexiest man she had ever laid eyes on. And damn it to hell... she wanted him.

26

*K*yle could see his own desire reflected in her expression. Her eyes big pools of shimmering green, her lips plump and sumptuous...*inviting him*. Damn his body! His fractured ribs, his broken arm, not to mention his fucked up leg, were major barriers to him taking what he wanted. His lack of control wasn't something he was used to or patient about. He was used to getting what he wanted, when he wanted it—instant gratification.

"Why do you have to be so damned sexy?" he said, voice low and gruff.

"Kyle, stop. The rules," Ella said in a whisper.

"The rules suck."

"Kyle..."

"You do know what I think of your rules don't you?" He grabbed her hand his thumb rubbing her inner wrist. "I'd like to shove everything off this table and take you right here and now."

She laughed at that, breaking the sexual tension. "Your waiter would really enjoy walking in on that, I'm sure."

He grinned. "He'd be discreet."

Their exchange was interrupted by the salad and first course, which was a welcome distraction. "You're getting quite good with that left hand of yours," Ella commented.

"Desperate times, desperate measures."

"I'm betting there isn't anything you can't do if you put your mind to it."

His lip quirked. "Arts and crafts?"

She choked on her wine, snorting with glee at the image of Kyle sitting over a needlepoint loom. "That image slays me," she said.

"As it should."

"What other hobbies does the mysterious Kyle Bennett do in his free time?"

"I have my pilot license and I own a small Cessna. My father's company also has a small private jet at our family's disposal. I love sailing, taking my boat out. I'm trained classically in piano."

"That sounds like a billionaires guide to fun," she said withdrawing her hand from his caress.

"I can travel 1200 miles in two hours just in my small Cessna. Opens up your options for date night."

"I'd say. Do you do sports?"

"I played baseball in college, almost went pro."

Ella sipped her wine, getting a nice little buzz. She felt more relaxed than she had since she had arrived. "What stopped you?"

"Dear old dad."

"That sucks. I'd have thought he'd have been proud to have a son so accomplished."

"He thought it was foolish. He wanted me to follow in his footsteps and take over the family business. I went to law school instead... my other dream and a little less risky. My younger brother opted out as well. Sis too. In my father's opinion he got screwed by all three of his offspring. Except now the company retains my legal services, so in the end I still work for him."

"I can totally see you as a baseball hero. Women throwing themselves at your feet. What do your sister and brother do besides travel?"

"Griffin, he's the youngest, is a playboy, lives off the family fortune. Hell of a golfer, was on the pro-circuit for a while, but that took too much of a commitment. Faye same, she flits around the world, a free spirit, and she is actually a very talented artist with an artist's soul to go with it. But you've met her, I'm sure that was obvious."

Their entree arrived and since it was fish Kyle easily tackled it without any help from Ella. "This is delicious," she said.

"I have an amazing chef. Speak of the devil."

"*Bonjour*, Mr. Bennett. *Mademoiselle*," he said bowing slightly as he held out his hand to Ella. She grasped it and he placed a kiss on the back of her hand. "How are you enjoying your dinner this evening?"

"Oh my God! Beyond delectable, really. One of the best meals in my entire life," Ella said sincerely.

"You are too kind. I will leave you to it."

"Thanks, Jacques," Kyle said.

"My pleasure. If you're ready we'll bring out your dessert, *crème brûlée.*"

Ella putting her hands on her stomach said, "Oh no, my favorite."

"This is a problem?" Jacques asked confused.

"Yes, because I'm ready to explode. I don't know where I'll put it."

He smiled. "Maybe you could save it for later, *penses-tu?*"

"I'm going to have to take up French if I hang around Mr. Bennett much longer," she said giggling.

"You are enchanting. Please, *bon appétit.*"

"Now that I understand, thank you so much."

"I think you have another conquest," Kyle said after the chef departed.

"He's just a flirt."

"I've entertained women here before and have never seen that kind of reaction. Jacques is usually a pretty cool character."

Flustered Ella quickly changed the subject. "Back to our previous conversation, you and baseball and career choices, and siblings."

"Enough about me and my fucked-up family. Will you teach me to paddle board after this broken body heals?" Kyle asked.

"You remembered," she said.

"Are you kidding me? I couldn't get the visual out of my brain. It gave me something to fantasize about while I was confined to my hospital bed. You in a bikini, standing on a board, smokin' hot!"

Her eyes lit up at the compliment. "I'd be happy to teach you."

"Deal. This near-death experience has given me a new perspective... or maybe just reminded me that there are other things besides work. Finn needs more of his dad even if I suck at it."

"I'm sure you don't suck as bad as you think you do. It's obvious that Finn adores you. Kids just need to know they're loved. And love is a verb. That's all I have to say."

"Jemma, his mother, was the best mom. She was straight-out-of-a-sappy-movie kind of mom. He was her world. She blossomed after Finn was born. Unfortunately, I wilted."

"It's daunting that's for sure."

Kyle stifled a yawn and said, "I'm embarrassed to say I'm exhausted."

"I'm not surprised. Get it through your head this is a marathon not a sprint. You almost died. Most of your external bruises have healed but you're still healing on the inside," Ella said.

The waiter entered with their dessert and Kyle asked for it to be wrapped for them to take back to their rooms. Kyle had difficulty standing after sitting for so long. He was sure Ella could tell he was in quite a bit of pain.

"I'm sorry I should have reminded you to stand up once in a while," she said confirming her watchful eye.

"I'm a big boy Ella, that's not your job."

"It kinda is," she muttered.

Returning with the packaged *crème brulée*, the waiter handed it to Ella. "Thank you so much. Everything was perfect," Ella said.

"You're welcome. I will see you soon, I am sure."

"Night."

Kyle was wincing in pain as he took his first steps. "I would almost welcome a wheelchair."

"As painful as the exercise is, you need it. Let's go."

"There's that sadistic nurse I've come to know."

"She's baacckk!" Ella joked.

"Tomorrow is a big day; my son arrives home."

"I know. I can't wait to see him."

"He's pretty damn cute, equally matched by his precociousness. I can't even take care of my fucking self; how the hell am I going to be able to keep a six-year-old entertained?"

"I can help. I'm feeling pretty useless most of the time. I'll feel less guilty, like you're getting your money's worth."

"A surrogate nanny?"

"Kinda sorta," she said smiling.

She had rested her hand on his lower back as guided support as he hobbled along, his limp much more pronounced than it had been on their way to dinner. "We'll get you tucked into your comfy bed, and I'll tell you a bedtime story while we eat our dessert."

"What kind of story? Little Engine That Could?"

She hooted with laughter. "And you'd be referring to what exactly?"

"As if you didn't know."

27

Kyle let out a sigh of relief when they finally reached his quarters. He sat on the bed reclining his upper body.

"Here let me get your shoes," Ella said, pulling off his loafers one at a time. She sat next to him in order to reach the buttons of his shirt. Kyle thought he would lose his mind as her fingers feathered against his skin, arousing him further. He tried to reach for her, but she stilled his hand and said, "No."

Dropping his hand, he watched her with an internal heat ready to combust. He loved the smell of her... musky... sexy, her soft hands, her playfulness, her confidence. She was wild, exotic, a woman comfortable in her own skin. Her hair, an unruly mass of cascading loose thick waves, made him fantasize of burying his fingers there while ravaging her mouth. As she unzipped his pants and tugged them off, he had to keep reminding himself that this was Ella the nurse not Ella the woman.

With difficulty, Kyle ignored his erection straining against the fabric of his underwear. The intimacy of the moment was driving him insane. He wanted her to kiss and lick her way down his body, starting with his lips and slowly continuing the whole way down until she reached his cock.

As if Ella read his mind, she licked her lips and said, "Um, maybe I should leave."

"Ella, you're driving me crazy. I want you under me, on top of me, behind me, in front of me, legs wrapped around my neck, limbs tangled."

Ella blushed, biting down hard on her lip. When their eyes locked, molten fire met unapologetic carnal lust.

Breathlessly Ella said, "Kyle I..."

"Ella, don't think, feel."

"I have to think!"

"Why? We're two consensual adults. Ella, I have to have you."

Those were exactly the wrong words because it looked like she'd been hit with a bucket of ice-cold water. She stiffened and tried to put distance between them. He grabbed her hand to stop her.

"No," she said forcefully. Kyle held her wrist firmly as she tried to pull away.

"You know that's where we're heading. Make no mistake, before this is all said and done, I'm going to feel your naked body writhing underneath mine and you're going to be begging me for it." He trailed his hand up her arm and used his fingers to grab her chin, forcing her to look at him. Her eyes glittered like faceted gems.

"A timely reminder that what Kyle Bennett wants he always gets," she said bitterly. "I may be your object of desire at the moment but are you so certain that I'll fall into bed simply because you snap your perfectly-manicured fingers?"

He didn't bother to respond. The moment had passed and he'd blown it.

"I'm going to bed. Thanks for dinner."

His voice still husky with desire he said, "I'll be here if you change your mind."

"Not going to happen."

"You never know."

"Give it up and get some rest. Oh! Your pain meds. Sorry, I forgot." She went into his bathroom to retrieve them.

Handing him a glass of water she shook out the pills into his open palm. "Goodnight Kyle."

"Goodnight Elle."

"See you in the morning. What time are they bringing Finn home?"

"Around ten."

28

He was casting a spell and it was working. She had to force herself to remember who she was dealing with, but that voice of reason became weaker by the minute. She left his room like the devil was at her heels.

The worst part of it was that as confident as he talked, there was a quality of loneliness that tugged at her heartstrings. He'd probably never admit it, but she could see it in his eyes. He wanted her, yes, but she also thought he needed to feel connected and alive instead of like an isolated invalid. She had to steel herself from giving in. God this man was complicated! How could he look so lost and vulnerable and so commanding at the same time? *Rules! Work only... remember Ella?*

She was restless and tempted to do some laps in the indoor pool but felt too full after the food and wine. She'd watch a little TV and hopefully settle down enough to sleep. *Geesh,* she was going to have to make an effort to leave the house occasionally. She felt like she was getting sucked into the Kyle vortex. What had happened to her safe boring life from a month ago? That restless itch she'd been aware of since she met Kyle, rather than diminishing, was full on...and demanding to be scratched.

She closed her bedroom door and leaned against it. Daisy greeted her, rubbing her whiskers against Ella's bare legs.

"What am I going to do? It's no fair." She took off her earrings as she slowly walked to the dresser. Looking at her reflection she thought she looked freshly fucked. Flushed cheeks, overly bright lustful eyes, wild hair... exotic almost. She needed to tread very carefully, or she'd regret it. Being seduced by a billionaire was ridiculously impossible unless one wanted to be. And she most certainly did not. *Liar!*

29

_K_yle was in his office reading _The New York Times_ online when he heard a loud commotion coming down the hall in the form of a six-year-old ball of energy...close on his heels was Faye.

"Finn slow down! Remember you have to be careful not to roughhouse with your dad."

"I know. Daddy!" Finn ran towards his father at full speed skidding to a stop when he reached Kyle's side.

"Hey buddy!" Kyle found himself fighting back emotion. "I've missed you so much."

"Me too. Grandma wouldn't let me come back to the hospital to see you again," he said.

"I know. Hospitals aren't for kids, but we did FaceTime."

Kyle reached out his good arm and held on to his son's hand. "Can I have a hug?"

"Faye said not to hug ya account of your ribs."

"It's okay as long as you don't squeeze too tight," Kyle said. He gathered him in for a hug and felt Finn melt into his arms.

Finn's eyes suddenly welled with tears. "Dad, I was scared."

"I know buddy, but everything is going to be all right. Your dad is going to be as good as new."

"Promise?"

"I promise." Kyle wiped a tear from Finn's cheek, then kissed the top of his head.

Kyle's voice was thick with emotion as he changed the subject. "What did you and your grandparents do for fun?"

"Lots of stuff."

"Like what?"

"Zoo, water park, games."

"A man of few words," Kyle said smiling.

Winking, Faye piped in, "You didn't tell him the biggest news of all!"

"What news?"

"Grandpa says he will buy me a puppy!"

Kyle tried to hide his irritation. This was not a new topic of conversation; they had discussed this on many occasions. "I thought we'd already talked about this Finn. I said it's not a good time for a puppy."

"Please Dad! I *need* a puppy."

"Finn," he said in a voice that brooked no argument.

"But Grandpa said..."

"Knock knock, am I interrupting?" Ella said entering the den.

"The more the merrier," Faye said warmly. Kyle and

Ella exchanged an intimate look which did not go unnoticed by Faye.

"Finn, remember my nurse, Ella?"

Finn looked up shyly at Ella. "Yes. You don't look like a nurse anymore."

Ella squatted down to be eye level with Finn. "Oh? And just what does a nurse look like?"

"Not like you," he replied. "You look like a princess."

Ella's eyes widened as she unconsciously put her hand against her heart. "That's the nicest thing anyone's ever said to me."

He grinned displaying the gap where his two front teeth had once been. "It's true, just like Belle from Beauty and the Beast."

Ella laughed delightedly. "I'll have to find a beast I guess," she said, unintentionally glancing sideways at Kyle.

"Daddy did you ask her?"

"Ask her what?" Kyle said.

"If Ella can be my new nanny."

Ella chuckled causing Finn to look a bit crestfallen.

"I'm not your forever nanny but I am your daddy's nurse and I'll be around to help out until your new nanny comes. Maybe we can be friends. How would you like that?"

He nodded, then impulsively grabbed Ella's hand and tugged on it as he tried to pull her along behind him. "I'm going to show her my room, come on Ella, follow me."

"Why don't we do that later?" Faye said.

"Nooo! Please, I want to show her something," he said.

"Okay but make it quick."

He flashed his toothless grin that melted everyone's heart every-single-time. "Come on Ella. Let's go."

---

30

*F*inn chose the spiral staircase over the elevator, and they practically jogged to the second floor. They made their way to the end of the corridor, turned right and then entered a room that could best be described as every kid's fantasy.

King sized bed with a colorful canopy and sheer multicolored panels draped around the perimeter, making it seem like a secret meeting place...sparking one's imagination. A playhouse the size of most children's bedrooms sat in the far west corner, next to a ten-foot bay window complete with the requisite cushioned window seat.

If she didn't know better, she would have sworn she had stepped into a toy store; there were shelves and toy boxes filled to the brim. An oil portrait of a beautiful young woman, holding Finn as a toddler, was unquestionably Finn's mother. Ella couldn't stop herself from staring.

"That's my mom," he said, matter-of-factly.

"I gathered. She's very beautiful. She's the one who looks like a princess," Ella said.

They both stood side-by-side continuing to study the painting together. "I'm afraid I'm going to forget her," he said his bottom lip quivering.

"You'll never forget her because she is always with you. She lives right here," she said touching his bony chest, "in your heart Finn; you will never lose that."

"I can't remember her voice, and grandma and dad won't let me watch any of the videos we have of her," he said.

"Maybe it's too hard for them right now. But when the time is right for them, they will. I think your dad knows what's best."

"I guess."

Changing the subject Ella said, "Anything else you want to show me?"

Running toward a display case he said excitedly, *"This!"*

Ella's eyes widened at the exhibition of model boats and airplanes. "Wow Finn, that is some collection you have," she said.

"I love boats and planes. This one is my favorite," he said opening the glass doors and reaching for a sailboat. He handed it to Ella, who studied the exquisite craftmanship. It was quite beautifully detailed.

"It's wonderful, Finn," she said.

"I'm not really allowed to play with them being as they're so expensive and breakable, but if I'm real careful I can hold them," he said proudly. "My dad has a big boat. Maybe we can take you sometime when he is all better."

"I'd love that." Looking at his collection she spied one and pulled it down from the shelf. "Now this one looks like a fancy yacht. And this one looks like a Viking vessel."

"Yep. Okay, let's go," he said, tearing ahead out of the room only to turn back and say, "Sorry."

"No need to apologize, you're excited that your dad's home I get it," Ella said, carefully placing the novelties back in the case. "Race you to the stairs!" She and Finn raced to the staircase.

His cheeks were flushed and he crowed, "I won!"

"You rascal, you left me in a cloud of dust."

She was already half in love with this little person. Why couldn't he have been an obnoxious brat. It sure would have made things easier on her heart strings.

When they made it back to the den, Faye and Kyle were in deep conversation but stopped abruptly when they spied Ella and Finn.

Kyle cocked an eyebrow and said, "Everything all right?"

"Yes, of course, why do you ask?"

"You looked deep in thought."

"Finn just showed me up in a race. I'll have to get back out on the trails."

"Did he now? That's my boy." Finn beamed at his dad's compliment.

"Listen, I was thinking about getting out of the house for a little while. Since Faye and Finn are here it's probably a good time to do that," Ella announced.

"Of course," Kyle said his frown at odds with his endorsement.

"I won't be gone long. Two hours at the most."

Faye grinned at Ella. "Don't let my brother bully you. He's used to getting his way. I'll stay until you get back. I don't have anything else to do."

"Thanks Faye, see you."

As Ella walked out, she smiled as she heard Finn say demandingly, "Why can't I have a puppy? Please!" She didn't hear Kyle's response. Looks like his child was growing up to be equally determined as he. *Ha!*

——————

$\mathcal{T}$he days flew by, and Ella realized she'd already been there two weeks. The three of them had settled into a very comfortable routine. They breakfasted together, then while Kyle worked with his physical therapist, Ella dropped Finn off at his private school; she had a couple of hours to herself before returning to pick him up. Kyle was growing stronger every day and the physical therapist was impressed with his progress. Stubbornness had its advantages.

Ella realized she was as attached to Finn as he was to her. Last night he had had another nightmare, his screams waking her out of a sound sleep. She had run to his bedroom and crawled into the bed, holding him tightly against her while his little body quaked with tremors and he wailed, "Mama, mama."

Kyle had shown up several minutes later and before joining them had stood for a long beat watching Ella rocking Finn in her arms. Sandwiching Finn between them, the three had ridden it out together, letting the healing tears flow, both offering soothing words of comfort until he cried himself back to sleep.

As they lay quietly listening to Finn's steady breath, the air suddenly became charged. Kyle had reached over the sleeping child and tucked Ella's hair behind her ear, then ran his thumb over her lips. He had continued his exquisite torture by brushing the backs of his fingers over her shoulder then tracing her collar bone. She'd been painfully aware of her nipples visibly erect through the skimpy fabric of the aqua nightie he had bought her. She'd felt an unbearable longing.

Ella whispered that she was going to sleep there the rest of the night and Kyle nodded. Silently getting off the bed, he leaned down and gently brushed his lips across hers before heading to his own room.

This morning at breakfast there had been an obvious warmth and greater intimacy between them. She knew they had both felt it. Throughout breakfast even with Finn's steady chatter, she could feel Kyle's gaze. Each time their eyes met the air practically crackled.

Kyle had decided that he felt strong enough to ease back into working a few hours a day from home. Ella had tried talking him out of it, but she knew it would sort itself out. He would find out soon enough what his body was up for. Pete Sullivan, his college friend and business partner, was coming over this afternoon to bring him up to date on their current caseload and give him the lowdown on what he had missed.

Having volunteered to take Finn for the afternoon she dressed for their outing while Richard helped Finn get ready. She slung her bag over one shoulder and went in search of them. She found Finn in Kyle's office petting Daisy, who now had the run of the house. He loved animals and was borderline obsessing about a dog. His grandpa had sure put gasoline to that fire. Personally, Ella thought it was a great idea, but so far had kept that opinion to herself.

"Ready Freddy?"

"Yep. Bye Daisy." He dashed to the door only to remember he had forgotten something and raced back to his father. Giving him a hug, he said, "Bye Dad."

Kyle's eyes crinkled as he laughed and said, "So now I'm just an afterthought. I get it."

He was so dang beautiful when he smiled that Ella's breath caught in her throat. His bruising was gone and the hours by the pool had restored his gorgeous tan, and he no longer wore that pained expression. It was miraculous just how far he'd come.

"I'm just the flavor of the day because I'm getting him out," Ella said reassuringly.

He winked and said, "I don't blame him a bit. Have fun and thanks for getting him out of the house for a few hours. You're sure you don't want to use my driver?"

"No way Dad! I want to ride in Ella's jeep. She's going to take the top off."

"He's right. We're good. We'll take the jeep. I've already put his booster seat in the back. Finn and I could use the open air. Thanks though."

He looked as if he wanted to say more but changed

his mind. "Hurry back." His warm gaze met hers, conveying a depth of meaning to that simple statement.

Tamping down the butterflies in her stomach, she said, "Yes, we'll be back in a couple of hours."

32

Kyle watched as Ella took Finn's hand in hers and felt an ache in his chest. Was he setting his son up for another heartbreak? Who was he kidding, more to the question, was he setting himself up as well? He liked Ella... a whole lot. She filled the house with joy. It had been so dark and gloomy after Jemma had died, and in the months preceding her death. Ella was bringing life and laughter here again, not to mention his permanent hard-on which he was beginning to doubt would ever be satisfied. *There should be a law against her wearing shorts. Damn she has the best legs I've ever laid eyes on.*

Rich appeared with Pete by his side.

"Hey pardner, how's my gimpy friend?" Pete said, his humor missing its mark.

"Where the hell have you been?" Kyle growled.

"I felt like it was best to stay away, or you'd be picking my brain and not following docs orders."

Kyle pinned his partner with a hard stare then shrugged. "Great excuse... but I suppose you were right. A phone call or two would have been nice, but what do I know."

"Not much," he said. "You're looking pretty good, no permanent scars on that perfect face of yours. Some guys have all the luck."

"I'd hardly call a near-fatal accident luck."

"You always manage to come out of everything smelling like a rose."

Kyle let it slide since he knew his college friend meant no harm. He had always been a smartass and slightly competitive. They had been roomies their freshman year of college, both intent on careers in law. They had attended the same law school and after passing the bar, Kyle on his first attempt, Pete on his third, had opened a practice together.

They currently had five attorneys working for them, a paralegal and two legal secretaries as well as Elenore, their office manager and assistant. Their firm practiced in several areas, mainly real estate, tax law, some divorce cases, and environmental litigation, which happened to be the area of law that Kyle was most passionate about.

"Pull up a chair."

Taking a seat Pete said, "Who was that babe walking out with Finn? I'd like a little piece of that action."

"Hands off. That's Ella, my live-in nurse."

Pete snickered. "Yeah right. Nurse by day, mistress by night."

Kyle glared at his friend. "Shut the fuck up, you have no idea what you're talking about."

"Hit a nerve, did I? I guess that means she's available then?"

"Keep your hands off."

"So, I was right the first time. Hey, no harm no foul, I'm jealous, she is damn fine! I'd be doing her too."

"I'm going to say it one more time so it can penetrate that thick skull of yours, Ella is off limits. You got that? You will talk about her with respect and leave your dick at home when you're around her. Understand? There is nothing going on. She's my nurse and she's helping out with Finn. End of story."

Pete held up his hands in mock surrender. "Okay already, got it. No need to get churlish."

"Can we change the subject? Let's get back to our main objective."

"I know you were told about the package delivery, turned out to be baking powder."

Kyle's brows drew together. "Any ideas?"

"None. It could be any number of disgruntled defendants we've prosecuted. Or even our own clients. We haven't won them all."

"Most," Kyle countered.

Sarcastically Pete replied, "Of course, we're the best. I've been thinking about it, first we've got that environmental group Earth's Saviors breathing down our necks over your father's development site where that old factory was torn down. The zoning commission is giving the developers all kinds of grief as well. Then to make matters worse, the neighborhood watch dogs got in on the act, clamoring about having to hold their noses before entering their gated community. Boy you rich folk sure don't want to share do ya?"

Kyle lifted an eyebrow, studying his friend. Something was off about Pete today. He couldn't put his finger on it but there was something...

"Everything all right with you?" Kyle asked.

Pete's jaw tightened. "Why wouldn't it be?"

"Just asking. You seem even darker than usual."

"I guess it's been a little rough without you at the helm this last month."

"I'm sure. I really appreciate you carrying the load. I'll make it up to you. You can take a long exotic vacation when I get back. On the firm's dime. Until then..."

"Yeah, let's get to it."

Kyle scrubbed his jaw. "I don't get it. Somethings not right about this. It's a solid plan, a win-win for everybody. An abandoned eyesore will be developed, and it will provide affordable housing for thirty plus families, effectively killing two birds with one stone," Kyle said.

"You're preaching to the choir. Damn it's good to have you back my friend. I've missed having you to bounce things off of. The class-action suit is moving forward and I'm really out of my element on that one. That's your specialty and I don't mind copping to it."

"Okay we'll start there, fill me in."

"Barclay Technology is trying to buy their way out of it. They claim that they didn't know that the chemicals they dumped into the ground were dangerous which is complete and utter bullshit! We contend that they lied to government regulators and knew all along what they were dumping," Pete said. "They're trying to intimidate the plaintiffs. Offering them settlements far below what they'd have to pay if they lost in court."

"Are they getting to them?"

"A few are waffling."

"All about greed. They just wanted to save money rather than do the right thing and put the safety of the environment and the citizens above their bottom line," Kyle said thoroughly disgusted. "When are these company heads going to realize that they have to live on this planet too? Their kids and grandkids are inheriting this mess. You can't eat or drink the all-mighty dollar."

"Yeah, but they can find a way to turn a profit if all the water is undrinkable, then they can purify and bottle it so only the moneyed can afford to drink," Pete chimed in equally disturbed. "In the meantime, the company is asking the judge to dismiss the lawsuit."

"On what grounds?"

"They claim we haven't shown irreparable harm."

"Jesus, what's it going to take?"

"I have a bad feeling about this one Kyle. They have the ear of some powerful local officials. They don't want the company pulling up stakes and moving elsewhere. Even at the expense of safe drinking water."

"That's where I'll start. I'll begin by reaching out to our clients and see if I can calm them down. What else?"

"My tires were slashed the other night and one of the junior partners had his house burglarized. Nothing taken just ransacked. Could be unrelated."

"Jesus, why didn't you tell me?"

"I'm telling you now. You can see why I'm a bit rattled."

"Man, I'm sorry."

"Yeah well, I'm just glad you're getting back into it.

"I am glad to be back to the land of the living. For a while I wasn't sure I'd ever get back to work."

"Dude, I'm sorry I've been MIA. After Brooke left last year, I kind of lost my head for a while, then your accident... but I'm back in the game," he grinned.

"Glad to hear it."

Pete opened his brief case and unloaded a stack of files plopping them down in front of Kyle. "Careful what ya wish for."

"Why don't you come back this Friday. After a short meeting then we can have a little social time."

"Sounds good to me. Will your *nurse,*" Pete mimicked quotation marks, "be joining us for the social hour?" he asked slyly.

"You don't give up do you? Yes, more than likely. I'll warn her ahead of time since I can't count on you to behave."

"Whatever became of the wild-ass ladies' man I used to know?"

"He grew up," Kyle said, chuckling.

"Damn shame. It's lonely here at the bottom. See ya Friday."

"Thanks Pete. You're a good friend. I appreciate all that you've been carrying."

"We're in this together. Always have been chief." He saluted then left Kyle sifting through the files, already engrossed in work.

33

*E*lla needed to pick up a few basic toiletries, so they stopped at a Family Dollar on their way home from the park. As she and Finn perused the aisle full of tacky cheap toys, she found herself thinking that Kyle had probably never stepped foot in a dollar store his entire life, therefore neither had Finn.

"This is the greatest!" Finn exclaimed; eyes wide as he touched every bright object on the toy shelves.

"Pick out what you want, my treat."

"Really? Can I have these swimming goggles and another noodle? Mine's old and disgusting."

"Sure. Why don't we get this kick ball and we can play in the backyard when we get home?"

"Ella?"

"Yes?"

He held up a tennis ball. "Can I get this ball for my puppy?"

Her brow furrowed. "But you don't have a puppy."

"Yet," he corrected grinning from ear to ear.

"You are something else, do you know that?"

"Is that a yes?"

"It's a yes. Just don't tell your dad it's for your dog or I'll have some splainin' to do," she said.

"I won't. I'll bet they have dog bowls here," he said jumping up and down excitedly.

"Finn, no. When the time comes, we'll go to a pet store, they'll have more to choose from. Okay?" She hated to see his little face wrinkle in disappointment. "We can buy a basket that you can put that ball in though. You can keep adding to the collection and by the time you get your pup, he'll have lots of toys. A tennis ball is a tennis ball, but you'll want to get quality toys that are safe for your buddy. You'll find those at pet stores. Do you have a name picked out?"

"I've been thinking. I like the name Charlie if it's a boy and Lucy for a girl."

"Those are great names, now we just have to work on your dad."

Finn was bouncing the plastic ball against the floor his face scrunched up in concentration. "Does this mean you'll help me talk dad into it?"

"I don't want to get your hopes up any higher, but I'll work on him."

"Cool! Thanks Ella." He dropped the ball and threw his arms around her waist hugging her tight.

She ruffled his hair and squeezed back. "Let's pay for our booty and get home. Your dad will be wondering where we are."

A man approached holding the bright orange ball Finn had been playing with. "Lose something kiddo?"

Ella looked on as Finn nodded his head reaching his arms out for the ball. The stranger had dark hair and a full dark beard, and he gave Ella the creeps. She felt a shiver run down her spine when his smile didn't quite reach his piercing cold eyes. And there was something about him that niggled the back of her mind, like she should know him or had seen him somewhere before. He squatted down to be at eye level with Finn. "I heard you say you were getting a dog."

Finn's whole face lit up, bashfulness evaporating as he enthusiastically replied, "Yes, if me and Ella can talk my dad into it."

"Ella, beautiful name for a beautiful woman," he said looking up at her.

Nervously, Ella said, "Okay Finn let's go, we're running late."

"Late for what?" Finn asked innocently.

Ella's cheeks turned pink. "We've got another errand to run and I'm sure you're getting hungry." She grabbed his hand as she pushed the cart toward the checkout line, trying to hustle Finn away from the stranger.

"Bye Ella and Finn."

"Bye Mister," Finn replied.

Ella didn't respond, completely spooked that he'd used their names with such familiarity. As they were checking out, she glanced back, and saw that he was still watching them. He quickly turned away when he realized she had caught him staring. She couldn't get out of there fast enough. After loading their packages in the jeep, she shook off her paranoia and told herself she was being ridiculous. *What is wrong with me? Maybe this is what parenting is like. Overprotective mama bear moments like these. Get a grip!*

~

*E*lla and Finn arrived home loaded down with packages. She had made a last minute, impulsive decision to take a detour to the pet store. Big mistake! Now she really had created a monster. Kyle was going to kill her. Reaching beyond her scope of employment she had purchased two goldfish for Finn. He was over the moon and had already named them Miley and Cyrus.

He ran ahead tearing into Kyle's office full speed yelling "D-A-D! Look what I got!"

Well, here goes nothing. She plastered a confident smile on her face and followed behind Finn, sizing up the temperature of the room. Kyle was bent down peering into the clear plastic bags at the newest editions to the family. "Miley and Cyrus huh?" he said.

"Yep, account a she is my favorite."

"Aren't you a little young to be into Miley Cyrus?"

"Natalie listened to her all the time," he said, giving his former nanny full credit.

"I see. Well, we'll have to get them set up in their new home, won't we?"

"You're going to help?" he asked in disbelief.

"If that's all right with you and Ella."

"Yes," he said pumping his little fist in the air as he pivoted and raced out of the room heading for the stairs.

"Hey, give me the fish! They'll think they're in a

hurricane," Ella said laughing as she took the fish from him.

Kyle's warm smile felt like a caress and made her toes curl. Sweeping his arm wide he said, "After you, *mademoiselle.*"

"*Merci,*" she responded, smiling back. He grabbed a package and his cane and headed for the elevator.

"You're not upset about the fish?"

"Nope. Hopefully that will be the end of the puppy conversation."

She cleared her throat. "Um about that, he already has puppy names picked out and full disclosure... I let him buy a tennis ball for Lucy/Charlie today at the dollar store."

Kyle rolled his eyes. "Great."

"Wait... that's it? That's all you're going to say?"

"Must be the head injury."

"I'd say."

"Or, maybe it has something to do with the present company. You bring out the best in me. Come to think about it, you bring out the best in everyone. How do you do that?"

"I wouldn't go that far. I've certainly seen your worst on many occasions."

"It's not healthy to hold grudges," he said, winking at her.

Kyle was barefoot and had on an old pair of faded jeans with an untucked unbuttoned white oxford shirt. *Oh God!* Day old stubble, hair a tousled mess... the combination had her pulse thundering for this man.

They stepped out of the elevator and of course Finn

had beaten them by a mile. "Can I hold them now? Please? I won't run."

"Let's put them on your desk and you can look at them while Ella and I get the tank set up."

"I'm going back to the car to get the rest of the stuff," Ella said.

"I'm sure we can find someone to do that for you, I'll page Richard."

"No, you won't. I'm perfectly capable of carrying in my own supplies from the car," she said.

"We'll be here, bonding with our belugas," he said, as she hurried off to unload the rest of their booty.

34

Kyle felt Finn eyeing him and raised his brow. "What?"

"You like Ella dontcha?"

"Of course, she's a great nurse who also happens to be a nice person."

He scrunched up his face. "No, I mean like-her like-her, you know, like marry her, like her," Finn said. "I think she likes you too."

"Finn, me thinks you think too much."

"Well, do you?"

"I told you I like her just fine. We're becoming friends."

"I want her to stay forever. Be part of our family."

Kyle took his time before responding. "Finn, I know you like Ella a lot, and she really likes you, but she has a job to go back to. She won't be here forever but that doesn't mean she won't be in your life."

"But why can't she be here forever? I know she likes

you. And you like her too." They were interrupted by Ella's return.

"Hey guys, here we go, Miley and Cyrus's new home. *Voilà!*" Ella called out cheerfully setting the aquarium on the table Kyle pointed to.

Finn clapped. "I can't wait!"

Kyle followed Ella into the bathroom to grab some towels and whispered, "Finn is playing matchmaker."

She raised her eyebrows in question.

"Me and you babe," he said, waggling his eyebrows.

"That kid is something. You're going to have your hands full. He is an exact replica of you, a mini-Kyle."

"God no!" he looked heavenward. "I think he's on to something though. He says you like me. Is that true?"

Flustered she said, "Now you're taking dating advice from a six-year-old?"

"Why not? He's pretty astute for six."

"Dad hurry up!"

"Coming," he said. He dropped a kiss on the tip of Ella's nose and her eyes went wide with surprise. Her mouth hung open for a few seconds and he chuckled before returning to the whale project.

35

The following Saturday, Ella volunteered for breakfast duty. Kyle watched as she put on an apron tying it around her slim waist. The awareness between them was crackling and Kyle wanted her with an intensity that was all consuming.

"Would you rather have pancakes or dippy eggs?" she asked.

"Pancakes please," Finn replied.

Eyebrows arched she turned to Kyle. "How about you?"

"Both. And bacon," he said, patting his ripped stomach, "I have to put some weight back on, the doc said as much."

Sitting side by side on bar stools facing Ella, Kyle nudged Finn, slyly winking as Finn chimed in, "Yeah, me too! I want both and bacon."

"Well, I can hardly argue with doctor's orders, or a growing kid, can I?"

Kyle and Finn exchanged smirks and watched as Ella pulled out a bowl for mixing up the pancake batter then began gathering the rest of her ingredients and lining them up on the massive granite countertop.

"I'd say Ella looks like she knows her way around a kitchen, what do ya think Finn?"

"Yeah, and I'm glad because I'm starving."

Kyle ruffled Finn's hair. "You're always starving."

Teasingly, Kyle continued his running commentary. "See how she expertly cracks those eggs, Finn? The wrist action is on point. It takes real skill to keep the shells out of the mix. And she handles that whisk like a master chef."

Finn catching on said, "Yeah giving Chef Jacques a run for his money, right Dad?"

"Ha ha a kitchen full of comedians, just wait' til you taste them. Pancakes are my specialty."

Kyle couldn't get enough of this show, Ella barefoot, wearing a pair of short cut-off jeans and a skimpy cropped tank top. She had her hair piled on top of her head, her skin was golden from the days by the pool and she looked radiant and fresh. It had been a long time since he had felt this alive or for that matter this attracted to someone. Even more endearing was the flour now streaked across one cheek.

"Ella, can I help?" Finn asked.

"I think I can put you to work. I'll pull the step stool up to the sink and you can wash the berries for me."

Kyle had a moment of melancholy watching the two of them together, but it was quickly eclipsed by Finn's delight. It was contagious and before long he was grabbing the bacon from the fridge to add to a skillet.

Ella's lips twitched. "The billionaire knows how to cook?"

"Hey, I had great nannies, what can I say." He grinned at her enjoying the easy banter. She had a mischievous sparkle in her eyes this morning and he was down for it. She was becoming harder and harder to resist.

With Finn busy at the sink and the bacon cooking, Kyle edged behind Ella bracketing his arms on either side of her while peering over her shoulder. He pressed his body against her back effectively pinning her against the counter. He was naked from the waist up and wore sweatpants that hung low and loose around his hips. He could feel the heat of her body through her skimpy cotton tank top.

"Great technique," he whispered in her ear as she whipped the cream with a mixer. "If there's any left-over whipped cream, I have a couple of ideas for it I'd like to share with you." Kyle breathed in her intoxicating scent and wanted more.

The cream now light and fluffy, she turned off the mixer and set it aside. She glanced over her shoulder. "Don't burn the bacon," she said her voice slightly breathless.

"Under control chef."

Ella slid out from between Kyle and the counter and went to see how the fruit was holding up. "How ya doing over here sport?"

"I'm almost done," Finn said. Ella glanced over at Kyle biting back a smile as she nodded at the mangled berries.

"It's about time for me to cook the eggs. Do you want to be in charge of the toast?" Ella asked Finn.

"Yes please," Finn replied.

She handed him several slices of bread and moved his step stool to the toaster. "When the toast pops up here is the knife and butter, maybe your dad and you can do that together?"

"Okay."

The intimacy was suddenly pierced by a sultry voice. "Well well well. Domestic bliss with the domestic help, charming."

Kyle stiffened then tried to tamp down his irritation. "Hey Charlene, what brings you out and about?"

Pursing her lips in a pout she complained, "Well since you never called me back yesterday, I thought I should come see for myself how you're really doing."

"How's my favorite little rug-rat?" she said. Finn ignored her.

"Finn, say hello to Charlene," Kyle directed.

Keeping his head down he gave a mumbled hi, clearly upset that she'd intruded.

"The nurse, right? What's your name again?" Charlene asked.

Scrubbing her palms on her apron before reaching out her hand in greeting Ella said, "Hello. Yes, we met briefly at the hospital."

Kyle made the introduction. "Ella, this is Charlene, an old family friend."

"Not so old but we do go way back. Our nannies took turns watching us while our parents held lavish soirées. When we got old enough, we were shipped off to boarding school together along with his sister and brother. I'm sure you've met them?"

"The sister Faye yes, but not Griffin," Ella said.

"He's always off jet-setting around the world. He inherited all of the charm in the family... of the males anyway." She gave a sly side glance at Kyle.

Ella's jaw dropped. "I totally disagree! Kyle has plenty of charm once you get to know him," she said, then as if realizing what she'd admitted to, clamped her hand over her mouth.

Kyle chuckled. "Thanks for the endorsement. Our families are in business together," Kyle explained further.

"Yes, and apparently after amassing their fortunes, a lifetime of working together wasn't enough so Daddy and Mother packed up and followed Kyle's parents to Palm Springs."

"Wow, that's some history. Lifelong friends," Ella said politely.

Charlene smirked. "With benefits."

Wrinkling his brow Finn asked, "What are benefits?"

Charlene laughed as Kyle steered the conversation to safer territory. "Buddy let's take our seat so we can eat."

"Have you eaten? We have plenty," Ella asked Charlene.

"No thanks. Just came by to check on this naughty man. He never seems to return my phone calls these days." Eyes narrowed she sized Ella up. "I didn't know cooking fell under the auspices of nursing," she said sounding annoyed.

Exasperated with her tone Kyle said, "Charlene did you come here just to bust my balls or is there something else?"

"Kyle darling, I've missed you. I know you're recovering but is there any reason why we couldn't take the boat out? After all, you do have a captain you could call on."

"I haven't even thought about taking the boat out. My limited energy is being used very strategically."

Charlene walked over to Kyle and planted a kiss right on his lips. Kyle neither encouraged nor discouraged the display, but he caught Ella rolling her eyes.

"Gross!" Finn said.

Ella snickered. "How many eggs does everyone want?" She had already piled the stack of pancakes onto a platter and had set them on the kitchen island. The toast was buttered, the whipped cream and berries waiting to complement the flapjacks, and the pitcher of juice ready to be poured.

"Two for me, one for Finn," Kyle said.

"Charlene are you sure?" Ella asked politely.

"None for me, I'll just eat a few berries with the cream."

"Help yourself."

Ella cracked the eggs onto the griddle. "Sunnyside or over-easy?"

"Over easy but very dippy," Kyle said.

"Me too," Finn echoed.

As Ella carefully flipped the eggs she said, "Charlene, the coffee is freshly brewed help yourself, cream's in the fridge."

"I'll get it for you, cream or sugar?" Kyle asked.

"You don't remember?"

Rolling his eyes, he said, "Well?"

"Black."

Kyle held on to Ella's shoulder for balance as he reached over her head to grab a coffee mug from the shelf. He intentionally rubbed against her and sniffed her hair appreciatively murmuring, "Why do you have to smell so damn good?"

Charlene's nose wrinkled in distaste. "You both look awfully chummy."

Kyle carefully walked over and handed Charlene her mug of coffee, his mouth twisting sardonically he replied, "Yes I'd say we're quite chummy."

Finn had become quiet and withdrawn, an obvious reversal from the lighthearted child he had been minutes before. Noticing, Kyle became determined that he wasn't going to let Charlene spoil this morning. He pinned Charlene with a hard stare which she ignored.

"Here's your egg, over easy, extra dippy, just the way you like it," Ella said, setting the plate in front of Finn. She bent down to give him a quick hug, ruffling his hair then went to grab Kyle's eggs. "*Bon appétit.*"

"Where's yours?" Kyle asked.

"I'm down for the pancakes," she said, smiling as she piled on the whipped cream and berries.

Charlene, rather than taking a seat, chose to stand next to Kyle her hip resting against his stool, shoulders touching. She reached down and placed her palm high on his thigh and squeezed.

Without making a scene, he removed her hand and scowled. Kyle wasn't quite sure how to save this morning from the wrecking ball that was Charlene.

Eyes narrowed, Charlene asked, "How much longer are you going to need a full-time nurse, or is she Finn's new nanny?"

His eyes flashed with irritation. "Thanks for your concern, Charlene, but mind your own business."

"Just curious. This must be a terrible inconvenience for Ella. I can't imagine disrupting my entire life for a complete stranger. But I should take into account who that stranger is. No doubt, a handsome rich bachelor must have sweetened the pot."

Ella stood abruptly and left the room without a word obviously fuming.

Finn's eyes welled with tears. "Can I be scused?"

"Yes, don't worry about your plate I'll clean up."

Without a word he ran after Ella like a bat out of hell.

"Really Charlene?"

"What?" Charlene asked, all wide-eyed innocence.

"You know what. Why do you always push people away? I know you'd like Ella if you gave her a chance."

"Doubtful."

"Only because you're so competitive and unreasonable."

"Well, I'm glad we can be alone for a few minutes. I never get to see you anymore. I've missed you."

"Charlene, why do you act so proprietary over me? It has to stop. You're my friend but let me be perfectly clear, there is no *we* as in couple. We fucked a couple of times, got our carnal needs satisfied. We were both aware of what it was and what it wasn't."

"How can you be so cold?"

"I'm being honest. We've been over this. Before and

after. We were on the same page, now suddenly you're trying to make us into something we aren't."

"We were fine until your accident...until Florence Nightingale stepped into the picture," she said.

"We hadn't had sex for ages prior to the accident."

"Only because you were always working."

"No, that's not the reason. We've been friends almost our entire lives. Had each other's backs through our lonely fucked up childhoods. I wouldn't have survived it without you. I never want anything to come between us. That's why it was a mistake for us to leave the friend zone. And I'm sorry. I really am. I believed you when you said you wanted a post-divorce fuck with no strings."

"I meant it darling, it's just you were such a great lay, how could I stop at a few? We are a good match, Kyle. Imagine if we merged our resources. Both of us are ambitious, not to mention animals in the bedroom. They always say marry your best friend." She ran her long scarlet fingernail down his nose. "Can you say you don't miss the sex, even a little?"

"Yes, I can say that. We're friends. Accept it or not, that's all I have to offer."

"This Hallmark movie starring your nurse will get old. You're not the domestic kind of guy. I'll be around when you tire of her."

"Give it a break Charlene. She has no interest in me."

She wrinkled her nose. "There must be something seriously wrong with her."

"I'd say she's discerning, wouldn't you agree?"

Charlene laughed out loud. "Part of your dubious

charm is your self-effacing demeanor—that is unless you're in the courtroom, then look out."

Kyle lifted an eyebrow and said, "And here I thought the charm gene skipped me entirely. Are we good then?"

"You know we'll always be good. Can't say I'm happy about you cutting me off but easy come, easy go. I'm just glad you didn't die on me. I would have been very pissed off."

He held out his arm and she leaned into him as he squeezed her tight.

"I'll see myself out. Bye darling." She flounced out of the room like she owned the world.

Kyle stood up stiffly, grabbed his cane and mentally rehearsed his damage control speech. He shook his head wondering how the hell Charlene always seemed to have impeccable timing when it came to Ella.

36

---

*E*lla stuffed Finn's spiderman PJs into his superman backpack and zipped it closed. "You're going to have so much fun with your Aunt Faye."

"Yeah, but what if Dad needs me?"

Ella sat on the bed and pulled him to her for a hug. "That's why I'm here, remember? Plus, he's getting stronger every day, soon he won't even need me."

Finn buried his head in her neck and in a muffled voice said, "But I'll still need you. I don't want you to leave, ever."

Her heart ached at his admission. This little guy had already lost so much in his short life, now another big transition. They were scheduling interviews this weekend for his replacement nanny.

"Buddy, I promise you that we'll always be friends. We'll make play dates and do lots of fun stuff together. Sound good?"

"It won't be the same."

"No, you're right it will be different, but who knows, maybe it'll be even better. You'll probably like your new nanny even more than me."

"Never!" he pushed away and grabbed his pack and ran out of the room.

Ella sighed, her chest heavy. This wasn't going to be easy all the way around. She had become very attached to this little person. All her maternal instincts had kicked in and she felt their destinies were now somehow intertwined.

Ella caught up with Finn in his father's office, sitting glumly on the floor with Daisy. Faye had already arrived and the energy in the room crackled with her vibrancy.

"Ella! Great to see you again." Faye looked radiant, her fair skin and features delicate, so different from her brother's dark complexion and hard angles. It was as if each of their parents got to have a replicated self, Kyle so much like his father and Faye a mirror image of her beautiful mother.

"Hey Faye. Finn and I were just discussing his apprehension about leaving his dad all night," Ella shared. "He's a bit worried he might be needed." She exchanged knowing looks with Faye and Kyle.

"I'll be fine, in fact I'm taking Ella out for a fancy dinner at The Yacht Club tonight."

Finn and Ella said simultaneously, "You are?"

"Yes. I figured it'd be good to have my nurse by my side for my first big outing."

"Clever of you to throw in the nursing card," Ella said dryly.

Finn jumped up from the floor, his little match-making self, delighted with this turn of events. "Yes!" he said his earlier upset forgotten.

"Ella, make sure to order the calamari, it is to die for!" Faye said.

"And you hafta dress up 'cause everyone is rich," Finn said making everyone laugh.

"But I don't have anything to wear," Ella said.

"Already taken care of. There is a dress hanging up in your room. Faye picked it up for me on her way here."

"Shoes..."

"Check. Size six-and-a-half, correct?"

"How did you know that?"

"Richard checked your tennis shoes for size." Kyle smiled seemingly quite pleased with himself.

"You've certainly thought of everything except for the most important part, asking me if I wanted to go."

"Ella, you *have* to go," Finn piped in. "My dad needs you; you heard him, he's scared to go out alone for the first time." He grinned at his dad mischievously holding his thumb up.

"I see how this is going. I'm outnumbered. I'm beginning to wonder which plan came first, Finn's sleepover with his aunt or the Yacht Club?"

"You'll have to continue to wonder," Kyle said grinning.

"I didn't know, I pinky swear," Finn said.

"I believe you," Ella said. "This sounds much more like something your father would concoct."

Brow furrowing Finn said, "What's concock?"

"She's implying that I was being sneaky."

"Oh, I get it. Well, were you?" he asked innocently.

"Kind of, how else am I going to get her to go out with me?" Kyle said. Finn nodded slowly then smiled conspiratorially at his dad.

"Let's go Finn, we've got places to go and things to do," Faye said.

"Can we go look at puppies?"

"No!" Kyle exclaimed.

"Wah," Finn said, rubbing his eyes comically.

"Go on get out of here you two, I've got a mountain of work to get through."

"Bye, love you," Finn called out as Faye pulled him along.

Finding themselves alone, Ella's heart began pounding. "It's awfully quiet," she said suddenly overcome with shyness.

Kyle studied her before replying, "Be ready by six o'clock, my driver will be waiting for us at the front door."

"Kyle..."

"Don't complicate this Ella, it's a thank you for everything you've done for Finn and me. I want to pamper you a little. Deal?"

"I guess so," she said reluctantly.

His warm smile had her responding in kind but the glint in Kyle's eyes did nothing to assuage her misgivings. She knew she was toast.

She shuffled her feet nervously then said, "Um... well I guess I'll let you get back to work."

He raked his hands through his already disheveled hair further mussing it up then he turned back to the file in front of him. Ella took her cue and turned on her heel and left.

---

37

*E*lla applied mascara with shaky hands, apprehensive about the evening ahead. She hadn't a clue how she was going to eat she felt so queasy. At least she was having a good hair day which helped bolster her confidence a little. There was a familiar knock at the door. *Déjà vu.* "Come in."

As before, Richard Drake entered and discreetly stood at the door until Ella motioned him in the rest of the way.

He held a long velvet jewelers' box in his hand and Ella eyed it warily. "What cha got there, Rich?"

"I suspect it is something to compliment your exquisite beauty Ms. Palmer."

Her hand fluttered to her chest. "I see." Taking the box, she lifted the lid and gasped when she saw the long string of pearls with matching earrings nestled inside.

"They're magnificent," she said in a hushed tone.

"Yes, truly. A fine choice to compliment your attire."

"Thank you. They will look lovely, are they on loan from a jeweler then?" she asked tentatively.

"No, Ms. Palmer. They are a gift from Mr. Bennett. He sincerely hopes you'll accept them as a token of his appreciation for your excellent care of him and his son."

Ella's forehead creased with doubt. "I don't know what to say."

"If you don't mind a bit of unsolicited advice, just say thank you."

Seeing her discomfort, he smiled warmly at Ella. "If it helps, while this gift may seem extravagant to you, for Mr. Bennett, it is most definitely not. Might I also add you are a vision Ms. Palmer. You are going to knock his socks off."

"Why thank you Richard."

"Have a lovely evening, and Ms. Palmer, try to have a good time. You look like the proverbial deer in the headlights."

Ella felt her cheeks grow warm; she smiled shyly and replied, "I'll give it my best shot."

"Goodnight." He quietly left Ella alone.

Ella slipped on the Jimmy Choo metallic pumps. Perfect fit. Taking the string of pearls from the box she fastened them around her neck. The necklace nestled in between her breasts and was the ideal accessory.

The short midnight blue chiffon dress had a vee neckline plunging daringly low in the front and the back. The sleeveless garment left her creamy shoulders and arms bare. The fabric flowed loosely. Going braless was her only option due to the extreme cut of the dress.

She dabbed a couple of drops from her twelve-thousand-dollar perfume bottle onto her inner wrists and behind her ears. Adding siren red lipstick as the finishing touch, she grabbed her matching Jimmy Choo clutch and headed out the door.

38

Kyle had just closed the bedroom door behind him when he saw Ella heading his way. His entire body suddenly felt warm as his eyes hungrily took in every inch of her. She was breathtakingly beautiful, moving gracefully like a goddess, long slim arms swinging easily by her sides, one hand gripping a glittery clutch.

As she approached, he could see the slight bounce of her breasts, free and unconfined by any undergarment. The long string of pearls he'd purchased rested tantalizingly in the vee of the dress. Ella's eyes sparkled with excitement. Her loose hair cascaded around her shoulders. It appeared almost black, so soft, so luxurious, it was all he could do to not ravish her on the spot. He let out a low whistle. Kyle had left his tie hanging around the collar of his white oxford since he couldn't do a knot one handed.

"Do you know how to knot a tie?" he asked, voice

low and husky.

"I can try," she said breathlessly. Setting her purse on a credenza, she walked up to him and grabbed his black tie, so close he could see his breath stir her hair. He felt her hands tremble as she fumbled with the knot. He lifted her chin until their eyes met. Hers a luminous pool of smoldering green. He leaned down and gently brushed his lips against hers.

"Kyle... I..."

"Shh, I have to, I can't stop myself," he said, voice low, almost daring her to protest. "Ella you are the most magnificent creature I've ever known." He scooped his palm underneath the weight of her hair, cupping the back of her head as he leaned down to take her lips again. This time he wasn't so gentle as he explored, taking, plunging, tasting, tongue parting her lips further. Breathing heavily, his voice shaky he said, "I want you naked in my bed."

The heat from her palms resting on his chest scorched through his clothing. At her bemused expression Kyle dipped down for another taste. He had never wanted anything as much as he wanted this woman. He was rock hard and the temptation to drag her back into his bedroom almost overrode his sensibilities. He felt a primal need and he smiled against her lips. *Me Tarzan you Jane.* He had no wish to scare her off, so he reluctantly pulled himself from the edge.

*E*lla was obviously flustered, her cheeks now a delightful pink, her red lipstick slightly smeared. He used his thumb to wipe the smudge. Her eyes darted up to meet his, burning with desire...*all for him*. It was heady and intoxicating. She took his breath away.

He had slicked his normally unruly mop of hair back, and her low and throaty laugh went straight to his cock when she reached up and ran her fingers through it.

"I like it wild and unruly," she said breathlessly.

He laughed and raked his hand through it returning it to its natural disarray. "Whatever you want. That's what I want to give you. Shall we?" he said, crooking his elbow as she slipped her hand through.

They exited the elevator together and walked out to the waiting limo. The driver opened their door and they slid into the quiet luxury of the Mercedes. Soft jazz filled the interior, creating a buffered cocoon-like ambience.

"Would you like a glass of wine?" he asked.

She looked dazed as she leaned her head against the soft leather seat and sighed. "Why not?"

Kyle pulled out two wine glasses and poured them each a glass of white. He raised his to hers and said, "Here's to me sweeping you off your feet."

A smile touched her lips. "Mission accomplished."

"I'm losing my battle with keeping you at arm's length. It's pretty obvious that I'm crazy about you Ella. Am I wrong to think you're beginning to like me just a little?"

Her flushed cheeks and wet lips were his undoing. He dipped down to lick the wine from her bottom lip. Lingering, he stilled when she slipped her tongue into his mouth, running the tip of it over his teeth.

"You wouldn't be wrong," she whispered.

Placing his glass in the holder, he splayed his palm around her throat as he kissed her. He could feel her pulse pounding beneath his thumb and he lost control. With mastery he hungrily demanded a response as their tongues danced and explored, giving, taking... only feeding his insatiable desire. Her breasts pressed against him, and he was painfully aware that there was little between him and her bare skin as he felt her nipples harden. He slid his hand under the fabric to cup her bare breast. She hissed. "Is this okay?" he asked hoarsely.

Hot with longing, his need for her surged when Ella nodded and responded by melting further into the plush leather seat, surrendering to his touch. He licked the tender spot right below her ear, desperate with want. "Beautiful Ella. I've never felt this way before. I need you. You're like kryptonite."

She looked at him so wantonly that he almost went over the edge. "Same," she whispered voice husky.

He groaned and pulled away kissing her forehead. "Damn, we're almost there already."

"Aren't you going to finish what you started?" she said, pulling his head back down to her lips.

He whispered against her mouth. "To be continued. Don't worry... I'll finish it."

She smiled against his lips. "I'm going to hold you to that."

Kyle closed his eyes, absorbing the sensations of her scent and her soft willing body and the whispered promise of her words.

39

"**M**r. Bennett, so glad that you'll be joining us this evening," the host said as they entered the posh country club.

"It's good to be out in the world again."

"We were sorry to hear about your accident. We have your usual waterfront table ready. Would you like to enjoy a cocktail in the lounge before being seated?"

"Yes, please. I understand you have a jazz pianist for entertainment tonight."

"Yes. He's very good."

"Ella does the lounge sound good to you?"

Eyes shining in anticipation she said, "Perfect."

Even with the stiff competition of moneyed guests, Kyle and Ella stood out. Kyle was indifferent to the stares they received but was fully aware that they made a striking couple. The private club afforded many perks for guests but also created a camaraderie amongst its members. Most either had yachts permanently docked there or rented vessels available through the club.

Many members were deep-sea fishing enthusiasts and entered competitions regularly. Kyle was one of them. Unfortunately, he would miss the annual Blue Marlin Tournament this June. It was great fun and he was disappointed that Finn would miss out as well. He had looked forward to the festivities this year thinking that Finn was finally old enough to enjoy the competition. They could still hang out and see the catches of the day being judged. The club had lots of activities for its members and their families so there would be plenty to do. Hopefully he'd be up for some of it.

A loud wolf whistle pierced the crowd as Pete, Kyle's law partner, unsteadily made his way over. "Wow! What the fuck man! You caught the most beautiful mermaid in the sea!"

"Have you met Ella? Ella Palmer meet, Pete Simon, my college friend and partner in crime."

Pete, obviously having imbibed too much alcohol, was laying it on thick as he bowed dramatically, kissing the back of her hand. Rather than releasing it, he held on, eyes burning with interest. "What are you doing hanging around with this low life when we could be dining together on his yacht?"

Ella laughed, going with the flow as she tried, unsuccessfully, to withdraw her hand from his grip.

Kyle glared at Pete and with steel in his voice said, "Down boy, this is *my* date."

"Only because she hasn't met me yet," he grinned wolfishly.

"Wine?" Kyle asked her.

"Yes please."

"It appears you're set, am I right Pete?"

"Sure partner. I'll keep your *date*," he said, winking at Ella, "company while you get the drinks."

"I'll go with Kyle, but thanks," Ella said, finally escaping his grasp. She hooked her hand through Kyle's arm and walked with him to the bar. He had intentionally left his cane in the limo and so far, hadn't needed it. Ella had told him she'd be his cane for the evening. Pete trailed along.

"When are you returning to the office? There are some important matters that need your attention."

"I get this damn cast off on Monday and I'm heading in straight from the doctor's appointment."

Kyle ordered quickly, keeping an eye on Pete in the mirror behind the bar. Pete wasn't being shy about ogling Ella—Kyle wouldn't have been at all surprised to see drool escape from his lips. Kyle turned with their drinks and Pete immediately lifted his gaze from her cleavage. Ella rolled her eyes to no one in particular.

Kyle was aware that he was with the most beautiful woman in the club. She had caught everyone's interest, in part because she was a knockout, but also because she was new to the club and people were always curious about his love life. As everyone's eyes kept straying to her, Pete seemed to become increasingly competitive for her attention. He reached out and ran his fingers down her slim arm as he complimented her outfit. "This dress looks like it was designed with you in mind."

"There you are!" An irritated female voice interrupted Pete.

"Andrea, look who I ran into."

"Kyle! So great to see you." Andrea stood on her tip toes to plant a light kiss on Kyle's cheek.

"Andrea, you look stunning as usual. This is Ella."

Andrea smiled warmly. "Hi, I'm with this guy," nodding her head toward Pete. "Nice to meet you."

"My pleasure."

"I hope Pete isn't being too naughty; since I'm the designated driver he's been hitting the martinis since happy hour." Pete looked annoyed but didn't respond to her comment.

Ella looked relieved to have Andrea near. "It happens to the best of us."

Kyle draped his arm across Ella's shoulders and said, "Let's go grab our table. I'm afraid I'll get pulled into work if I hang around this guy any longer."

"Sounds good to me, I'm famished."

"See you Monday, Pete. Andrea, pleasure as always."

"Kyle, can I have a minute before you go?" Peter asked. Kyle reluctantly agreed, stepping away from Ella.

"I'll give you thirty seconds because I'm dying to get Ella off in an intimate corner and have her all to myself."

"I'll talk fast." Pete looked over at Ella and said, "Bro, you better lock this one down. Damn but she is fine!"

"You're eating into your thirty seconds, speak," Kyle demanded.

Pete rolled his eyes but did start talking.

40

*E*lla missed the warmth of Kyle's body next to hers. He appeared to be listening intently to Peter, but his eyes never strayed from Ella.

Catching her gaze, he flashed a grin. She bit her bottom lip as her belly flip-flopped with excitement.

Andrea touched Ella's arm grabbing her attention. "It's so nice meeting you Ella. How long have you known Kyle?"

"Several months. I was his ICU nurse."

Andrea glanced pointedly at Kyle, who was still watching Ella and said, "I think a certain someone is utterly captivated. I've never seen him so gaga."

"Really? I'd have thought a bachelor in his position would be beating the beauties off with a club."

"It's a fact...but I've never seen him look at any of them the way he's looking at you."

Secretly thrilled, Ella played it cool, shrugging her shoulders she said, "New toy in the toybox."

"I doubt it's just that, but anyway, I'm certain I'll see you around. We come here quite a bit."

The men finished their discussion and Kyle appeared somewhat preoccupied as he led Ella back to the maître d' who waited to seat them.

"Everything all right?" Ella asked.

"I'm sure it will be. Some disturbing things are happening at the office. I'll get to the bottom of them next week. Until then, I'm not wasting another second on anything but the sumptuous babe I'm lucky enough to have as my date."

She rubbed her cheek against his shoulder and wove her fingers through his as they were led to their table. Large urns filled with fragrant flowers were scattered around along with hanging baskets of ferns. It was dusk and the tiki torches had already been lit, the white tablecloths adorned with fresh flowers and individual candles glowing within their hurricane lanterns. Kyle had reserved the table off by itself at the far end of the deck.

Ella inhaled the briny smell of the ocean air. The view of the marina was spectacular, the quiet occasionally ruffled by the low rumble of a yacht returning to dock, their colorful lights reflecting off the water. They could hear the piano chords drifting from the inside dining room. Perfect balmy weather, calm and pleasant. The night sky was clear and soon to be filled with twinkling stars. Ella sighed, enchanted with the restaurant, the marina, the ambience but mostly with the company. *How had she let this happen?*

After being seated and placing their drink and appetizer orders, Ella slipped off her shoes and hooked a foot around Kyle's lower leg rubbing her toes against him. He scorched her with a smoldering look no longer trying to hide his desire. He reached across the table and took her hand in his, rubbing his thumb against the inside of her wrist. She couldn't look away. Her pulse skittered as she unconsciously licked her lips.

"Oh baby, don't look at me like that or we might not make it through dinner," Kyle said softly.

"Kyle..."

"Ella..." He was interrupted by the waiter.

"Good evening Mr. Bennett, I'm sure the maître d' told you about our specials this evening, do you have any questions about the menu?"

"No, I think we're ready to order. Do you mind me ordering for you?" Kyle asked.

"No please do."

"We'll both have a cup of the she-crab soup, followed by catch of the day, flounder I believe, with the lobster risotto and asparagus."

Taking their menus, the waiter said, "Very good sir," and left them alone again.

"Talk to me. I feel like I know you and yet I don't know that much about you. You mentioned being a foster kid, what was that like?" Kyle said.

"Pretty awful, until I ended up with the family that later adopted me."

"So, you lost your parents when you were four, just like Finn."

"Yes, except they weren't ill. They died in a plane crash."

"No! Commercial or private?"

"Commercial. Coming back from a business trip.

Mom happened to go along with my dad that time, and the plane went down in bad weather."

"I'm sorry, I can't imagine, that must have been really tough on a four-year-old child."

"Yes, and it didn't help that there wasn't any close family to take me in. I was staying with my mom's second cousin while they traveled, she couldn't take me on, so I was put into the foster system almost immediately."

"Orphaned and in shock, I'm sure."

"I don't remember a whole lot about that first year. I was in shock, I'm sure. Later I held on to whatever memories I had of my parents... my mom's perfume, her holding me, singing to me at night...reading me stories. My dad teaching me to swim... going out boating with them. I was sad for a very long time."

Kyle put his hand to his chest and said, "That hurts my heart."

"It was a long time ago. I'm fine now... all grown up."

"And yet our experiences become part of who we are. They never really leave us," he said quietly.

A momentary sadness creeped in. "After five years of being shuffled around from foster to foster, I landed with an older couple, he was the pastor of a church. They had already raised a family and wanted to give something back. They met me during my week at their summer church camp. They inquired about me and my circumstances and ended up taking me on. It wasn't meant to be permanent, but they fell in love with me and I with them."

"You were lucky you found each other. Fate is a funny thing."

"Fate, is that what you think it was?"

"What else?"

"Coincidence?"

"I thought I was supposed to be the cynical one," Kyle said lightly.

"Not cynical, just realistic. When your parents fall out of the sky you tend to stop believing in miracles and mysticism."

"And yet your adoptive father was a minister."

"Yep, ironic, isn't it? I'm not saying I have no faith, but I stopped believing in happily-ever-after a long time ago. Life is cruel and not discerning about who it crushes. Kids, rich, poor, no one is immune."

"Yes, I can personally attest to that."

The waiter arrived with a breadbasket and poured some olive oil on a plate, shaving some fresh parmesan cheese and ground fresh pepper on top. "I'll be back momentarily with your soup."

"Thanks."

The warm bread smelled yeasty and delicious and Ella wasted no time grabbing a piece and dipping it in the oil concoction. Rolling her eyes heavenward she moaned, "Hmm, so good."

Kyle's eyes crinkled as he smiled warmly at Ella. Tearing a slice in half he dabbed his own bread, turning it over to coat both sides and stuck the whole thing in his mouth. "Oh yeah, that's what I'm talking about," he said while chewing.

"Your soup. Please enjoy." The waiter refilled their

wine goblets and motioned to a young staffer to top off their water glasses.

Kyle leaned back in his seat and studied Ella. Aware of his intense gaze she said, "What? Do I have oil dripping down my chin?" She self-consciously wiped her chin with her napkin.

He chuckled. "No nothing like that. Just admiring the view."

"I'm full already," she said.

"You'd better jump up and down to make room then, you don't want to miss out on their daily catch. It's always amazing."

As if he had conjured it up, their meals arrived. He was right—it was scrumptious, and Ella practically licked her plate clean. Her cheeks felt flushed from the wine and the company.

"That was phenomenal. Thank you, Kyle."

He nodded his head in response. "Let's blow this joint," he said. "We can walk around the marina, and I can show you my boat." He slipped several large bills into the leather folder and stood up.

"Are you sure you're up for it?"

"I'm sure." He stood and waited while she slipped her pumps back on.

"My feet aren't too happy. The minute we get out of here its barefoot for the rest of the evening."

Kyle rested his warm hand at the small of her back as they left the club and headed toward the docks where the vessels were moored.

"Here she is," Kyle said as they approached.

"What a beauty! She's huge."

"Not really, a forty-footer is relatively modest for a

yacht, but don't let that fool you, she has plenty of amenities. Good for day trips, cruising, fishing, it has sleeping quarters. We use it to butter up clients and for personal pleasure. It's manageable for two people which makes it perfect in my opinion. I don't want to always have to rely on my captain to take out my own fucking boat."

"Sounds like fun."

"We'll take her out soon. You, me and Finn."

"I'd love that."

Kyle leaned down and gave Ella a soft lingering kiss, smiling against her lips as he felt her breath quicken. He lifted his head, and she was stirred by the hunger in his eyes.

"I want you Ella, as much as I've ever wanted anything in my life. I'd like to pick you up and carry you onto my boat, but I'm afraid my body has a different agenda. I think we'd better head back, my leg is starting to ache."

Her brows drew together with concern. "This is the most you've done outside of your physical therapy since your accident. I'm not surprised you're tired."

"It catches me off guard. It doesn't seem like it takes much to exhaust me."

"You're doing great, think of how far you've come!"

"My impatience rearing its head again," he said. "I'm just glad to be here, enjoying this night with you."

Ella carried her shoes and clutch in one hand and held Kyles hand in the other. The stars were now out on full display and the water lapping at the hull of the boats was at once both comforting and peaceful. Perfect evening.

41

The limo door had barely shut when Kyle pulled her into his arms and began kissing her neck. Whispering in her ear as he held her against him, he said, "Your skin is so soft. I want to kiss every inch of your body. I want to make love to you."

Ella looked up at him as Kyle traced the curve of her cheeks then ran the pad of his thumb over her lips. Her breasts pressed against him, and he skimmed his fingers down her shoulder taking her dress with it... slowly... planting a trail of kisses as he went. *So soft.*

Ella's skin was like silk and Kyle finally got to kiss the tiny mole that had been driving him crazy for weeks. He pushed her bodice aside and her breasts spilled out full and ripe. He circled her lush pink nipple with his tongue before drawing it into his mouth and suckling, pressing his palm into the curve of her low back to hold her steady.

When he had her panting, he lifted his head and

took her lips commanding a response. Skimming his fingers down her torso he moved lower to lift her skirt, stroking her inner thigh all the way to her panties. She vibrated under his touch. He brushed his thumb over her clit while she arched her pelvis against him. When he pressed harder, she moaned with pleasure. He slipped his finger under the elastic and found her warm wet center and dipped inside. He shoved her dress up higher as she rocked against his hand, her eyes glazed with passion.

Kyle wanted to satisfy her and bring her to a climax right here and now. Continuing his assault on her senses he began tugging, nipping, suckling on her nipples like he was drinking of her nectar... long hard pulls... taking complete control. She was moaning his name as she gripped his hair in tight fists and began to rock wildly against him.

He smothered her lips with his own, kissing her wildly, as if he could devour her, holding her while her body began to tremble. He rubbed her clit furiously increasing his tempo as she shuddered in his arms. Her fingers stayed tangled in his hair as she held his lips to hers. She suddenly stiffened them moaned as she climaxed. Their tongues explored and pulsated in an erotic rhythm causing Kyle's tight rein on his dick to unravel.

"Babe, touch me," he murmured against her lips.

Ella reached for him still in the grip of her orgasm. She rubbed him through his slacks, but it wasn't enough. He needed skin on skin. "More, I need your hand on my cock," he ground out thickly.

She quickly unbuckled him then pulled his zipper

down. Straining against the last barrier between them, his cock sprang free from the confines of his pants. She lowered his slacks below his hips and gripped him igniting a fire he had nothing to compare to. He needed her touch... he craved it... he desperately called out her name and jerked like he was being tortured. She gripped him harder then slid her hand up and down using his arousal to moisten his length. She stroked slowly until he was bucking with the need for release. She ran her other hand up his shirt teasing his nipples and sifting through the hair on his pecs.

She bent down and took him into her mouth. She licked and teased the head of his cock while cupping his balls in her other hand. Then she took him deep inside her hot wet mouth and he thought he'd die. It was everything. "Elle... I... I'm not going to last. I'm about to come." He tried to pull her head up, but she didn't pull away. "Elle... I mean it..." He suddenly stiffened then let out a long shuddering breath and climaxed.

After the earthquake subsided, they continued to lay sprawled out together in the back seat of his limo, both languid and satiated. He had his arm around Ella while she snuggled against him. Kyle suddenly realized that the car was no longer moving.

Giggling into his chest Ella said, "Are you sure this thing is soundproof?'

"Soundproof? I didn't say it was soundproof."

She gasped, her eyes wide, then she glared, playfully swatting at him. "You are so bad."

"And *you*, are so damn good. You feel so right in my arms."

Ella suddenly bashful, buried her face against his chest.

"Are you blushing?" he said teasingly.

She nodded into his shirt. Her voice muffled she said, "I hate it."

Kyle tilted her head up with his knuckles then kissed the tip of her nose. "You're adorable."

Her nose crinkled. "I'm glad you think so."

Smiling he said, "Its sexy as hell when you blush, and you wear it well."

"We'd better make ourselves decent," Ella said. She tugged the bodice of her dress up before attending to Kyle's pants. As her hands brushed against his belly, his cock immediately responded. Laughing she said, "Down boy," and zipped him up quickly. He watched as she slipped her pumps back on and combed her fingers through her wild tangled hair before pulling her dress back down around her thighs.

Kyle chuckled. "Your eyes say you've been thoroughly fucked."

"You should see yourself. You're not in much better shape."

With a lopsided grin, Kyle raked his hand through his hair. "Fortunately, all of my staff are discreet. No need to worry about it."

They climbed out of the limo and walked toward the house, and he hated that he had to lean so heavily on his cane. *Probably overdid it.*

Ella gave him a worried look. "I hope we didn't push it too far."

"I'll be fine. You ready for dessert?"

"Didn't we already have that?" Ella teased. "What do you have in mind?"

"Ice cream."

"I'm in."

They wound up in the kitchen, their shoes came off first, followed by Kyle's shirt, belt and tie. He felt an overwhelming need to please her, to be enough. Like the lyrics from an old Rolling Stones tune Beast of Burden, was he smart enough, rich enough, sexy enough? He wanted to be all of that for her. He saw her eyes darken as they sized each other up, almost like circling one another. He saw lust there but something else as well, he couldn't quite put his finger on. *Doubt... need...longing?*

Her dress had slipped down around her shoulder, tempting him to kiss the exposed skin. As if her eyes drew him in, he found himself moving toward her. He brushed her hair away from the creamy curve of her neck, then leaned down and kissed her there. All feminine, soft curves, strong yet fragile. Nipping her skin with his teeth he licked her, tasting her sweetness, the feminine scent of her intoxicating. He understood he would never get enough of her.

Her arms wrapped around his waist pulling his hips against hers. He ran his hand down the length of her back and cupped her buttocks. Kyle flinched then shifted to his uninjured leg. As Ella pulled away, he missed her warmth.

"You need to rest you've been on your feet too long. Sit at the counter and I'll dish out some ice cream."

"I guess I can't argue with my nurse, I'll have one scoop of vanilla and one of chocolate."

Licking her spoon a few minutes later, eyes narrowed, she asked, "What comes next?"

"Next?"

"You know, next, as in you're not in need of my nursing services any longer, especially after your cast comes off, you're heading back to work on Monday, you're interviewing nannies all day tomorrow...where do we go from here?"

"I'm hoping we continue getting to know each other. It's kind of been accelerated due to our circumstances. I'd like to see more of you, have you in my life, Finn's too. What do you want?"

"I'm not sure. I'm not going to lie to you, your wealth intimidates me. You can have anything and anyone you want. Where do I fit in? I'm from the other side of the tracks. I've had to work my ass off for everything I've ever gotten. I'm not sure how well we'd fit in the real world."

A flash of hurt pierced him. "You don't think this is real?"

"Of course, it's real." Ella touched his thigh resting against hers. "What I meant is that we've been insulated here in this fairytale castle, away from the rest of the world, it hasn't prepared us for outside influences."

"Ella I'm not afraid for *us*, my only fear is that you'll leave me before giving us a chance."

She swiveled her stool to face him and trailed her fingertips softly across his bare chest. "Let's take it slow. I've agreed to stay on another week to care for Finn until your new nanny is on board. Then we'll figure out where we go from there. I'm not ready to let you go either. I'm just super cautious. I'm out of my league and smart enough to know it."

He tried to tamp down his irritation. "League? Really? What are we, in high school? You can't be *that* bright if you truly believe that load of bullshit."

"You know what I mean."

"No, I don't."

"I think you do but can we please change the subject? I just want to lay in bed together and snuggle and make love and snuggle again. Is that too much to ask?" she wheedled.

"No more talking about leagues or comparing our financial portfolios. I'm inspired by everything about you, your brains, your passion, how engaged you are with life, your killer bod..." he waggled his eyebrows.

"You're laying it on a bit thick, but I like it."

"And I like you." Yawning loudly, he stood up and took their empty bowls to the sink to rinse out. "Are you ready for bed? It's been so long since I've held a woman in my arms all night... I didn't realize how much I'd missed it."

"I hope you don't snore," she said.

"I hope *you* don't snore."

"After you Mr. Bennett."

His eyes smoldered. "*Mademoiselle.*"

42

---

*K*yle sat sprawled on a club chair beside the bedroom fireplace waiting for Ella to finish in the bathroom. His eyes were closed but his fatigue had disappeared, and his body tingled with anticipation. Rather than feeling satiated from their earlier exploration in the limo, he felt like that had merely been a taste of what was to come.

She got to him like no one ever had. Yes, she was beautiful, but beyond that she had depth and a keen intelligence. She was interesting, exciting, warm, and fully engaged with life. Rather than break her, her difficult childhood had made her grab life by the balls and go for what she wanted. He admired her resiliency and that her humor had stayed intact.

"I'm all yours," Ella said standing in front of him, her eyes lively and bright with expectation. He cracked his eyes open and raked her body from head to toe. She still had her dress on but now that she had captured his full attention, she began to undress in front of him...*correction,* she began to strip.

Smiling seductively, she bent over to kiss him. When he reached for her, she backed away, index finger to her lips, and shook her head no. Ella slowly began to undress, running her hands down her hips before reaching around to unzip her dress, then playfully pulling the top down one shoulder at a time. Meeting his gaze, she tugged at the bodice and her full rounded breasts spilled out, pink nipples engorged. He thought he was going to come right then.

She turned her back to him and took her time bending forward to gracefully step out of the dress, making sure he had a tantalizing view of her fine as fuck ass. She added some extra wiggle as she straightened and tossed the garment aside.

Standing naked except for her lacy white panties, she bit her lip suddenly looking unsure and a delicate pink bloomed on her cheeks. Kyle groaned. "Don't stop now," he said his voice thick with desire.

He watched her uncertainty vanish, her lips turning up, confidence restored. Her seductive dance continued, hips swaying as she slowly approached him. The moves meant to drive him insane, were working.

His nostrils flared as he stared at her perfect body. "I'm going to explode, come over here."

She stood in front of him, taking her time to slide the panties off inch by torturous inch, her breasts round and firm as she bent over. She kicked the lace aside and knelt on the floor at his feet. She buried her face in his lap and nuzzled him through his slacks. He brushed his hand through her thick curls as she looked up at him through her lashes. Now Ella was back to her confident, daring, self. Kyle thought he couldn't get any harder, but she'd just proved him wrong.

Ella pulled his pants down over his muscular thighs, slinging them to the side. She smoothed her hands up his inner thighs her mouth following where her hands had been. When she reached his angry scar she murmured, "My poor baby," then tenderly kissed his healing wound. His heart contracted and he felt a deep longing and with it the startling realization that he had always felt alone until Ella.

"F-u-c-k," he groaned, "that feels so good!"

She finally reached his erection and mouthed him through his briefs. "You're killing me," he said gripping her hair.

Putting an end to his torture, she pulled off the last remaining barrier of clothing. "Condoms are in the drawer," Kyle ground out.

She reached into the nightstand drawer and grabbed a foil packet, looking sexy as hell as she tore the wrapper open with her teeth. Gripping the base of his cock she rolled the condom over his hard length. Her hips swayed as she straddled him, allowing just the tip of him inside her wet center, before lifting her pelvis teasingly. *Teasing... torturing...* just a taste. Each time she would sit a little lower her tightness engulfing him.

He captured a nipple, circling with his tongue as he drew it in to suckle hard. She cried out, suddenly lowering herself all the way taking his whole length inside of her. *Warm...wet...wild...*

Her arms encircled his neck as she rocked her hips, riding him slowly, pinning him with her lustful gaze.

He slid his hand down her flat belly and rubbed his thumb against her sweet spot. He was mesmerized by the hunger in her eyes as she picked up her tempo and rode him harder. Her breath quickened and she threw her head back when he pinched a nipple. Lifting her pelvis, she thrust down harder... taking him deeper inside.

He knew he couldn't hold out much longer but wanted to wait for her. When she began to moan he knew she was close to climaxing so he let go of his own control and released, ejaculating hard. The orgasm rocked him to his very core and only intensified when he felt her tightness pulsating around him as she cried out with abandon. Her body melted into his as their breathing returned to normal, and they landed some-where between ecstasy and exhaustion.

43

———

They lay sprawled in the chair, spent. Ella didn't want to move... didn't want him to slip out. Cradled against his chest, her lips pressed against his throat, tongue darting out to lick his salty skin. She'd never felt this wanton in her entire life. Her body was hot where his fingertips caressed her back, from her neck to her buttocks and back up again. If she were a cat she would be purring. Kyle buried his nose in her hair.

"Ella," he said kissing her neck, "that was amazing... *you* are amazing. I want to be enough for you. Stay with me, don't go back to your condo." She stilled, her breath hitching.

"I feel so alive when I'm with you."

She was touched by his vulnerability yet at the same time left feeling like she was the one with the most to lose. She had been ripped apart before and wasn't sure she was ready to take that risk again. He seemed to be holding all the cards; she was already half in love with him and that felt like a freefall into the abyss.

She was silent for so long that she felt Kyle stiffen. She finally responded. "But for how long? I'm a new shiny object Kyle. The newness will eventually wear off, then what?"

"Then we go deeper."

"You say that now, but what happens when you've grown tired of me? You've had everything you've ever wanted for your entire life. I can't compete with that. How do I know that once you get what you want, you'll no longer want me? The excitement will wear off, trust me. I've been there, done that. There will always be another beautiful woman waiting in the wings." Ella got up from his lap and moved to the bed, sitting cross legged she tucked her hair behind her ears.

Kyle followed her to the bed and lay down on his side facing her, running his fingers softly up and down her thigh. "I could say the same about you. You have your share of admirers. I think that's fear talking. You're still living in the past."

"I was that girl, the *IT* girl. The chief surgeon put his sights on me. Like you, he could have anyone he wanted—rich, gorgeous, successful, and he wanted *me*. I was the new bright shiny object. He chased me relentlessly, seduced, cajoled, until finally I broke my very own cardinal rule and mixed my personal and professional lives."

"You can't paint all successful men with the same brush Ella."

"Look, I resisted for a while, just like I did with you.

Then I caved...it was all downhill from there. Once he had me, it didn't take long before he no longer wanted me. I was devastated Kyle. I didn't think I'd ever get over the heartbreak and humiliation. I was stigmatized at my job, and I still had to make myself get up every day, go in to work, and hold my head high."

"I'm sorry that happened to you but life does have risks. Relationships are a gamble. My marriage wasn't perfect by a long shot, but I got Finn out of it. My wife and I loved each other; we just weren't *in* love. Then she got sick, and we fought hard together. Jemma wanted to live, so bad." His voice broke. "I'm not the same man that I was before. I've learned not to take anything for granted. I don't know why Jemma died and I was spared. She deserves to be here."

Brushing his hair back from his brow she said, "I'm glad you're here. Finn needs you, don't ever forget that!"

Sadness clouded his features. "Bottom line, I'm here, she isn't. Jemma doesn't get to see her amazing little boy grow up. He was the love of her life. Her whole world revolved around him."

Ella tenderly cupped his face. "He had her for those first formative years, she's a part of who he is and who he will become. That's why he's doing so well. He's always been loved."

"I hope you're right and I hope it's enough."

"Are you kidding me? Your face lights up whenever you look at your son. And you are his hero. You're both going to be just fine."

"When I'm with you I believe that...like everything is going to be all right. How do you do that?" He pulled her head down and nibbled on her lower lip.

"I just speak the truth," she said.

"Ella, I don't pretend to know much of anything when it comes to relationships, but I can promise you that I am in this one hundred percent. There is no one else."

She searched his eyes looking for answers and reassurance. She knew he meant what he was saying in the moment and for now that had to be enough. She kissed him on the nose then got up and returned to the bathroom to brush her teeth. She still felt like she was in way over her head. She could only hope he was falling at least half as hard as she was.

⁓

*I*n the early pre-dawn hours, Ella woke up conscious of Kyle's arm slung across her waist and a feeling of safety and connection settled in her heart. Still half asleep she snuggled into his warmth at her back. Kyle was breathing slowly and evenly in sleep, his breath stirring her hair. She smiled contentedly then fell back asleep.

⁓

*H*earing a door slam from somewhere downstairs they both jerked awake then laughingly scrambled out from beneath their warm cocoon of blankets.

"Lock the door, quick," he said, "you're faster than I am."

Ella raced to the door and turned the lock, giggling.

"I feel like I'm about twelve years old right now," Kyle said.

"Me too. So much for showering together."

"We could still try."

"I'm going to slip on my dress and high tail it back to my room. I've got to feed Daisy anyway. She's probably confused and wondering where the hell I am."

Kyle grabbed Ella's hand and pulled her back onto the bed hugging her tight. "That was the best night of my entire life. From start to finish."

"Mine too." She yawned stretching sensuously before extricating herself from his arms. Climbing out of bed she grabbed her dress off the floor, still lying where she had tossed it the night before and slipped it over her head.

"Here let me zip you up," Kyle said. She sat beside him so he could reach. He pulled her hair aside to nuzzle the back of her neck. She melted for a second then remembered again that she was in a hurry and grabbed her panties, not bothering to put them back on she left him with a sweet kiss. "Later."

44

Kyle waited on his last nanny applicant to show up, feeling utterly discouraged. He hoped to hell this interview surpassed the last several. Although he thought the first person he'd interviewed was adequate, he knew she would be a little too stiff and formal for Finn's liking. He glanced up as Richard led an attractive twenty-something woman into his office.

Standing, Kyle reached his hand across the desk and greeted her. "Hi, I'm Kyle Bennett."

"I'm Lindsey Jones. Nice to meet you."

He motioned to the chair in front of him and said, "Have a seat."

She perched on the edge, knuckles white as she clutched her portfolio tightly on her lap.

"Can you tell me a little about yourself? What made you decide to become a live-in nanny?'

"I come from a large family, I'm the oldest, and I

practically raised my four younger siblings. I love kids. It seemed a natural career choice for me."

"Tell me about the last family you worked for, why did you leave?"

"They had two little boys, a four- and six-year-old, both parents were professionals with demanding careers, they both worked fifty plus hours a week. I loved the family, but unfortunately the wife took a job in England and I didn't want to move out of the country, so I resigned."

"That must have been hard, I'm sure you'd grown attached."

"Heartbreaking really. I not only loved the children, but I loved the parents too... not to mention their dog. They were like family."

"Lindsey, I'd like to bring in a friend of mine who has been my temporary nanny while I've been recovering. I'd like her to meet you, if that's all right."

"Sure."

~

*E*lla smiled warmly at Lindsey. "I won't bite I promise. I hate interviews. They're the worst."

Visibly relaxing Lindsey said, "They really are."

Kyle made the introductions then invited Ella to ask any questions she thought might be helpful.

Ella smiled and leaned forward. "Remember there are no right or wrong answers."

Lindsey bit her bottom lip. "Okay."

Continuing Ella said, "Finn has been through so

much... losing his mom, then his dad getting hurt, he sometimes wakes up with nightmares, how would you handle that?"

"Well, first I'd hold him and let him cry it out. Then I'd read him a story or tell him something funny... my youngest brother had nightmares, so I'm used to it."

"Do you think of yourself as flexible or are you more organized and routine-oriented?"

"I'd have to say both. I think routine, like same bedtimes and mealtimes, stuff like that, makes kids feel secure, but I think play time and being off the clock are equally important."

Ella exchanged an approving look with Kyle. Kyle liked that Lindsey was articulate and confident as well as sensible. He also thought her age would be an advantage; young enough to keep a six-year-old entertained but mature enough to be level-headed when necessary.

"You're young and I'm sure you have a boyfriend or will have at some point, how do you work with that? Do you compartmentalize, on the clock and off the clock?" Kyle asked.

Her smile slipped for a moment before answering. "Um, yes exactly, just like any other job. I try to keep my personal life separate from my work... for the most part. It's not to say they never cross over, but most of the time, I see my boyfriend when I'm off-duty."

Kyle studied her for a moment then said, "If you decide to have a guest here, they have to be cleared by our security team first."

"Of course."

"Anything else you can think of Ella?"

"Nope."

"If you get the job how soon could you start?" Kyle asked.

"I'm crashing at a friend's house right now so I could start almost immediately. I don't have a lot of stuff so there isn't a whole lot for me to move."

"I'll get back to you with my decision by tomorrow afternoon. But first I'd like you to meet Finn. I'll page my house manager."

"No, don't bother Richard—I'll go get him," Ella said.

"Okay, that will give Lindsey a chance to ask me some questions."

"I'll be right back."

_____

45

Much later, Ella and Kyle were supervising while Finn splashed around in the pool with Monique, a little friend from school.

Lying prone, stretched out on a chaise lounge next to Kyle, Ella said, "I liked Lindsey; I thought she seemed a little unsure of herself at first, but most importantly Finn liked her."

Kyle's forehead creased. "Yes, she seems to have it all, including a stellar resumé."

"Why the frown?"

"It's such a big decision and she is a little young. Can't put my finger on it, maybe I was hoping to find someone a little more granny-like," he said grinning.

"Well, you had several interviews, didn't anyone fit that criterion?"

Kyle laughed. "Yes, and she was stiff as hell! Finn would have a meltdown."

"There's your answer, unless you want to have a second day of interviews."

"Hell no! That was exhausting."

"Sounds like you've made up your mind."

"I guess I have." Kyle reached over and stroked her back, running his fingers down her spine, he glanced over to make sure the kids were occupied.

"Ella, please stay. You don't have to go just because I've hired a nanny. Live with us. You'll be off at work, I'll be working, we'll come together, we can be a family."

With her cheek resting on her forearm, she sighed. "It sounds so easy when you say it, but it's too soon. We just became intimate... we don't even know how we'll be when life returns to normal. Things will change."

"Things are always changing, that's called life."

"I know, it's just that I'm the one with everything to lose. I'm the one uprooting and taking all of the risks."

"Babe, there are no guarantees about anything, but I want you here, with me and Finn. You won't have to let go of your condo; I'll pay for all of your expenses while we figure things out. So, what's the risk?"

Ella huffed. "As if I'd let you pay my bills!"

"It would be more than worth it to me to have you here. I didn't even know how fucking lonely I was until you came along."

"Same here, but that doesn't mean we should jump into living together, that's a huge step."

"I hate to tell you this but we're already living together."

She pushed herself up and swung around to face him. "Kyle, I really like you a lot. In fact, I'm crazy about you and I'm head over heels in love with your son."

"I want you to be head over heels for me too."

Her heart melted. "Even if I am, I'm not admitting it."

"Ella, I'm crazy about you too. I'm not afraid to follow where this leads us. Let me take care of you, shelter you, make love to you every night and wakeup next to you every morning."

"It's a lot to take in, I need time to think. I need to go back to my condo and have some space...to get my bearings."

Kyle's jaw tightened and Ella could tell that he was becoming frustrated with her, which only strengthened her resolve. She had almost forgotten his stubborn streak and determination, along with his domineering personality. But she could be just as resolute as he.

"I can tell you're getting angry; I'm sorry, but did Mr. Bennett just snap his fingers and not get his way?"

"Don't twist this around," he said. "You're just as much of a butt head as I am...maybe more so."

"Puleeze! Spare me. I've never seen the likes of somcone as used to calling the shots as you are."

"Daddy, Ella, watch this!" Finn yelled, effectively derailing their bickering.

"We're watching," Kyle called back. Finn stood at the side of the pool while Monique held a plastic tube steady in the water. He took a leap and jumped right in the center.

Clapping her hands, Ella said, "Yay! Way to go Finn."

"That was impressive son."

Still irritated, Ella stood up and grabbed her beach

towel wrapping it around herself and strode toward the house.

"Ella where are you going?" Finn called out.

"In to take a shower, you guys should get out and dry off. I have to take Monique home soon."

"Darn!" Finn said.

"It's almost dinner time... listen to Ella," Kyle said.

Ella felt his stare burning holes in her back as she marched off.

46

*R*ich had given Kyle a ride to work and had dropped him off at the door to his office building. He felt grumpy as he grappled with both his briefcase and his cane limping to the elevator. He stepped on and rode it to the ninth floor of the luxurious office suites of Bennett and Sullivan. Although he had warned his staff that he was coming in, everyone in the front office did a double take when he entered. They all greeted him like a long-lost friend, and he felt warmed by their enthusiastic welcome.

He knew he could be difficult to work for. He demanded the best from everyone, but he also expected it from himself. He had always sought to be fair and didn't ask for more than he was willing to give. One hundred percent and nothing less. It appeared that he wasn't perceived as the ogre he had thought he was, if his reception was any indication.

"Mr. Bennett! So great to see you back. You gave us quite a scare!" His secretary Gillian said.

"I heard you had a scare of your own. Thanks for dealing with that delivery so professionally, Gillian."

She beamed with pleasure at the compliment. "You're welcome. It was nothing."

"It was a lot. I really appreciate it. Could you call everyone into the conference room for a brief meeting in thirty minutes please?"

"Yes, of course Mr. Bennett."

"I'll be in my office until then."

His office had an ocean view, one entire wall made up of floor to ceiling windows. Another wall had bookcases. He had a dart board in the corner of the room that he used when he needed to clear his head. There was a piece of tape on the floor, regulation distance from the target.

The only personal memento he had was a framed photograph of Jemma and Finn, taken on their last family vacation before Jemma had become sick. He walked over and picked it up to study their joyful faces. Finn was only three in the snapshot, so innocent, all of them in the dark about what was to come only a year later. He set the picture back down on his massive desk which someone had kindly organized while he was away. His assistant Elenore, he was sure; she was the best.

It felt weird to be back in his office. Before the accident everything work-related had seemed of utmost importance, and now... nothing seemed urgent. The wheeling and dealing of his law practice had somehow lost its import. An early morning phone call from the construction foreman had left him with a headache and a feeling of dread. They could no longer pretend that the sabotage was just mischief; things were amping up...and were much more ominous. Someone meant business.

He also felt frustration with Ella and wondered where their relationship was headed. They had made love that morning, both subdued. She was moving back to her condo this coming weekend. Lindsey had accepted the job offer and was moving in on Friday.

So much change. His old pattern was to bury himself in his work and avoid all feelings. The wake-up call of his accident had given him the break he had needed to see the error of his ways. He owed it to Finn to become the father he had never had. Hell, he owed it to himself.

Ella. He felt a hollowness in his gut thinking of her moving out this weekend. She had dug her heels in, and nothing was going to convince her otherwise. Maybe she'd miss him so badly that she'd cave. He was not a patient man, but he had a feeling he was about to learn a thing or two about that.

"Knock knock," Pete said, sticking his head in the doorway. "Heard you called a meeting."

"Come on in. Missed ya big guy!"

"Sure, you did. With that goddess under your roof? I doubt it, but seriously—thank God you're back."

"Anything I should know before the meeting?"

"Naw nothing you don't already know."

Kyle walked to the door and he and Pete headed towards the conference room. Some of their team was already seated around the long table. Kyle took his seat and his assistant Elenore took her seat beside him, pen and notebook in hand.

Looking around at the engaged faces of his colleagues, Kyle felt a sense of camaraderie that was unfamiliar to him. He cleared his throat. "First, on a personal note, I want to thank you all for your dedication to this firm and your willingness to go above and beyond. It is greatly appreciated and noted. As you are all aware, it's a miracle that I'm even sitting here right now. Thank you for the get-well cards and words of encouragement. They meant a lot."

Gillian piped in, "We're so glad you're back, sir. It was such a shock."

"I'm glad to be back, thank you. I'd like to go around the table and give everyone a few minutes to brief me on your cases...any issues you'd like help with, any concerns." Smiling Kyle said, "Let's start with you John, what do you have for us?"

Everyone took turns sharing and Kyle was satisfied that none of their current cases had anything to do with either the vandalism and sabotage of his father's development or the anthrax scare.

"Does anyone have any ideas about who could be trying to threaten our firm?" Everyone looked concerned as they shook their heads no.

"Pete, would you fill everyone in on the latest?"

"Sometime in the wee hours of the morning, there was more machinery vandalized at the Bennett construction site. Kyle got the call about an hour ago. I drove by on my way here and right now, we have two separate groups picketing the site. Earths Saviors and the neighboring billionaires club. Fun times."

Kyle's eyebrows drew together, his jaw tight. "I'm very concerned. I can't stress enough the seriousness of this. People, you come first. I want everyone here to be extra vigilant. I'm not trying to scare anyone, but we can't assume that they won't escalate their attacks, I'm sorry," Kyle said.

Pete continued, "Two pieces of heavy equipment were targeted. A grader, about a five-hundred-thousand-dollar proposition, and excavator valued around two-hundred-thousand dollars. Someone broke into the mobile office and took the keys to the excavator and spun it around crashing into the bulldozer next to it. Turned it over and crushed the cab. Then, not satisfied, they poured tar in the fuel tank of the grader and all over the interior of the office, almost impossible to clean up. Ruined for all practical purposes. Some serious tampering going on."

Kyle added, "Couple that with the powder delivery and the random slashed tires and burglary, we've got a big problem. I've hired extra security for the office. We're having more surveillance cameras installed in and around the building and parking lot," Kyle said.

"At least they're targeting things and not people," one of the paralegals offered hopefully.

"Yes, there is that, however we don't want to assume anything. If you have any concerns or see anything suspicious let Pete or me know immediately, and don't hesitate to call the police. Any questions? Okay, so I'll only be in the office a couple hours a day until I build up my stamina. Everyone knows how to reach me. Thanks for your time," Kyle said. He stood up and shook a few hands as the group filed out of the room.

Elenore lingered behind, concern etched on her face. "You look so pale, are you sure you're ready to jump back in?"

Kyle smiled kindly at her and said, "I'm only going to be here another hour or so then I'm heading home. Don't worry about me, you've got enough to worry about just keeping this damn place going."

"Don't push it. Remember what you said, people first, that includes yourself." She turned on her heel and left him standing there with Pete.

"She's right. Why don't you go home? You look like hell."

"Gee thanks."

"I know I was pushing you to return, but we've got it covered. You can deal with your old man from home. I'll let you have that honor."

"Just shoot me, will ya?" Kyle knew how that conversation was going to go. He would somehow be to blame for the problems at the construction site. "I've just got a few things to finish up and then I'll head out of here."

"Back into the arms of your sexy nurse for hire. Maybe I could retain her services. I've been a little under the weather lately." He grinned wolfishly.

Gritting his teeth Kyle said, "Her name is Ella. And she'll be returning to the hospital, this was a one and done."

"One and done huh? Money talks. Only the best for the Bennett family."

"What the fuck is your problem?" Kyle asked.

"No problem. Did you develop a thin skin while you were convalescing?"

"No but I'm thinking maybe your sensitivity chip got misplaced while I was recovering."

Touching his hand to his forehead in a mock salute, Peter said, "Good one chief. You must have confused me with someone else. Never had one of those chips to begin with. I've got to run, see you tomorrow."

"I thought you said you had it covered. How are you going to do that if you're not around?"

"It's not like our staff need us hovering over them to do their jobs."

"There has to be a leader or things start to fall apart," Kyle said.

"Well, since I'm the leader now you'll have to let me decide whether or not I need to be here. It's been a very long nine weeks buddy."

"Wow, really? Get the fuck out of here then."

"I'll be back in a couple of hours. Don't sweat it."

Kyle ignored his last statement and turned toward his office. He shut his door forcefully behind him. He was fuming. If the situations were reversed, he would have gladly picked up the slack, in fact he had carried most of the weight of the practice since the beginning. *I guess you find out who your friends are.* Maybe Pete had always been this self-*centered* and he just hadn't noticed. *Maybe I'm the one who has changed.*

Ella and Finn were outside playing kickball when Kyle returned home. Their laughter pierced the air and he felt himself relax from the sound of it.

Finn spotted him. "Daddy!" Running full speed towards Kyle, he stopped just short of barreling right into him.

"Looks like you two are having fun."

"Yep, and I'm winning."

Kyle eyed Ella warily as she approached, waiting to see what the weather conditions between them were going to be this afternoon.

Eyes downcast she said quietly, "Hey."

"Hey yourself."

"How was your first day back?"

He lifted her chin with his fingers and looked piercingly into her liquid green eyes. "Lonely."

"Me too."

Tears shimmered in her eyes which was his undoing. Tenderly he said, "Come here you." Pulling her tightly to his chest, he inhaled her intoxicating scent. "I'm sorry."

Her voice was muffled against his chest as she replied, "I'm sorry too."

He whispered softly in her ear, "Could you repeat that."

He felt her smile against his chest her arms wrapped tightly around his waist.

Finn snuggled his way in and sandwiched himself between them. Kyle felt an ache in his chest and his throat tightened with emotion. *I'm in real trouble here. How the hell did this happen?*

47

---

*E*lla was struggling with how vulnerable she felt. When she had looked up from their ball game and saw Kyle standing there in his suit coat and dress shirt untucked and unbuttoned, her heart had literally flip-flopped. Her earlier anger had vanished and was replaced with a deep longing. Hell, she didn't want to leave, but she knew it was the sensible thing to do. Things had moved so quickly between them and giving herself a breather seemed like the right thing to do. So why did she feel like bawling her eyes out?

As if reading her mind Finn looked up, eyes brimming with tears, and said, "Dad says you're leaving but why do you have to go? Why can't you stay and live with us forever? Daisy doesn't want to go either."

"She doesn't?"

He solemnly shook his head no. "Besides, me and dad love you, you're our family now."

Ella's eyes widened and she burst out in laughter as Kyle joined in.

"What's so funny?" Finn asked bewildered.

"Nothing you little munchkin," Kyle said squeezing him tight. "You've got it all figured out. Way ahead of us adults."

"I know," he said impishly.

"How does ice cream sound?" Kyle asked.

"Yes!" Finn said.

"Let's go. Ella, will you drive us? It's a jeep kind of excursion."

"Sure."

They held hands while Finn raced ahead to the six-car garage where her vehicle was parked right next to the Porsche 918 Spyder. He hadn't replaced his Ferrari yet but most of the garage stalls were full. Parked next to his Porsche was a gorgeous Harley-Davidson bike which made Ella practically drool with envy.

"I can't wait until you can take me for a ride on your bike."

"Me either." He leaned down and kissed her lightly on the lips.

Finn crawled in the back of the jeep, sitting in the booster seat that had become a permanent fixture, and Kyle sat in the front passenger seat.

"Buckle up," Ella said cheerfully.

Finn called out, "I love this jeep!" He stuck his hand out the side before pulling it back in at Ella's sharp glance.

Ella hung back while the gates swung inward and then she took off. She put in a classic CD of Derek and The Dominos, and Bell Bottom Blues blared out from the speakers. She glanced over at Kyle and warmth spread through her body at seeing his look of contentment. Lately, except for their disagreement over her moving in, it really was easy between them. The sexual tension was always there but that was exhilarating and made everything seem brighter and more alive.

When she glanced over again, she caught him studying her. His eyes were the color of lapis lazuli today and when he raised an eyebrow along with a suggestive grin, her lady parts throbbed. She honestly couldn't remember ever feeling this happy. The wind in her hair, her man by her side, the love of her life strapped in the back seat...

Kyle started singing along, *"If I could choose a place to die it would be in your arms."*

"Here we are!" Finn yelled as Ella pulled into the parking lot of the ice cream parlor.

Kyle reached for Finn's hand and grabbed Ella's with the other as the three of them strolled in together. After ordering some god-awful concoction for Finn that looked like a candy machine had exploded, Kyle chose two scoops of chocolate, and she a scoop of butter pecan. They sat outside at a picnic table under a shade tree. Licking her cone delicately while Kyle and Finn slurped like cattle, she flashed Kyle an amused grin.

"What's so funny?" Kyle asked.

"Oh nothing," she said then giggled.

"Finn what do you think?"

"I think she's hiding something."

"I was just admiring your synchronized attacks on your ice cream cones."

"Oh really? And you found that amusing, did you?"

Ella snickered and said, "Yeah like watching two cows at a salt lick."

"Finny, are we going to let her get away with insulting us like that?"

"No way!"

"Hey, what do you have against cows? It could be a compliment," Ella said.

"Yeah Dad, what's wrong with looking like a cow anyway? I love cows," Finn said taking the last bite of his cone. Kyle tossed him a napkin.

"I guess we have to wait while miss dainty-pants slooowly finishes her one dip," Kyle said teasingly.

"Like a cat," Finn said.

She winked at Finn as she bit into the crunchy cone, tucking her hair behind one ear. He beamed back at her. She peeked at Kyle, who returned her glance with an intense gaze of his own. She could almost read his mind. His eyes told her that he wanted to feel her tongue lapping at him like that damn ice cream cone. Warmth shot through her at the thought. Finn's bedtime couldn't get here fast enough.

They sat for a few minutes before loading up and headed for home, completely oblivious of the car parked across the street that immediately started up and pulled away from the curb.

48

That evening, the three of them were sprawled out on the sectional sofa in the theater room watching *Finding Nemo*. Kyle lay on his side his head in Ella's lap, and she had her arm around Finn as he snuggled against her on the other side. She ran her fingers through Kyle's hair then traced his face and neck. He rubbed his head against her lap, one hand resting on her thigh. Her body was practically humming, and she couldn't wait for the movie to end.

Finn's eyes were heavy, and he looked like he was about to fall asleep. She wanted to feel Kyle's hands on her body so badly she was ready to crawl out of her skin. Not that she wasn't enjoying the time spent with the three of them, but being in such close proximity to Kyle, feeling his warm skin on her bare thighs, having his head so close to her womanhood, was taking its toll. He turned to look up at her and his eyes burned with desire. *Good.*

The End. Finally! Kyle picked his sleeping son up from the couch and carried him to the elevator and on to bed. Ella rode up with them then went to her room to brush her teeth and slip into a nightie. Kyle had bought her a plunging black lace teddy that she hadn't worn yet, so she decided to surprise him. Dabbing a hundred dollar's-worth of perfume behind her ears, she smiled wryly, remembering how angry she had been when she'd googled the price point. It seemed like months ago. She fluffed out her hair then adding a touch of lip gloss, threw on a robe and headed to his bedroom.

Kyle was brushing his teeth as she wrapped her arms around his waist from behind and watched him in the mirror. She trailed kisses along his back and shoulders, then rubbed her cheek against him. Their eyes met and his were liquid fire. She trembled with need. Slipping her hands into his boxers she fondled him. Her palm gripped him firmly as she slowly moved up and down his rock-hard shaft while the other hand cupped his roundness from behind. He braced both hands on the vanity to gain purchase.

Ella paused long enough to pull down his shorts and he stepped out of them. As she trailed her finger down the cleft of his buttocks, he turned and unbelted her robe, gasping when he saw her in the sexy lingerie. She knew he could see her nipples through the lace and the swell of her cleavage in the lowcut halter of the bodice. The bottoms were lacey high cut panties which left some of her rounded butt exposed.

His voice was husky, and her pulse fluttered when he whispered her name, before pulling her roughly to him, plundering her mouth. Her skin felt seared where his hands splayed across her ass. She trembled as he squeezed and massaged while holding her pelvis tight against his own. His assault was unrelenting, and she matched it thrust for thrust. Their tongues danced and explored. She curled her hands into his hair and gripped tightly as she held his mouth to hers.

Ella felt breathless when he grabbed her hand and pulled her along to his bed. He climbed on top of her rubbing his length between her thighs, poking against the flimsy fabric driving her crazy with longing. He was all male, skilled, confident, strong...he buried his fingers in her tangled hair fanned out around the pillow, his eyes burning with desire.

Swooping down he covered her parted lips and took what she was offering. He hovered over her, peppering kisses all over her face. She was throbbing as he slowly kissed his way downward, lingering at the hollow of her throat before continuing on his path.

He nuzzled her breasts then pulled the lace aside to take her nipple into his mouth sucking hard. She bucked under him, every pull sending shock waves through her body. He guided his erection beneath her panties and was now rubbing against her, he teasingly dipped the tip of his cock in, before pulling back out. Again and again going a little deeper each time until she moaned.

Bending her knees, she spread her legs wider, coaxing him to enter her fully. "I need to feel you inside of me now!" He reached in the bedside table and pulled out a condom. After rolling it over his shaft, he thrust, *hard,* deep inside of her. Taking total control, he rocked his pelvis driving deep. She was hot and wet and ready.

Sweat glistened on his furrowed brow and she watched his beautiful face as he rode her, plunging in and out. He held her hands prisoners stretched above her head and his hungry gaze was pinned on her. She could feel her breasts bouncing with every thrust.

"I—don't know—how—much longer—I can... *I'm coming,*" he groaned as they climaxed at the same time. She moaned and shuddered beneath him as she felt his body racked by the waves of his orgasm.

Ella loved the weight of Kyle's body pressing hers into the mattress. His lips trailed kisses along her neck, nibbling tenderly. She ran her hands down his back cupping his butt and squeezing. "Well, that was amazing," she said, her voice husky with sex.

"Babe, you have no idea..."

Kyle rolled off Ella and turned onto his side facing her. He traced his finger across her lips as her teeth caught it and bit down. "Ouch, you wench, that hurt!"

She stretched her arms overhead, squirming like a cat, still half in half out of her skimpy lace nightie. He pulled it down the rest of the way and undressed her. She lay naked and vulnerable under his intense stare. "Ella, beautiful Ella. I'm tangled up in your web."

She arched an eyebrow. "So, you're comparing me to a spider?"

He grinned. "As a matter of fact, yes, a black widow." He dove between her legs and nuzzled the soft hair on her mound before gently licking her vulva. She shuddered. He used the pad of his thumb to press against her sweet spot while inserting his finger inside her.

She breathlessly said, "What are you doing to me?"

"I'm trying to make it impossible for you to leave me."

She took hold of each ear and tugged him up to her face. "Can we please not talk about that tonight?"

"Why not? You know this is right. Why are you being so stubborn?"

He should have taken her hint when she glared, but in his usual pushy style he continued, "We have something special here. You know it, I know it, even Finn knows it. Are you sure you're not just trying to prove a point that I can't have everything I want?"

"You know what...you can go screw yourself. I asked you not to ruin our night by pressuring me. And yes, you always get your way, maybe it's time you learned the art of accepting the word no."

"That's just what I thought. How immature can you get. You're willing to take a risk of losing us, just to prove a fucking point. Great."

"Grow up Kyle. I have to return to work next week. Imagine the dragon lady hearing that I am now shacked up with the billionaire who paid for my services. That would be a real fun time for me."

"That's what this is all about? What other people might think?"

"A bit of an oversimplification, don't you think? My reputation happens to mean something to me, I'm sorry if that seems shallow to you. I happen to be self-made; nothing was given to me."

Kyle jerked his head back and glared. "You know

what I think? You're a snob. That's what I think. You think you're better than me because you had to "work for everything" and I'm just some dumb schmuck born with a silver spoon in his mouth and of no value as a person."

"That's ridiculous."

"Is it? You seem to be the only one hung up on my money. Let me ask you this, if I weren't rich would you stay with me?"

"That's not fair. How would I know. It would certainly be easier that's for sure."

"There, you just answered it." Kyle got up and went to the bathroom.

Seeing him standing there naked bent over pulling up his briefs made her heart turn over. She knew he was hurt but she couldn't explain her feelings. "Kyle I'm not trying to punish you for something you had no control over. It's just that the inequality of our situations puts me at a disadvantage. It's probably impossible for you to understand. For one you're a man and therefore judged on a completely different playing field and two you've always had money and power."

"Money yes, power no," he said quietly.

"Societally, you've always had power, that's not to say you've always felt powerful."

"You say tomotto I say tomato." With eyes narrowed he said, "I'm going downstairs for a shot of whisky. Then maybe a dip in the pool to cool off. You want to join me?"

"No thank you. I'm going to go to sleep."

"Fine," he huffed, forgetting his cane in his haste to get away. Ella sat there wondering what the hell just happened. She felt like she just suffered a whiplash. How could things have gone south so quickly. She was tempted to return to her own bedroom but that seemed childish, so she got under the duvet cover and turned on her side; reaching for the bedside lamp, she switched it off. Soon she fell into a restless slumber.

Sometime much later she awoke to Kyle slipping into bed beside her, turning on his side with his back to her. She could smell the bourbon and figured more than one shot was involved. She felt hurt and lonely. She had hoped that when he returned to bed, he would have cooled off and come to his senses. Apparently not. *Spoiled brat.* She sighed.

"Are you going to pout all night?" Ella asked quietly.

"Who's pouting?"

Ella rolled over to face him and snuggled up against his back. He stiffened for a moment then softened and relaxed into her. "Goodnight," she said kissing him on the back of his neck and slinging her arm around his waist.

"Night."

~

The following morning, she woke up to the sound of Kyle taking a shower. She lay there, still half asleep, missing the warmth of him next to her. She rolled onto her belly and buried her head in the pillow. Hearing the water shut off she glanced through the open door of the bathroom and watched him towel off.

What a magnificent creature he was. Every girl's

fantasy. She admired his broad shoulders and sculpted back; his defined muscles taut as he vigorously towel dried his hair. His ass, *oh my God*, his hamstrings. Warmth pooled in her belly. He glanced in the mirror and met her gaze. He didn't say anything, but his eyes flickered with some emotion he was determined to keep to himself.

"You're up early," she ventured.

Silence.

"I guess you're not talking to me?"

"You're pretty quick," he snapped.

"He does speak. Kyle..."

Kyle interrupted her, "Ella I don't want to hear it. You've made yourself perfectly clear. I guess I was no more than a fuck for you. I get it. You're afraid of losing yourself. You're afraid of being hurt again. You're afraid of hospital gossip, I get that, but what I don't get is your lack of courage. Why not try facing your fears instead of running from them."

"Who's the one running now and last night?"

Kyle shoved a leg into his jeans. "I invited you to join me."

Ella sat up covering herself with the sheet. "Yes, you did—after you tried bullying me to go against my own better judgement."

Zipping his jeans, he said, "And after you told me I'm a sexist pig that would never be able to understand."

"I said no such thing!"

"It's what you didn't say. I can read between the lines, babe."

"Apparently not. Hey, I've got an idea, why don't you

go out and buy me some expensive jewelry or perfume, that might convince me."

He pulled a tee-shirt over his head. "You're unbelievable. You know I finally figured you out. You really are the one with the problem. You have a poverty complex."

Ella glared. "You're practicing without a license there Freud."

Striding toward the door he said, "I'll take Finn to school this morning. I'm heading into the office anyway. Lindsey starts tomorrow. I guess that means your nanny obligation is fulfilled."

Ella fought back tears as she said, "How dare you twist this around. Finn has never been just an obligation to me. I love him. I have loved every single second of my time spent with him." Ella stood up with her chin in the air; with the sheet wrapped around her she gracefully strode to retrieve her robe from the bathroom.

"I guess since I'm out of a job here, I'll pack up today and be on my way."

"Ella..."

She raised her eyebrows, hand on her hip, waiting to see what he was going to say.

His nostrils flared as he glared at her. "Nothing," he said and walked towards the door.

"Don't forget your cane," she said. He glared then left without it. She threw herself on top of the bed and sobbed like her heart was broken, because it was. Was that really the best he had?

49

*I*t was a typical Monday morning and Ella's first day back at the hospital. It had been almost a week since she'd moved out of Kyle's place. When she arrived at work this morning, she had been welcomed enthusiastically by her colleagues but had yet to run into the head nurse. She dreaded it. Deb had filled Ella in on the latest gossip and brought her up to date about the patients Ella would be covering that day.

Before Deb had clocked out, she had looked Ella up and down, forehead creased with concern, and commented about her appearance. Ella had been surprised it was so obvious. She knew she hadn't been sleeping but she thought her makeup would conceal it. Deb's empathy touched her and was almost her undoing. She would rather stay numb. Ella shut her out and felt bad at the look of hurt on her friend's face. She just couldn't. Not here, not at work...maybe not anywhere.

Kyle had tried calling the first several days after she

had left, and Ella had let it go straight to voice mail. Then he had stopped. She'd stayed busy exhausting herself with obsessively cleaning and exercise. That had worked in the past. It hadn't this time. *Damn him!*

She had just finished sponge bathing her patient when Delores popped her head in. Rattled, she missed a step as she was carrying the tub of water and spilled half of it on the floor.

"That will be a slipping hazard. Clean that up immediately! You should be more careful." Ella's cheeks reddened and she secretly fumed but said nothing.

"Come to my office when you finish up here."

Ella nodded her head yes and continued cleaning up. Deloris stood in the doorway, arms crossed watching her, wearing her permanent scowl. Exasperated Ella said, "Is there anything else I can do for you?"

"No. Carry on."

Anger flashed through Ella and Deloris smiled knowingly, her lips twisting in a satisfied smirk as she exited the room.

Her patient, a charming senior on the other side of eighty, patted her hand as she took his blood pressure. "She's a real piece of work that one is."

Ella smiled warmly and winked. "Ya think?"

"I know. What a dour and unpleasant woman. I take it she's your boss?"

"Yes, but don't worry about me, I can handle it."

"I'm here if you want to talk about it. I don't think I'll be going anywhere in the near future," he said, looking hopelessly tiny and frail.

"I might just take you up on that Mr. Fogarty."

His smile lit up his weathered face. "Good. I hope you mean it."

"You're all set for now. I'll be back soon to check on you. Try to get some rest."

"Don't let that witch push you around."

"I won't." She plumped his pillow and adjusted his covers before heading into the viper's den.

～

*E*lla knocked lightly. "Enter," Deloris said.

Ella stood just inside the door, hands clasped waiting for her instructions.

"Sit." She did.

"Well, well, well, I'm surprised you came back."

Ella's lips tightened and her eyes narrowed, daring her to go there. "You called me in for a reason I presume?"

"Yes. Tonya called in sick, so I need you to fill in for her today."

Her voice shaky Ella said, "You're pulling me from my nursing duties to be an aide?"

"Exactly."

"Are you sure this isn't punishment for my time off?"

"Don't be dramatic. You know, six weeks is a long time to go short-handed. We had to hire a replacement and she is just starting to catch on. I would hate to pull her when she is still learning the ropes."

"I would think with my seniority, you would! She could learn quite a bit as an aide. I've paid my dues. I have the most seniority on this unit."

"And I am your supervisor. As my subordinate I expect you to comply without argument. End of story."

Delores continued, "I'm sure you're not going to like this either but tomorrow I'm transferring you to another floor. They had someone quit unexpectedly. Better prepare yourself, you could be floating for a couple of days or it could even turn into weeks. Their unit needs you and ICU doesn't."

"We'll see about this!" Ella said seething.

"I hope you're not thinking about running to your billionaire lover to rescue you."

Tears shimmered in Ella's eyes as she said quietly, "Is that all then?"

"One more thing... I had better not hear any gossip come back to me that you've been complaining to your peers; we want to keep morale up and disgruntled employees have no place in nursing. Do we understand one another?"

"Completely." Turning on her heel she stormed out of the office and headed to the restroom. Locking herself in, she let the tears come. She felt humiliated and outraged at the same time. *That bitch!* But Deloris had called her bluff when she brought Kyle into the equation. She knew Ella wouldn't lower her pride and ask Kyle to intervene on her behalf.

She stopped in to inform Mr. Fogarty that she had a change of duty and she wouldn't be his nurse, but she'd still be in and out as an aide.

"You're telling me that woman demoted you to emptying catheter bags and bedpans?" Mr. Fogarty said incredulously.

"Now Mr. Fogarty, it's not so bad. Aides are a very important part of a patient's care. I'm happy to serve."

"I may put in a complaint."

"Please no!" she said panicked.

"If you don't want me to I won't."

"Please. It would only make the situation worse. But thank you. Let's just keep this between you and me, okay?"

"I will."

Ella erased her name from the white board and entered the new nurse's name. "Your new nurse's name is Sarah. She'll be in soon to check on you. Get some rest. That's an order," she said with a smile.

When Ella turned to leave Dr. Thompson entered the room.

His eyes widened when he saw her. "Ella! Great to have you back. How is my favorite patient here doing?"

"Ornery," she said smiling.

"How do you feel Mr. Fogarty, on a scale of one to ten what is your pain level today?"

"I'd say a three."

Dr. Thompson smiled. "I'm leaving for the day and had to check on another patient, so I thought I'd stop in to see you on my way out."

"Thanks."

Andy looked at Ella. "Could you join me in the hallway for a sec?"

"Sure. See you later Mr. Fogarty. I'll be popping in."

As they exited the patient's room, Andy smiled warmly at Ella and said, "Will you walk me to the stairwell?"

"Yes."

"I've missed you, Ella. I'm glad you're back. Please don't take this the wrong way...you know how hospitals are, but I have to ask, are you involved with somebody?"

"Not at the moment."

"But you were? The patient you were caring for?"

"It wasn't like that..."

"I'm not here to judge, I just thought we had something... I thought you were attracted to me. Was I just imagining that it went both ways?"

"No, I was... am attracted to you, it's just that I don't date doctors anymore, remember?"

"And what about patients?"

Ella winced. "That's not judging?"

"I'm sorry. I really, really like you, Ella. If you tell me nothing's going on, I'll believe you. Please consider letting me take you out. You won't regret it."

"Andy, let's revisit this another time. I'm having a very bad day. I promise I'll get back with you."

"As long as you promise." He reached out and tenderly brushed a loose tendril of hair from her cheek. That simple act of kindness almost sent her over the edge.

"I've got to go; I'm subbing for an aide today and it's one of me to ten patients."

He frowned but didn't comment. "I'll check back in with you another time then."

"Okay. Thanks Andy."

His eyes were intent, and it seemed like he wanted to say more but stopped himself. "Bye Ella."

50

*E*lla was exhausted after running up and down the unit all day caring for ten patients. The ratio of aides to patients sucked. She didn't know how the aides did it day after day. Her feet were killing her, and her low back ached after having to do several transfers of larger patients at the end of her long day.

As she turned the corner onto her street, she spied a cherry red sports car sitting in her drive and her heart skipped several beats. Her stomach roiled and she hoped she didn't throw up. She pulled in and saw Kyle sitting on the top step of her front stoop holding a bouquet of flowers.

Turning off her jeep, she sat there for a minute, taking several calming breaths before getting out to confront her unexpected guest. His tie was undone and hung loosely around his neck. He had taken off his jacket and unbuttoned his shirt halfway down his chest. His hair was unruly, and he looked tired. She softened for a moment until she recalled the day she had just spent at work, thanks to him.

He stood up, hesitantly offering the flowers, which she ignored. Walking around him she stuck her key in the lock. She went inside leaving the door wide open. He hesitantly stepped inside, seemingly unsure if it was an invitation or not.

Ella put her bag down and turned to face Kyle, glaring, with hands on her hips. "Well?"

"Ella why won't you return my calls?"

"What's the point? We're miles apart. This is a one-sided relationship. It's all about you!"

"No, that's not true." He approached, setting the flowers on the counter as he reached for her hand. She jerked it away.

"Don't touch me!"

Kyle took a deep steadying breath. "We had a fight. Couples do that you know. Why are you making this out to be more than it is?"

"Let me tell you a little story. You know what I was greeted with today, thanks to your intrusion into my life?"

"No, but I'm sure you're about to tell me."

"I was assigned to sub for a nurses' aide who called in sick, despite my seniority. That means instead of one to two patients I had ten. Instead of using my nursing skills to save lives, I changed catheters and bedpans. I changed bedding, I cleaned up vomit. Not that I'm above any of that—it's an important job, but this was assigned out of spite just because she can!"

"Ella..."

She held up her hand. "I'm not finished! You know

what I'll be doing tomorrow and for the foreseeable future? I'll be floating, which means I'm being pulled from ICU, and moved to another unit that needs me. Completely new routine, I'll have to deal with the hierarchy and cliques, I'll get the crappy assignments and the difficult patients—you know, the whiners and complainers, the ones whose call lights are going off continuously. Floaters aren't typically treated that well."

"Ella, I'm sorry, I had no idea..." Kyle trailed off.

"No of course you didn't, because you're a spoiled self-centered man who always gets his way. You plow over anyone in your path."

"How could I know my request would lead to all of that?"

"That's not the point. If you had respected me and listened to the word no from the beginning, none of this would have happened."

"You know what, I'm going to say something that will get me further in trouble, but what the hell! I'm not sorry." Her eyes widened. "If I hadn't insisted you come work for me, I wouldn't have gotten to know you. I would never have held you in my arms, made love to you... so no, I'm not sorry."

Ella felt her eyes sting with tears and looked away.

"But I *am* sorry that you're being punished for my actions. I never saw that coming. How could I?"

This time when he reached for her hand, she didn't pull away. He brought it to his lips and kissed her palm. "Ella, I've missed you. I'm lonely without you. I need you in my life. So does Finn. Please forgive me. I promise not to pressure you anymore about moving in with us."

She squeezed her eyes shut, causing her tears to spill out and run down her cheeks. Kyle groaned and pulled her to his chest. He kissed the top of her head. "Oh baby, I'm so sorry. I never meant for you to get hurt. I'll talk to Joe; I'm sure he's unaware of what a bitch your supervisor is."

Her hands rested on his hips, sniffling against his chest she said, "No please, it would only make things worse. I'll get through this. I'm tough. It was just a rude reentry. I love my unit and working in ICU, but I'll adjust and hopefully I won't be a floater forever."

He tilted her chin up and used his thumbs to tenderly wipe the tears from her cheeks. Then he kissed both eyelids, the tip of her nose, finally settling on her lips. He didn't press, his lips lingered there. The rasp of his afternoon stubble against her chin, the sensation of his soft lips hovering, the scent of his expensive aftershave, his breath against her skin, were all familiar and welcome. She parted her mouth, and still his lips remained motionless. His hands burrowed into her thick mane of hair. Her breath quickened. She reached up and wrapped her hands behind his head pulling him closer as she licked into his mouth.

That was all it took to unleash him. The inferno erupted and he began to ravage her mouth. His thirst seemed unquenchable. Separating he pulled her scrubs over her head and unclasped her bra, inhaling sharply when her breasts spilled out. Pulling her pants down he kissed her flat belly... her mound... her thighs... she steadied herself, hanging on to his shoulders as she stepped out of her slacks. She stood before him in a skimpy lace bikini bottom, feeling raw and vulnerable.

Still squatting, he ran his hands up her inner thighs and kissed his way up her parted thighs. Nestling his nose against her mound, she rocked against him as she braced against the counter behind her. He opened mouth kissed her there and she could feel the heat through her panties. He nuzzled and Ella moaned his name.

Standing, he ripped off his dress shirt and unbuckled his pants then slid them off kicking them aside. He turned her around to face the counter and she arched her back, looking over her shoulder willingly parting her legs for him. His eyes were blazing as he hungrily raked over her, lingering on her ass. Reaching down he rummaged through the pockets of his discarded slacks and pulled out a condom. He ripped it open and rolled it over his thick hard cock.

He gripped one hip while positioning his cock at her entrance with the other. He entered from behind and she cried out with pleasure as he filled her wet center. Holding her steady with both hands his fingers dug into her as he pistoned his hips, plunging deeply inside, slowly at first, then faster and harder, pounding against her buttocks. The sounds of groaning and flesh slapping against flesh were carnal and erotic. He used his foot to spread her legs further and pulled her tighter into him as he rode her.

With each push he stimulated her G-spot. When he reached around and squeezed her breasts, she exploded throwing her head back while she cried out.

Grasping the counter-top she rode wave after wave as she spasmed around his big cock.

"Oh baby, you feel so good. I love how warm and tight you are." Ella could feel herself pulsating around his cock. He groaned, erupting violently, coming inside of her, pumping wildly into her receptive womb. She felt his slick chest as he draped himself against her, one arm wrapped around her waist, his palm pressed against her flat belly. He grunted with each surge of ejaculation. When the storm calmed, he withdrew and discarded the condom before turning Ella to face him and pulling her into his arms.

Ella, still feverish from their passion, could barely move. She sucked and nibbled his neck as her breath returned to normal, her fingers stroking the damp curls on his chest. She practically purred when he ran his hands down the length of her back, settling only when he reached her buttocks, cupping them.

Ella found her voice. "Kyle, that was...the best makeup sex I've ever had."

He smiled into her hair, squeezing her tightly against him. "Promise me you'll never leave me like that again."

She cradled his face between her palms and peered deeply into his blue eyes. "I promise. Kyle I..."

"You?"

"I... I'm crazy about you."

"I'm more than crazy about you, you know that don't you?"

"Yes, I think I do."

"Unfortunately, I've got to get home and relieve the nanny, who by the way is working out well."

"I've been wondering how that was going. I'm relieved to hear it."

"Finn is already becoming attached. But that doesn't let you off the hook, he misses you terribly."

"I miss him too."

"He's spending the weekend with Faye; she is picking him up Friday afternoon and he'll be there through Sunday. Wanna come over and stay with me?"

"Yes!"

He hugged her tightly. "Good answer. Maybe you can drop in to see Finn one night this week. He'd really like that."

"I will."

While Kyle got dressed, Ella went to grab a robe before seeing him out. She stood on her tip toes and pecked him on the lips.

"You're so beautiful," Kyle said.

"You are looking pretty hot yourself. See you soon," she said smiling shyly before closing the door.

51

*K*yle was completely immersed in the work piled on top of his desk when his father stormed in without warning. "Why the hell didn't you call me about this latest clusterfuck?"

"Hello to you too Dad. What brings you to town?"

"I'm considering dumping the whole damn development. It's costing me way too much and the local law enforcement doesn't seem to be concerned about solving it."

"There is only so much they can do. They assure me they're on it."

His father glared. "Don't you have any connections?"

"Yes, but it takes time. It's not like pulling a rabbit out of the hat."

"As our attorney I'd like your opinion about our options."

"After the last round of vandalism, things have been

quiet. The Earth Saviors are still picketing but have backed off since development has ground to a screeching halt. Have a seat." Kyle motioned to a chair.

He thought his dad was looking old and haggard. When had that happened? He'd always been virile and as healthy as a horse. He stayed in shape, golfed five days a week, lifted weights, walked regularly, he and his mother always on the go.

In a moment of weakness, he let his guard down with his father. "Dad, you look tired. Everything okay?"

He pinned Kyle with a hard look. "Why wouldn't it be? Other than the fact that my oldest son can't seem to manage one tiny aspect of the family business, it's all just hunky dory."

Kyle's mouth twisted and he forced himself not to go for the bait. "Dad what would you have me do?"

"Now I'm supposed to tell you how to be an attorney? Why in the hell did I pay for you to go to an Ivy League law school? So, I could hold your hand?"

Despite his father's browbeating, Kyle still sensed something was off with him. "How's Mom?"

"She's fine. Spending money like there's no tomorrow... per usual."

"She has to get something out of it for putting up with you."

"I would agree."

Kyle raised his eyebrows in surprise. "Wow, did I hear right? You agreed with something I said. That's a first." He looked at his watch, "It only took thirty-four years, six months, twelve hours and three minutes for that to happen, very impressive."

His father waved his hand impatiently. "I asked for

your advice. Cut my losses and pull out or move forward?"

"For now, I'd say lay low and see if things settle down. Stop everything temporarily and reevaluate in a month."

"That's what we'll do then."

"Did Mom fly in with you?"

"No, I flew solo."

"Why not? Is she feeling okay?"

"Yes, why the sudden concern about us?"

"You're my parents."

"That's never held much weight before."

"Maybe I'm softening," Kyle said.

"Doubtful. Regardless, your mom is fine. So am I. I'm just under some added stress. I needed some time alone, but nothing I can't handle."

"Let me know if there's anything I can do to help," Kyle offered.

"Just stay on top of this clusterfuck going on here."

"Are you staying with Faye?"

"No, I booked a hotel. I'm here on business."

"You know you're always welcome to stay with me and Finn. It's not like there's a lack of space."

"I appreciate it." Standing he said, "I've got to get going. I'll notify the foreman of my decision."

"I think it's your best course of action."

As he reached the door, Kyle's father turned, his brows drew together and he said, "You know Kyle, I love your mother, I always have."

Kyle waited for him to say more but instead he turned and left, leaving Kyle to ponder that obscure statement. *Where the hell did that come from?* He'd have to call his mom later and check in to see if everything really was all right.

Kyle dove back into his case load and the moment was quickly forgotten.

*K*yle came down the staircase just as Lindsey was leaving. Since Finn was gone, she had the entire weekend off and had informed them she'd be gone until Sunday evening. A man stood waiting just inside the door next to Richard. Kyle gave a salute and continued on to his office. He would have to check with Richard to see if Lindsey had obtained security clearance for her guest as he had instructed her to do. The man had seemed to be staring rather boldly at Kyle, almost challengingly.

Kyle shook it off, chalking it up to his imagination. He didn't entertain strangers at his home and was unused to coming upon someone standing in his foyer. Natalie had never invited anyone on the premises and that had suited Kyle just fine. He might make that a new rule. He'd have a talk with Lindsey on Monday and clarify a few things.

As Rich was passing by his office, he called him in. "Hey Rich, did Lindsey happen to get security clearance for her visitor?"

"No sir, not that I am aware of. She didn't request it from me."

"Me either." Kyle rubbed his jaw. "I'm pretty sure I mentioned it. I'll discuss it with her on Monday."

"Yes sir."

"Ella will be spending the weekend here. She'll be here any minute."

Richard Drake practically beamed. "Very glad to hear it! I'll watch for her."

Kyle smiled. *Apparently, none of us are immune to Ella's charm.*

A few minutes later the bell chimed signaling that Ella had arrived. Kyle stuffed his files back into his briefcase and went to meet her. Richard was there exchanging words with her when Kyle approached. She had on short cut-off jeans that hugged her hips, a red tank crop top which exposed her toned arms and flat stomach, and her customary flip-flops.

He stripped Ella bare, his eyes roaming greedily over her with intensity, leaving no question about his level of desire. Richard discreetly slipped away as Kyle pulled her into his arms kissing her hungrily. Talking against her lips he said, "What took you so long?"

Breathlessly she said, "I've missed you."

"Where's Daisy?"

"My friend Deb is going to check in on her."

"Next time bring her along. I've grown quite attached."

"Deal."

He grabbed her hand and tugged her along. "Come on I have something to show you."

"What?"

"It's a surprise."

Ella let Kyle pull her along. He was in his normal stay-at-home garb, barefoot, old, faded jeans and a white tee shirt. He slowed down when she had to skip a couple of steps to keep up. Kyle was as excited as a little kid.

Ella said, "I can't believe how well you're getting around. You've come a long way."

He nodded. "I'm pretty lucky." They went outside and he made her cover her eyes. "Let me lead you from here. Can I trust you to keep your eyes shut?"

"Yes."

The automatic garage doors made little sound as they opened smoothly. Ella wrinkled her nose. "Do I hear garage doors opening?"

"Quit guessing."

"The suspense is killing me!"

"One more second." He pulled her a few more steps. "You can open them now."

She did and her eyes went wide with shock making Kyle grin. She gaped, staring at the black and chrome Harley Street Sportster with a wide pink ribbon wrapped around the entire bike and a big pink bow on the handlebars. She looked at him and squealed, "For me?"

"Yes, do you like it?"

"Like it? I love it! But I don't know how to ride."

"I'll teach you this weekend!"

"Really?"

"Really," he said, his gaze warm with affection.

"Can I get on?" He nodded, so she straddled the bike and looked up at him laughing joyfully. "Motor-cycle mama! Can we go now?"

"Let me show you a few things first, but yeah we can take them up and down the road a few times before dinner."

She wiggled her index finger at him seductively. "Come over here."

He walked over and stared down at her, utterly enchanted with her unspoiled delight. He felt sad that he had never really experienced that. He'd always had *things*...but they'd never made him this happy. It made his chest tighten to see her so excited. He leaned down and kissed her full on the lips. He held nothing back and neither did she. The fire between them had only increased with their growing intimacy; he would never get enough of her. It dawned on him that this must be what it felt like to be in love, which hit him like a ton of bricks. *I'm in love! Well, I'll be damned.*

Ella felt him freeze for a moment and wondered if his pain was back. "Are you okay?'

"Yeah, I'm fine."

"You look a little bewildered. Are you sure you're not in pain?"

"No nothing like that. Let's go over the basics. I'll give you a tutorial on the bike then we can go for a short ride."

"Sounds good to me."

He had her get off so he could sit on the bike and explain all the gadgets, bells and whistles. The bike was loaded. He guessed his early assessment had been incorrect; he was just as excited as she was. Her joy was rubbing off.

52

*E*lla looked at him and suddenly choked up. With a jolt she realized she had fallen in love with this man. Hook, line and sinker. He was so earnest as he patiently explained the rules of the road and stressed putting safety first. It was so new and tender that she knew she would keep her discovery to herself for the time being. She felt hopeful, scared, shaken, but she couldn't help the warmth that flooded her heart.

Much later, lying in bed after making love, Ella snuggled against her man, enjoying everything about him—his smell, his laugh, his intelligence, his quick wit, even his alpha maleness. Thinking about his accident and how critical his condition had been when she first saw him in the ICU, she slid down under the covers to kiss his inner thigh where his angry scar remained. It was the only physical reminder of his close encounter with death. She nuzzled his spent maleness, loving the soft skin surrounded by coarse hair, the intoxicatingly *musky... male...sexy...scent of him.*

"I couldn't even if I wanted to. You're wearing me out," Kyle said lazily already half asleep.

She kissed her way back up and planted a wet one on his lips. "Nothing like that, I just wanted to smell you."

"You're weird." He grinned, keeping his eyes closed.

"Maybe so but I love the smell of sex."

"Go to sleep."

"I will. Good night, my love," she said quietly, but Kyle was already snoring, fast asleep.

~

The weekend seemed to fly by. She and Kyle were enjoying Sunday brunch by the pool, when Finn appeared, running out to greet them excitedly. "Ella! Dad! I'm home!"

"We can see that," Kyle said, smiling indulgently.

Finn threw himself onto Ella's lap and she held on tight. "How's my favorite kid?" she asked.

"I'm so glad you're back. My dad was really grumpy after you left. But I knew it was accounta that he likes you and he was missing you."

Ruffling his hair, she said, "How did you get to be so smart?"

He grinned and shrugged. "Lucky I guess."

"I missed you guys too," Ella said.

"How's Daisy?"

"Good, no doubt wondering where you are. How are Miley and Cyrus doing?"

"Great but I still need a dog. You promised you'd work on Dad," he said.

"I kept my promise and I think we're making some headway."

His eyes went round. "Is that true Dad?"

"I'm considering it. Ella and I thought we could all go to the animal shelter and see if there are any puppies that would be a good fit. There are a few rescue places to check out as well."

"*Really?*"

"Yes really."

"When?"

"This week."

Finn spun around and around until he got dizzy and plopped down on the ground at their feet. "My dream is finally coming true."

Faye joined them carrying a plate of fruit she had helped herself to.

"Aunt Faye, guess what?"

"Tell me."

"Dad said I can get a puppy!"

"It's about time."

"I know, right?"

They all laughed.

"I've got an appointment with a realtor to look at a property," Faye said tentatively.

"What kind of property?" Kyle asked.

"A bar, right on the marina."

"You wouldn't happen to be talking about Skully's old place, would you?" Ella asked.

"Yes! Do you know it?"

"I spent most of my early twenties sidled up to the bar there...when I wasn't cramming for an exam."

"I love it!"

"Wait a minute Sis, are you trying to tell me you want to own and operate a bar?"

"Yes, and serve bar food and have live entertainment on the weekends."

"But you don't know anything about running a business."

"Don't be a killjoy. I can learn."

"Just the liability of owning a bar in your position makes me nervous," Kyle said.

Waving her hand dismissively, Faye said, "Says the attorney."

"Your point?"

"Why are you being so negative? Dad is harassing me about being a freeloading trust fund baby and now I come up with a plan and everyone is slamming it. I can't win!"

"I think it's a wonderful idea Faye," Ella offered.

"You do?"

"Yes, I do. It sounds like loads of fun too. I'm sure the initial investment is exorbitant but it's sure to pay off. As they say, location, location, location."

"That's what I think."

"Me too, Aunt Faye. I can help," Finn said. "Can I bring Lucy or Charlie?"

"Who?"

Ella laughed at Faye's puzzled expression. "He already has the names picked out for his puppy."

She chuckled ruffling her nephew's hair affectionately. "Sure."

"I guess I'm overruled here. What can I do to help?" Kyle said.

Faye threw her arms around her big brother and said, "Thank you! I knew you'd be there for me. If I decide to go for it, I need you to go over the sales contract for me...make sure everything looks legit. Then I'd like you to handle the deed prep, closing, all that legalese stuff."

"I can do that."

Faye finished the last ripe strawberry on her plate and got up to leave. Giving Ella a hug she said, "A little advice for you big brother... you'd better hold on tight to this one!"

Ella's cheeks turned pink as she met Kyle's smoldering eyes. "That's the plan. Now, do you have any suggestions on how to go about it?" he asked.

"Treat her the way you want to be treated...be romantic, surprise her regularly, don't be afraid to admit when you're wrong, don't be a butthead."

"Got it!" he winked at Ella.

"You left out the part about waiting on me hand and foot and daily massages," Ella said.

"That just goes without saying... I'll let you know how this showing goes, my realtor's probably already there. Gotta fly."

"See you soon, I hope," Ella called out.

"Bye, Sis," Kyle said.

"Bye, Aunt Faye. Can we go to the pet store now?"

Kyle and Ella exchanged glances. "Sure," Kyle said.

"Ella, can we take your jeep?"

"Does your puppy already have a name?" Ella quipped.

Finn looking puzzled said, "You know them already."

"Sorry, it's a tricky way of saying yes. You know, answer a question with a question, and both answers are yes."

Seeing Finn's expression made them laugh out loud. "I told you that you're weird," Kyle said.

A moment later Finn exclaimed, "I get it!"

Smugly Ella smirked at Kyle. "You were saying?"

"Weirdo."

She punched him on the arm. "I'll go get my keys and purse."

As she walked away, she heard Finn chattering about what essentials he'd need for Lucy/Charlie. This was going to be so much fun. The family was growing. She stopped dead in her tracks. *Family.* It had been so long since she had felt like a part of a family. It terrified her. She'd lost everyone she'd ever loved; she sent up a silent prayer for their protection.

53

*K*yle was frustrated at how long it was taking to regain the hand strength and dexterity required to play the piano like he could before the accident. He kept messing up and missing keys, discordant sounds that grated on his last nerve. These exercises brought out the worst of his perfectionism. Impatiently he started again. To anyone but him, the music probably sounded pleasing, but he was his own worst critic.

"Hey Mr. Bennett, Mr. Drake said you wanted to see me," Lindsey said.

Impatient at being interrupted, he replied curtly, "Not now. In my office, twenty minutes."

She turned bright red and mumbled, "I'm sorry to interrupt, excuse me. Twenty minutes." She hurried out of the room.

Kyle raked his hands through his hair and cursed under his breath for lashing out at Lindsey. That was a signal it was time to quit practice for the day. Glancing at his Rolex, he paged Rich and requested a pot of coffee, a plate of cold-cuts, cheese and crackers to be brought to his office promptly.

As he waited for Lindsey to show up, he quickly glanced over the contract Faye had forwarded to him. Everything appeared to be aboveboard. He didn't spot any red flags. He had advised Faye to offer full asking price since it was currently a sellers' market. Her realtor had suggested the same.

Lindsey poked her head in the door. "Are you ready for me?"

"Yes, come in."

"I'm sorry for interrupting you earlier."

"It's fine. You caught me at the height of my frustration."

"Sorry. It sounded beautiful."

"Hardly, but thanks."

"Is everything okay? I hope you're happy with my job performance so far."

"Yes, Finn really likes you. I called this meeting because I clearly instructed you to get security clearance for any guests you invited onto the premises. I checked with Richard and my security crew and there have been none issued from you."

"No, sir."

"And yet, you had someone here on Friday picking you up. I saw him in the foyer."

Lindsey fidgeted in her chair. "Yes, but that was just my boyfriend."

Kyle scowled. "And?"

Her eyes widened in surprise. "And what? You wanted me to get clearance for my boyfriend?"

"Wouldn't you consider him a guest?"

She shrugged. "Not really, he's my boyfriend."

"I accept that you made a mistake, but from now on anyone, and I mean anyone, even your mother, is required to be cleared through my security team, are we clear on that?"

She looked down at the ground, her cheeks bright red. "Yes, Mr. Bennett."

"Now if you'd submit your boyfriend's name and address to Mr. Drake, he will pass on that information to my security team for clearance. Problem solved."

Mr. Drake appeared with the food tray and pot of coffee and set them down on a side table. "Thanks Rich."

"You're most welcome. Would you like me to pour your coffee, sir?"

"No thanks."

Richard nodded to Lindsey and backed out of the room.

"Are you hungry? Help yourself," Kyle offered.

"Okay."

"Coffee?"

"No thanks."

Kyle poured himself a mug full, added cream, then loaded up a small plate for himself and sat back down. Lindsey filled a plate too.

Stirring his coffee, he said, "Since we're already here how are things going for you? Do you have any questions or concerns? Any observations about my son you'd care to share?"

Her face lit up with a smile. "He's adorable. He's kind and loving, I am very happy here."

"Good. Finn seems to be adjusting well. I like the way you engage with him. Other than the security issue I have no complaints. Keep up the good work. I think the nightmares are under control...to my knowledge I'm not aware that he's had any recently."

"No. You didn't miss anything. He hasn't had any."

Kyle smiled. "You're free to go unless you have any questions."

"No, thank you. I'm so happy to be working here Mr. Bennett. I already love Finn. It's a privilege. Thank you for entrusting me with your son."

"I'm glad it's working out for all of us." He glanced at his watch. "It's just about time for you to pick him up from school so I won't keep you any longer. Oh, I almost forgot, I've promised Finn a puppy. Do you have any objections? I know it will be extra work for you, but you mentioned your last family had a dog."

"I love dogs! That would be awesome. I'll help housebreak him."

"Great. I was hoping you'd be agreeable."

"I'll see you later Mr. Bennett. I'm sorry about my boyfriend."

"No harm done it was a misunderstanding. I guess I didn't make myself clear."

"Well, you have now, that's for sure."

"Good. I'll be heading back to my office. Tell Finn I'll be home in time for dinner."

"Will do. Bye."

Kyle shook his head, feeling old for thinking that young people just didn't seem to have common sense these days. That's something you didn't pick up from a book. He didn't understand how Lindsey had arrived at the conclusion that somehow her boyfriend was exempt, but what the hell, she knew now. *Geesh I am getting old.*

54

Ella, Kyle and Finn sat in a circle on the floor of a small visiting room at the local animal shelter with a half dozen lab mix puppies in the center.

"I want them all!" Finn said.

"Since you can't have them all, let's just observe for a few minutes and see what personality traits show up," Kyle said.

Ella chimed in, "Yeah, Finn look for things like which one is the most playful or laid back, the one who is curious, shy, aggressive, friendly, then we'll decide which of those personality types fit the household the best. But it's not a decision to be made just from thinking, you have to listen to your heart."

Finn giggled as a black puppy kept jumping up trying to lick his face. "I think this one likes me!"

"He does," Ella said.

Kyle grabbed a blond pup and held the small squirming bundle saying, "This one is a little girl."

"What's this one?" Finn asked about the puppy still climbing all over him. Ella checked and announced that it was a boy.

"Charlie," Finn said.

Ella met Kyle's warm gaze, her heart doing a little flip-flop. He was so damn sexy sitting there holding that tiny little puppy to his face while it chewed on his nose. Her heart melted.

"What about this one?" Ella said pointing to a shy chocolate pup that appeared to be the runt of the litter.

"Girl or boy?" Finn asked.

"Girl."

"Lucy," Finn said.

"Let's narrow the field here. Why don't you pick your three favorites and we'll have them take the rest away? Then we'll get a better idea of each one's personality."

Finn chose one of each color, the blonde, the chocolate runt, and the friendly black puppy. The assistant took the rest back to their pen.

"Two girls and a boy," Kyle said.

They observed them playing together and with only three pups, the runt seemed to come out of her shell and was now holding her own with her rough and tumble siblings.

"Dad, you know I was thinking, it'd be sad for Charlie not to have a sister or brother. He might get lonely."

Ella's heart ached, the casual remark possibly reflecting his own feelings about not having siblings. "But he'll have you, Finn. You can sleep and play together."

"But what about when I'm in school?"

"Son, you've got to pick one. That was our agreement."

Finn's face scrunched up in concentration. "Well, I like them all, but it seems like Charlie picked me."

Ella held the chocolate lab while Finn deliberated. The pup fell asleep in her arms. Kyle slung his arm across her shoulders and nibbled on her ear. "Lucky puppy," he whispered.

She glanced up and caught him staring and gave him a wide smile, her heart full. He leaned down and kissed her softly on her lips. "You're so beautiful."

She whispered, "Kyle, what if I took Lucy here and you and Finn take Charlie. Then they could have play dates and they won't be lonely."

His laugh lines crinkled around his eyes. "I knew it. I called this one the minute we sat down."

She laughed. "You did not!"

"I swear."

"What's so funny?" Finn asked.

"Looks like Charlie doesn't have to be lonely after all. Ms. Softy here thinks she would like to take Lucy home with us as well."

Finn jumped up and threw his arms around Ella waking the sleeping puppy. "I love you so much Ella! Lucy ya hear that? You're coming home with us too!"

"Well, I guess we've made our decision. Let's get out of here before we end up with three," Kyle said.

On the way home Finn sat in the back talking to Charlie, telling him all about his new home and the adventures they would have together. Ella held Lucy, asleep in her lap. Kyle reached over for Ella's hand and interlaced their fingers squeezing tight. She squeezed back.

Ella was having an inner battle. *It's scary to feel this deeply.* She had yet to mention the L word out loud. Did Kyle feel the same? Was she fooling herself to think that this was more than an affair? He was the sexiest, smartest, most beautiful man she had ever known who also happened to be a billionaire. She wished he wasn't. Why couldn't he be some average Joe? How could she ever hope to hold the interest of this man? She knew Kyle held her heart in the palm of his hand and if this ended tomorrow, she would never be the same.

She had to work up her courage to have a serious conversation sometime soon. But not tonight. She didn't want this to end yet. She wasn't ready to hear that he didn't feel the same. For now, she'd be content to live in the moment. It was too late anyway. She was already in the deepest of waters, she just hoped that she didn't drown.

55

*D*eb and Ella sat on her living room floor playing tug of war with Lucy and an old sock. She was growling and flinging her head from side to side like a real badass, all ten pounds of her.

"She is adorable!" Deb said.

"I think my old hound Bernie is smiling down on us."

"He's probably thinking, *it's about time, Mom.*"

"In a few months Lucy will be able to go on my runs with me."

"So, catch me up on the billionaire."

Ella blew out a big breath. "Do you have to remind me that he's rich? I'm trying to forget."

"Why?"

"I can't cope."

"Sure, you can."

"Really, I can't."

Ella stretched out on the carpet propping one arm

behind her head. Lucy crawled on top of her and sat on her chest while Ella scratched her behind the ears. "I know it's my issue, but the juxtaposition of growing up in foster with nothing, to mansions, Ferrari's and twelve-thousand-dollar bottles of perfume, how the hell am I supposed to feel?"

"I get it, but he can't change how he grew up."

"I know all that, it's just that I'm not sure where I fit in his life. The sex is great, I love his son, we're coasting along, he wants me to move in with him...but I'm afraid it'll change things."

"Have you ever thought that it could change things for the better? Besides maybe he's afraid too."

"No way. He has it all, looks, money, prestige, power, confidence, he's not afraid of anything."

"Everyone's afraid of something. Have you ever asked him?"

Burying her nose in the puppies fur she said, "To answer your question, no, I haven't asked him specifically if he's afraid... but we have talked about our relationship we just haven't defined it."

"No time like the present. Everyone feels vulnerable at some time or another. He lost a wife to brain cancer; he's been touched by life. He has a son. That changes a person. Give him a chance. Take a risk and ask him where he sees your relationship going. Nothing risked nothing gained."

"I guess I'm afraid that I care more about him than he does about me."

She scoffed. "Personally, I think the guy is head over heels in love with you. Why would he let you into his son's life the way he has...into his own life? He's invited you to share his world. He wouldn't do that if he weren't serious."

"I suppose. I don't feel like I'm just a booty call, but I'm not sure what I am."

"All you have to do is ask. I'd rather know. Uncertainty is a buzzkill."

"You're right, I'll do it."

"Good. Jump in, next time you see him."

"We're going to spend Saturday at the Marlin Tournament. Finn too. His yacht club has lots of festivities planned and stuff for the kids as well. The marina is right there, so we'll get to see the catch coming in and being weighed and judged. Afterwards Lucy and I are spending the night. I'll bring it up then, I promise."

"Girl, you only have to promise yourself, I'm not here to judge."

"I needed to say it out loud to keep it one-hundred-percent."

"I better be the maid of honor, that's all I'm saying."

Ella laughed. "Who said anything about marriage?"

"Me. Then I get to say I told you so. I've got to skedaddle. Call me."

"I will, thanks Deb." Ella followed her to the door.

"No problem. That's what BFF's are for."

Ella shut the door behind her friend and poured herself a glass of wine.

"Lucy it's popcorn, wine and Netflix tonight, what do you think girl?" Lucy wagged her tail enthusiastically. Daisy had decided to come out of hiding, making her dramatic appearance by jumping over Lucy onto the back of the couch. Lucy started barking at her which wasn't helping their relationship one bit. Daisy ignored her. She hadn't warmed up to Lucy yet, but at least she wasn't hissing at her anymore. Progress.

"I'll feed you two then we're all going to crash on the couch...together, you got that?" Daisy yawned then began grooming, making her point.

Maybe it was the liquid courage from the wine and her friends support, but now that she had decided to have the dreaded *relationship* talk, she felt better already.

56

"Baby you in that sundress, I won't be able to concentrate on anything else today," Kyle said. He kissed her bare shoulder then trailed kisses along her jawline. Settling on her lips he said, "It's been too damn long."

She kissed him back. "I know. I need to spoon with you. I can't sleep anymore if you're not next to me."

Her short flirty dress was perfect for sneaking his hand up her thigh, which he did now, his palm clasping her butt.

"I love when you wear thong underwear."

"Just for you, totally unselfish of me," she said grinning.

"Florence Nightingale, all the way."

They heard Finn coming so she quickly straightened her dress and pulled out her gloss to reapply.

"Hi Ella, where's Lucy?"

"Mr. Drake took her. He's going to watch the pups while we're gone."

"Can I go see her before we leave?"

"Sure, go ahead. Meet us in the music room," Kyle said.

"Okay."

Kyle took her hand and led her to the music room. He pulled the piano bench out and sat, patting the space beside him for her to sit. She scooched in next to him and he dipped his head to kiss her.

His strong tanned fingers hovered over the keys then he began to play. The opening chords from Carol King's classic *Will You Still Love Me Tomorrow* floated in the air like a kiss.

Then he began to sing. His voice had a smoky quality to it that was sexy as hell. Low and mesmerizing. He sang the love song like it was written just for her and Ella wondered for a moment if she was dreaming.

Holding her breath, her body tense and trembling with emotion, she feared she would break down sobbing. It touched her so deeply; it was without a doubt...nothing even came close...the most romantic thing anyone had ever done for her. A tear slipped out and ran down her cheek.

He finished the song and turned toward her eagerly. "Well? What do you think? It's a new song for me, I've been practicing all week."

Her eyes were stinging as she nodded her head.

"Hey baby, are you crying?"

She nodded again and buried her face against his shoulder.

"Babe, I didn't want to make you cry. I wanted to seduce you," Kyle said chuckling softly.

"Score," she mumbled into his shirt.

"Well, that's good then. Kiss me."

She lifted her head and he tilted her face up kissing the salty tears from her cheeks before tenderly pressing his lips to hers.

"Hey, Dad, Ella, you should have seen Charlie and Lucy just now."

Ella gave Kyle a watery smile then turned toward Finn.

Finn blinked and his brow furrowed. He ran over to hug Ella around the waist. "Why are you crying?"

"I'm okay Finn. Your dad just played a song that was so beautiful it made me cry."

"Is it that one he keeps playing over and over? All that love stuff?" He grinned up at her.

"That would be the one," she said.

"Well did you like it? Dad said he was learning it to surprise you."

"I loved it."

"Good, now maybe he'll play something else."

Kyle laughed heartily, the sound warm and intimate, making Ella's toes curl.

"You're something else, kid," Kyle said, pulling Finn in for a group hug.

They all squeezed together for a brief moment before Finn said, "Can we go now?"

"Yes. Shall we?" Kyle said pulling Ella up from the bench. "My ride or yours?"

"Jeep!" Finn called. "Race ya!"

Finn had a head start, Ella close behind. They raced

across the marble floors through the mansion's wide corridors and out the front doors where she had parked in the circular round-about.

"Do you want to drive?" Ella said, challengingly.

"You're trusting me with your baby?" Kyle asked, surprised.

"Why not?"

Grabbing the keys from her he got behind the wheel, Finn crawled in back and Ella buckled in beside Kyle. He adjusted the rearview mirror then gave them a thumbs-up putting it into gear. A minute later they were cruising along.

"A family that plays together stays together!" Kyle shouted over the noise from driving with the top off. Ella glanced in the back and her heart squeezed at the pure joy on Finn's face. *Life is good.*

57

*I*t was a gorgeous sunny day, the sky a periwinkle blue, the air festive and lively. There were food trucks and art vendors selling pottery, colorful paintings, framed photography, handmade jewelry, and booths with tee-shirts ranging from tacky touristy screen printing to artful hand-dyed batiks.

Ella stopped to look at a pair of handmade silver earrings and held one up to her ear, inspecting herself in the small hand mirror. Kyle came up behind her and slipped his arms around her waist, nuzzling her neck. She leaned back into him, her body melting into his. She had never felt so alive, her whole-body vibrating with anticipation.

"You like those?" he asked.

"I do but what do you think?"

"I think I love you."

She froze eyes widening, she gaped at him through the mirror.

Voice strangled she said, "Excuse me?"

He turned her to face him, laugh lines fanning out around his eyes, he played innocent. "They were made for you."

"No, I'm talking about the other part."

"You mean the 'I love you' part?"

She nodded. "Yes, that part."

"I love you, Ella Palmer."

She searched his twinkling eyes, which matched the navy polo shirt he had on today. "I love you too." She stood on her tip toes and pulled his head down for a kiss.

A loud voice interrupted them. "Get a room!"

It was Pete.

"Great timing, dude," Kyle complained.

"Hey, don't you two get enough time for that when you're alone? You don't have to subject the rest of us to your nauseating happiness."

"Jealousy is not a good look on you," Kyle replied.

"Hey, did you see that forty-six-footer at the end of the marina?"

"No, we haven't got that far. We just got here."

"Take a look, makes yours look like a row-boat."

Ella inwardly rolled her eyes. *Could he be any more obnoxious?* She knew he was Kyle's partner and best friend but *geesh, what an asshole.*

"And how is Ella today?" he asked her.

It annoyed her to no end when someone talked in third person like that. "Ella is fine. And how is Pete today?" Her sarcasm was wasted on him.

"Great! How could I not be? It's a perfect Carolina

day. Just wait until the boats start coming in with their trophies. It's exciting. Quite the zoo today. Great turnout."

"It gets bigger every year. I kind of miss the old days when it wasn't so well attended," Kyle said.

"Me too, except there are more hot chicks to ogle than there used to be. I have reservations for dinner at the club, are you two interested in joining us?"

"Can't," Kyle said. "The nanny is off this weekend and we have Finn."

"Where is the little turd?"

"He was just here." Kyle looked around and spied him watching some young teenagers painting faces the next booth over. Kyle waved catching Finn's attention and motioned him back.

"Buddy, you stay close, there are too many people for you to be wandering off without us."

"Okay."

Kyle paid for the earrings then asked Ella if she wanted to wear them now or have the artist bag them. "I'd like to wear them, please."

She gathered up her hair and held it back from her face and Kyle slipped the wires through her earlobes. His knuckles grazed her neck and sent shivers down her spine. It felt like an insatiable longing which was both intoxicating and painful.

"Quit looking at me like that. Man that toothy smile of yours...that gap... gets me every time," he whispered huskily.

Finn tugged on Ella's skirt. "Can we go now?"

"Yep, all set."

They returned with Finn to the face painting booth. The young girls were raising money for a local coastal conservation project. There were a number of kids lined up and at Finn's insistence they joined them.

"I want to be a dog," he said.

"Finn look, over there, that little girl looks like a cat," Ella pointed out a youngster sitting in a chair, getting her face painted.

"Cool, but I want to look like Charlie."

"He'll like that."

"Hey, if you two don't mind I'm going to walk with Pete to look at that Yacht," Kyle said.

"No problem. Looks like we'll be here a while."

"Remember what I said Finn. If I'm not back before you're done make sure you hold onto Ella's hand in the crowds." Kyle glanced at his platinum Rolex to check the time. "I'll try to be back in twenty minutes."

"Don't worry about us, take your time," Ella said.

Ella watched as he walked away, his jeans accentuating his tight butt, polo shirt tucked in, broad shoulders tapering to his slim waist. His limp was barely perceptible and probably only to her. His body relaxed; a man comfortable in his own skin. His beauty and air of confidence attracted the attention of a few hopeful women as he passed. She could hear his faint laughter at something Pete had said. *He loved her!* A warmth filled her chest and her heart fluttered just thinking about that moment.

"You're up, Finn."

He sat on the stool chattering away with the cute girl wielding the face paint, sitting patiently while she worked her magic. She finally stepped back and grabbed a mirror so Finn could see the transformation. Clapping his hands with glee he said, "Thanks, wait til my dad sees me! He will be shocked."

"Great job! Thanks." Ella handed her a very generous donation and they followed in the direction Kyle had been heading.

"Ella!" She turned toward the familiar voice calling out her name.

"Artie! I didn't expect to see you here."

"Not staying long. Too many people for me and Ralph. Where have ya been? I was beginning to wonder if you were dead."

"Paddle boarding has kind of been on the back burner lately, but I'll be out soon." Finn was petting old Ralph whose tail wagged slow but steady.

Kyle appeared and Ella made the introductions. "This is my old friend Artie, a real pirate."

"I live on my boat; I'm hardly a pirate, but I am the son of a sailor," he said shaking Kyle's hand.

Ella thought she caught a glimpse of Lindsey in the crowd. "Hey Kyle, isn't that Lindsey over there?"

"Where?" He looked to where Ella was pointing but if she had been there, she'd been sucked up by the throngs of people.

"It might not have been her, but a strong resemblance anyway."

"Nice to meet you Kyle, I think I know now why I haven't seen Ella out on the water lately. You're one lucky man."

Kyle slipped his arm around Ella's waist. "Don't I know it."

"Hope to see you around."

"Count on it," Kyle said.

"Bye Ralph," Finn said ruffling the dog's head.

58

Kyle had picked up a festival pamphlet with the activities and booths listed. "Finn, it says here that they have a bounce house. Would you be interested in trying that?"

"Yes! For sure. That girl that painted my face told me about it."

"According to this map it's back by the club."

"Come on let's go!" Finn tugged at their hands, pulling them both along.

"We're coming."

Kyle bought the ticket and they both watched as Finn disappeared into the gigantic inflatable room. They could see Finn tentatively jump up and down. After a few minutes he was leaping into the air and flopping around like a rag doll. He had already made a friend and they were laughing and bouncing together.

Kyle put his arm around Ella and held her tightly

against his side. "Back to our earlier conversation, was that just an obligatory response to my declaration?"

Suddenly feeling bashful she couldn't meet his intense gaze. "No, I was planning on talking to you tonight when we got home."

He faced her, tucking her hair behind one ear. "You were? What were you planning to talk about?" He kissed the tip of her nose.

"Us."

"What about us?"

"You know, stuff."

"Can you elaborate?"

"Like where do you see this going? Where do I fit in?"

"If you'll remember, I promised not to pressure you about moving in, but the offer still stands."

"It does?"

"Yes. I want it more than anything Ella. You, me, Finn, Lucy, Charlie, Daisy."

"Don't forget about Cyrus and Miley."

"Didn't I tell you? I flushed them."

Her mouth hung open until she realized he was teasing then she said, "You're such a brat!"

"And you're still the most exquisite creature I've ever laid eyes on."

He glanced at his watch again. "Are you hungry?"

"Starving."

"Let's grab Finn and get a bite to eat from one of the food trucks."

Kyle and Ella approached the enormous bouncy house. Kyle popped his head inside the inflatable play-house and called out Finn's name several times. There was so much screeching, laughter and screaming that there wasn't much chance of being heard over the clamor.

He turned to Ella. "I don't see him in there. Want to double check for me?" he said, his jaw tight.

"Sure. Don't worry I'm sure he's around here somewhere. Maybe he went off with his new friend." She squeezed his arm.

"I told him he had to stay with us."

She rolled her eyes. "He's a kid."

Ella looked in through the clear plastic windows. No Finn. She walked around the whole perimeter, becoming increasingly anxious. "Finn! Finn!" she called out.

She returned to Kyle's side. The color had drained out of his face and he was holding a piece of paper.

"What? Kyle what is it?"

He thrust the note toward her and with dread she took it from him and read.

We have your son. Do not call the police. Do not notify the authorities or you will never see him again. Go home and wait for instructions. Don't do anything stupid.

Ella felt the blood drain from her face. "Oh my God! Where did this come from?"

"A kid riding a skateboard handed it to me and took off."

"We have to notify the police."

"No!" Kyle said sharply. "You read the note!"

"But..."

He held up his hand. "Stop talking, I've got to think."

Ella felt like she'd been slapped. "Kyle, listen to me, time is of essence, they couldn't have gotten very far. He was only out of our sight for a minute!"

Raking his hands through his hair he said, "Ella just shut up, give me a minute, will you?"

Her eyes welled up, but she knew this wasn't the time to collapse into emotion. She had to keep a clear head for Kyle but more importantly for Finn. *Finn! Oh my God please no! Let him be all right. Please let him walk up laughing and sharing a funny story.*

But he never came.

Ella's legs felt wooden as they ran to the jeep. Her heart was racing, and she felt bile rising up in her throat. Kyle seemed to be an island unto himself, isolated...alone. It hurt that he was shutting her out, but this wasn't about her. Ella hopped into the driver's seat and Kyle climbed in, robotically fastening his seat belt.

59

---

*K*yle hunched forward and buried his face in his hands. *My fault, I put myself before my son, I shouldn't have been distracted...* He couldn't even comprehend what was happening. As if from a long distance away, he heard Ella talking but he couldn't understand what she was saying to him. It felt like he was living in a nightmare...his worst nightmare, but unfortunately, he was wide awake.

~

*W*hen they arrived home, Kyle contacted Dave Adams, a retired navy seal and the head of his personal security team, who immediately sprang into action. He made it there in record time and they gathered in Kyle's office, waiting to hear from the kidnappers. Richard, who had also been filled in, was doing his part to help, entering the war-room with a pot of coffee and mugs.

One look at Kyle's anguished face told him all he needed to know. Richard asked, "Would you like me to stay sir?" Kyle just nodded his head yes.

Kyle rubbed his hands across his haggard face. "Should I call my father for help? He's still in town on business. He may have some connections that I don't."

Dave said, "Yes, I think that's a good idea."

Richard offered to make the call and Kyle accepted gratefully, "Yes, thanks Rich."

Ella sat quietly, available if needed. Richard stepped out for a moment to make the call to James Bennett.

"Ella, I want you to think about the last several weeks. Has anything unusual happened, anything out of place, even if you think it's unrelated or insignificant?" Dave asked.

"No, nothing that I can think of. There have been lots of changes lately. I'm sure as head of security, you're aware that I'd been living here until two weeks ago, as a temporary nanny and Kyle's nurse. I was with Finn a lot. We had some outings but mostly hung out around here after he got home from school."

"Any unexpected visitors?"

"The only visitors I saw were Kyle's law partner Pete, his sister Faye, and a childhood friend of the Bennetts' Charlene. I never entertained any guests here myself."

"Kyle this could be about your father's development. You've got people vehemently opposed to it. The construction site has been sabotaged repeatedly, who's to say they haven't decided to escalate?" Dave said.

"I'd thought of that, the only problem I see with that theory is that as far as they're concerned, they've won. We've halted all construction. Pulled the foreman off the job and he's been reassigned. I just don't see it."

"What about the anthrax scare? That was pretty sinister."

"Yes, and we still don't have any answers," Kyle said.

Ella's forehead creased. "I hate to bring this up, really I do, but I've been getting a really bad vibe from your partner Pete. He seems so angry and bitter. I know you'll probably hate me for saying this, but has anyone checked out his alibi for the vandalism and anthrax prank?" She bit her lip nervously. "While you were laid up, he certainly had opportunity, not sure about motive though."

"He has been more of an asshole than usual, but this? I don't believe it," Kyle said.

"But he was there today... at the festival."

"So were a million other people."

They all seemed to be at an impasse. Nothing made any sense.

"Kyle, Pete was at the helm while you were recovering from your accident. Could he be in some kind of trouble...trying to cover up something else?" Dave said, warming to the idea. "Does he have money problems? Gambling addictions?"

"He likes to gamble but I wouldn't classify it as an addiction."

"Maybe I'm barking up the wrong tree, but he'd be one of the first people I'd look at," Ella said.

Dave took notes; looking up he added, "We have to consider him, Kyle. Ella, I asked for you to mention anything that you thought could be significant. Don't feel bad for speaking up. It's important that we all think outside of the box. The sooner we find our suspect the better."

Ella now on a roll said, "And another thing, did anyone ever check to see if there was more to your accident? I know the other driver ran a stop sign but wouldn't you have had time to stop? I mean you had to be going pretty fast. You told me the cops said that there were no signs of skid marks at the scene. Did anyone do forensics on your car?"

"Not to my knowledge. Dave?"

"No. It seemed straight forward. In hindsight with everything that has been happening with your firm we should have insisted."

A vague memory was niggling the back of Kyle's brain, a dream he'd had several times since the accident...one where he put his foot on the brakes, and they went straight to the floor. Was it only a dream or was it his subconscious trying to tell him something?

Dave had been clicking away on his computer and suddenly said, "Shit!"

"What?" Kyle said.

"Looks like your partner is in debt up to his eyeballs. That would be motive."

"Like how much in debt?" Kyle asked.

"To the tune of three and a half million. His house is in foreclosure...I'd say that moves him up a few notches. I think it's worth checking him out. I'll send one of my men over to his house and pay him a surprise visit. If there is something to find out, Chaz will get it out of him. Meanwhile we sit tight and brain-storm some more."

60

Ella wanted to climb out of her skin and volunteered to check on the puppies who were in an outdoor round pen set up in the back yard. Anything to keep busy.

"I'll be right back," she told Kyle.

When she saw Charlie, she burst into tears. All she could think about was Finn's little face, his grin showing two missing front teeth, his joy when he finally got his wish and brought home his puppy. Something nagged the back of her brain, but she just couldn't access it. It had something to do with Charlie. Hopefully it'd come back to her if it was important. She spent a little time with the pups but was anxious to return to Kyle.

～

yle's phone signaled that a text message had been delivered and he quickly swiped the screen as he and Dave bent over to read it. Kyle read it out loud so everyone could hear.

TEXT: Five Million deposited in an offshore account by noon tomorrow. Instructions to follow. Reply: AGREED

"What should I do?" Kyle asked Dave.

"Tell them that you need to see proof that they have your son."

KYLE: I need to see that my son is safe. Send a photo.
TEXT: I call the shots asshole.
KYLE: You want the money or not?

An image of Finn with his face paint came through Kyle's phone, he choked back a sob holding it up for all of them to see. Ella felt a sick dread in her belly. She was terrified.

Kyle choked out, "That's him... today...he had his face painted like a dog at the festival right before he disappeared."

"Okay that's good news. He's alive. Now we just have to get him back. Text him that you agree with the five million."

KYLE: AGREED, where?
TEXT: Instructions to follow. Remember no police

or you won't see your son again.
KYLE: Agreed

Kyle was as white as a sheet. All the color drained from his face. Ella could see the sweat beading his brow and he was practically hyperventilating. She walked to him and put her hand on his shoulder. "We'll find him."

"How do you know?" he snapped. "I'm not stupid. We all know the odds aren't in Finn's favor. The chances of them figuring this out or the kidnappers returning my son are slim to none."

"You have to fight. Now is not the time to give up," Ella said.

Her voice was thick and nasal from crying and he looked up at her for the first time. He went to her pulling her into his arms and held her close. "I'm sorry I snapped at you Ella. It's just that the guilt is eating me alive. If I hadn't been distracted, this never would have happened. I'm a shitty father and I'm a shitty human in general. Finn deserves better so do you. Please forgive me."

Her heart lurched with fear. Voice shaky she said, "Nothing to forgive. This is a nightmare. We're all doing the best we can under the circumstances." She looked at the image of Finn again and shuddered. Seeing that photograph ripped her wide open. She squeezed Kyle tightly while soaking his tee-shirt with fresh tears.

Kyle handed Ella a Kleenex. After drying her eyes, she blew her nose, "Now what?"

"We wait for more instructions or for a miracle, whichever comes first," Dave said.

61

Kyle and Dave waited outside in their vehicle while Chaz, another security personnel on Kyle's payroll, went inside Pete's house. He was wired so they could hear everything from the van. Chaz knocked on the door and Kyle heard Pete say, "I'm glad you came ba...who the hell are *you*?" It was quickly apparent that Pete had consumed a few too many martinis. He sounded quite drunk.

They watched Chaz push his way inside and shut the door behind him. "Who were you expecting?" Chaz said.

"What the hell?"

"Have a seat."

"This is my house, who do you...*hey!*" Pete yelled out.

"Here are the rules. I ask the questions you supply the answers. Got it?" Chaz said.

"I don't have to answer anything."

"You don't have to do anything but trust me you don't want to find out what happens if you don't cooperate."

"Who the hell sent you?"

Kyle could tell Chaz was enjoying his role of a cat playing with a mouse. "Guess."

"I told Frank I'd have the money by Tuesday."

Kyle's brows rose as he and Dave exchanged a puzzled look. "And where's this money going to come from?" Chaz played along.

"I have my ways."

"Frank needs a little more detail than that."

"I can't give it to him."

They could hear rustling then, "You want to keep that pretty face perfect don't ya?"

Pete cried out, "Put that knife away."

"Where is he?"

"Who? What are you talking about?"

"Don't fuck around, I'm only going to ask nicely one more time... what did you do with the kid?"

"I don't fucking know what you're talking about I swear, please don't cut me," he whined.

"Let's try this again, how are you going to come up with enough money to pay Frank—what do ya owe him now anyway?"

"I was able to borrow again from my firm. I'll have it by Tuesday, I've got collateral." Kyle's fists clenched. He wanted to kill the sniveling traitor.

"Collateral huh? What's this collateral you're talking about?" As he said this, Pete screamed out in pain.

"Stop! You're hurting me! Ow! Please, okay, I'll tell you."

"You were saying?"

"Our firm is representing my partner's father James Bennett on his latest development. There are some very powerful people who want to see that it never happens. I was promised a hefty sum of money to make sure the project was halted. I succeeded and now I'm going to collect."

"What's the collateral?"

"A very large insurance check that the Bennetts aren't aware of for the equipment destroyed by vandals. Since I'm a partner in the firm and the son has been laid up, I've been overseeing this case. When the cat's away..."

"You're telling me you've been embezzling from your own law firm?"

"Borrowing, I'll pay it back. My lucks going to turn. Frank gets paid back first, of course, then I'll reinvest a little, just enough to cover my ass. No one will be out anything," he said.

"Anything else you'd like to confess to?"

"That's it. Frank will get his money, I'll parlay the rest, pay back Kyle's father, and no one will be the wiser."

"Stay put. I'm going to make a quick phone call. Don't move!" Chaz said. "See this?" Just know that I'm an excellent marksman."

Dave's phone rang and he picked up. "Did ya get all that?"

"Loud and clear."

"What do you want me to do with him?"

"Come on back, we've got bigger fish to fry, we'll

deal with him later. Let him think you're cool with his promise, so he doesn't spook."

"Got it."

Chaz disconnected then said, "Frank says to tell ya you'd better not be fucking with him, he expects the full payment by Tuesday."

"Yes, he'll have it. Thank you!"

Chaz slammed the door behind him and headed to the van.

62

They drove back to Kyles where Ella and Richard waited for them.

"Pete doesn't have Finn but the fucker has been embezzling from our company." Ella's eyes widened. "As in...?"

"As in stealing from his own firm to pay off gambling debt."

"Oh my God! That's terrible!"

"We'll deal with him later. Now that we can check him off the list let's get our heads back in the game," Kyle said.

Dave pinched the bridge of his nose. "Other than the nanny, no new staff have been hired recently?"

Kyle shook his head. "No."

"How about at your firm?"

"No. You did the security clearance for Lindsey, she checked out, right?" Kyle asked.

"Yes, clean as Mary Poppins. Great references from her previous employers."

"I should mention that I did have to come down on Lindsey. After clearly telling her about my guest policy, she ignored my directive. She was told that if she was going to have visitors, they first had to be cleared through security. Richard, you remember her boyfriend coming last week?"

"Yes, I do. He was a bit off putting if I may say so."

"She didn't tell anyone that he was arriving to pick her up," Kyle continued.

"As a matter of fact, he let himself in as if he lived here," Richard stated. "I assumed Lindsey had instructed him to do so. I just happened to glance at the security camera as he entered and went to meet him."

Dave jumped on that. "So, there's footage? You mentioned he was odd, in what way?"

"A little too interested in his surroundings, as if he were sizing things up. Unfriendly. He didn't seem like Lindsey's type, but I don't really know her well. A bit old for her, in my opinion," Richard said.

"He did have a rather aggressive manner, I only saw him from a distance, but he was unabashedly staring. It struck me as odd," Kyle said.

"Any idea who this character is? Has she ever mentioned him by name?" Dave asked.

"No, not to me," Kyle said. Both Richard and Ella were shaking their heads as well.

"Do you remember the date and time that he picked her up? I'll review the security footage from that day."

"Yes, it was the Friday before last, Finn stayed with my sister and Lindsey had the weekend off."

"Great, that's a start."

The doorbell chimed and Richard went to greet Kyle's dad.

James Bennett entered the room in his usual commanding style. He exuded power, a true force of nature. "Son, tell me what happened. Tell me everything from the beginning."

"We were at the Marlin festival, Ella, Finn and me. Finn had been playing in the bounce house," at his fathers puzzled expression he explained, "It's basically an inflatable playground, the kids go inside and bounce around. He had been in there for about twenty minutes and when I went to grab him to get a bite to eat, he had vanished, no trace of him."

"Jesus, Kyle." James's face went ashen.

"While Ella was circling the area, a kid thrust an envelope at me and then took off. Inside was a note stating they had Finn and for me to not contact authorities and go home and wait for instructions."

Ella stood up abruptly, agitated. "Dave, I just remembered something. I thought I saw Lindsey at the festival a few minutes before this all happened. I had mentioned it to Kyle, but she had disappeared in the crowd before he could catch a glimpse."

Dave held up his hand, "Hold onto that thought. Here's the footage, a little grainy but clear enough."

They all peered over Dave's shoulder and Ella sucked in her breath sharply.

"I've seen that guy before. A few weeks ago, Kyle

you remember, the day Finn and I brought home the fish, he was there!"

"Where?"

"I'm sorry, in the dollar store. He creeped me out because he was staring at us and then he called us by our names when I hustled Finn away to the checkout counter. I couldn't get away fast enough. There was something familiar about him, but I was sure I'd never met him before."

James had remained quiet but now he began to talk. "I have a confession to make. I told everyone I was back here on business, which is only part of the story. I am being blackmailed for five million dollars. I refused to give in to the demands and now I'm wondering if this is all my fault. Maybe, since I wouldn't pay up, they went for my grandson."

"That's what they are demanding of me, five million," Kyle said grimly.

"That would be a pretty big coincidence for those two demands to not be connected," Dave said.

"What are you being blackmailed for?" Kyle asked suspiciously.

"An old accusation from thirty-five years ago which was completely unfounded then and remains a preposterous work of fiction today."

"Do you know who is blackmailing you? With your security and connections, I'm sure you've had someone looking into it," Kyle said.

"Yes, I do, and I have a name. Marcus Anderson. I also have an address. I hired a private investigator to find him. He has no idea that I know who he is, or that I know where to find him."

"Thank God!" Ella said. "That will give us a good head start and we'll have an advantage because he won't be expecting us."

"Let's go," Kyle said standing abruptly, his body coiled tight and ready for action.

Dave held up his hands. "Wait slow down. We have to come up with a plan first."

"We can't waste any more time," Kyle said impatiently.

"We can't be impulsive—the cost is too high," Dave countered.

Kyle's readiness deflated as if he suddenly remembered the danger Finn was in. "Dave you're the leader here. Tell us what we should do."

"We google the address. Then we do a reconnaissance of the area, then stake out the address. We wait until after dark then we go in. We have no proof that he is the one who took your son, but it's the only lead we have at this point and a pretty solid one. And no guarantee he has your son there. He could be holding him anywhere."

Kyle began to pace, his energy practically bouncing off the walls. "Were you ever going to fill your family in on this blackmail attempt?" Kyle asked his father.

James didn't reply.

"Did it ever occur to you that your decision to keep this information hidden from your family could put us in danger? We could have taken extra steps to keep ourselves safe."

A muscle in his father's jaw twitched as he replied, "I never even considered that my silence could harm my family."

Kyle's lips drew back in a snarl. "Of course you didn't. You're the king of our dynasty, why would you even think to include us in any decisions?"

"Enough!" his father rebuked Kyle vehemently.

"Fuck you! You're no longer the ruler, I will say whatever I damn well please in my own house. Your selfishness may have just cost my son his life!" Kyle's voice cracked and he buried his face in his hands.

Kyle knew Ella had put her hands on his shoulders but it barely registered. He felt broken but knew he had to pull himself together for Finn's sake.

63

*D*ave was calling the shots and currently he along with Kyle, Ella, and Chaz, were parked down the road from the suspect's house, waiting for the cover of darkness. The house was isolated, the closest neighbor a half mile down the road. Kyle lowered his binoculars for the thousandth time and leaned his head back against the seat. He reached for Ella's hand and held it; she squeezed in silent support.

Kyle appreciated Ella's quiet strength and calm demeanor more than she would ever know. Zero drama, he felt bathed in her love and didn't think he could have kept his sanity thus far without her. His entire world had turned on a dime and he felt stranded in the middle of the ocean. *Finn. Please let us find him safe and sound.*

Shortly after dusk Dave said, "Everyone ready to rock and roll?"

"Ready as we'll ever be," Kyle said. The plan was

that Chaz, Dave and Kyle would do a preliminary exploration of the property and see if they could gain access inside. They were hoping they'd get lucky and be able to see inside the house and locate Finn. Dave and Chaz were armed, and they were counting on the surprise element working in their favor.

Kyle brushed his thumb over her cheeks seeing his own fears reflected in Ella's eyes. The three men dressed entirely in black disappeared into the night.

~

*D*ave silently motioned Kyle over to where he was standing. He had a clear view of what appeared to be the living room. There was a big screen television on with a cartoon playing. Dave pointed at the TV then gave a thumbs up sign and Kyle nodded. Kyle closed his eyes in relief. Now he was certain that Finn was in there. He jerked his head toward the back of the house and Dave knew to follow him.

There was a walk out cellar door that had been padlocked, but they had come prepared. Chaz pulled out a pair of wire cutters and snapped the rusty lock. Now they had to open the old metal door silently, without giving themselves away. It creaked loudly when Kyle tried it, Dave held up his hand for him to stop. Kyle's heart was racing, and his hands were clammy, terrified of making a fatal mistake. Kyle signaled to Chaz to try lifting one end at the same time as he lifted the other to minimize the noise. Every sound was magnified but it was a definite improvement.

Dave pointed to himself and Chaz and indicated that they were going to enter through the cellar and that Kyle should stay outside. Kyle nodded his understanding. They slid through the opening and disappeared. Kyle, not about to sit it out, went to explore other entry options. By standing on an air conditioning unit, he was able to see into a room at the back of the house. It was a bedroom. He saw Lindsey bent over, reaching for something from inside a closet. His heart pounded.

He heard Finn before he saw him, calling out for Lindsey as he entered the room. Kyle almost collapsed with relief. Finn appeared to be fine. He was smiling at Lindsey, although he looked tired, he didn't appear to be frightened.

Lindsey apparently finding what she had come for, straightened then took ahold of Finn's hand and led him out of the room. She glanced back in and Kyle froze, then she turned the light out and shut the door behind her. Fate had just smiled upon him.

The screen was latched but Kyle's pocketknife cut easily across it. He pulled himself up and through the window dangling halfway in and out. It was a tight fit and he wiggled himself slowly through the opening. There was a slight thud when he hit the floor and he cringed. Crouching down behind the bed he stayed there until enough time had passed that he was sure he hadn't given himself away.

He put his ear to the door straining to hear anything. He could make out the sound of the TV and a male voice talking, but not the actual conversation. He cracked the door and silently inched his way down the long hallway. When he was halfway there, he stopped when the living room came into view. He could see Lindsey; she was sitting on a sectional sofa facing the television set with her back to him. He assumed Finn was sitting next to her, hidden by the couch. He wished that he could communicate his location to Dave but unfortunately, he was on his own.

Finn jumped up from the couch and rubbed his eyes with balled-up fists, his exhaustion obvious. This enraged Kyle and made him want to kill. His adrenalin was making him feel twitchy and he knew it could lead to him fucking up if he wasn't careful. Taking several deep steadying breaths, he prayed that Finn wouldn't spot him. He dared not move to bring any attention to himself. It was damn near impossible to remain still with his heart pounding out of his chest, but he willed himself into submission.

"I want to go home now Lindsey," Finn said. Kyle could hear him clearly.

"I know but your dad asked me to keep you overnight remember?"

"But why?"

"Because he had an emergency at work. We've already been over this."

"But that doesn't mean we can't go home."

"This is my day off and I'm doing your dad a favor. I want to be here with my boyfriend. He gets lonely here without me."

Kyle could see Finn look behind them, his expression doubtful. "But Mr. Drake could watch me, or Ella would."

He heard a loud male voice coming from the direction Finn had just glanced, "Stop complaining. Here are your choices, shut up or go to bed."

Finn's lips quivered, Kyle was sure he didn't know what to think, since he had never been talked to that way. Kyle wanted to roar at the top of his lungs! He knew he needed to duck into a room just in case they made Finn go to bed. As he started to creep backward Finn must have caught the movement because his eyes suddenly widened. Kyle shook his head frantically and placed his finger against his lips to silence him. Finn glanced toward that same corner and back at his dad, then sat down next to Lindsey. Kyle was drenched in nervous sweat. Thank God his kid was so damn smart. That could have had deadly consequences.

Kyle knew he had one shot at it. He had to risk it sooner or later, so he stealthily continued down the hall. When he reached the end, he charged full speed toward the adjoining room. Marcus had his back to Kyle, so he easily tackled him to the floor. Marcus recovered quickly and began fighting back. Kyle was on top of him pummeling his face. "You son of a bitch! No one fucks with my son; I'm going to kill you with my bare hands."

Marcus managed to grab Kyle's fist on the next swing bending his wrist back painfully. Since it was the same wrist that had been injured in his accident, he was at a disadvantage. Marcus kicked at Kyle as they both struggled for the upper hand.

Dave and Chaz burst through the basement door and hurled themselves into the fray, quickly subduing Marcus and twisting his arms behind his back to cuff him.

Kyle stood and immediately sought out Finn. The front door was wide open, and he could see Lindsey running toward her vehicle pulling a resisting Finn along behind her. Suddenly Ella appeared out of nowhere and threw herself at Lindsey. Screaming like a banshee she wrapped her arm around Lindsey's neck putting her in a choke hold.

"Run Finn, go get in that white SUV over there! Lock the door." Finn ran as fast as he could then climbed into the vehicle. Chaz ran out to help Ella while Dave phoned the police leaving Kyle to guard their prisoner until the police arrived.

64

Marcus had blood pouring out of his nose and his lip was split wide open. He still managed to sneer at Kyle as they stood facing one another. Kyle's jaw was clenched, eyes blazing with fury.

As he stared into the eyes of his enemy, he suddenly had a sick realization about why this stranger had looked so familiar. It was like he was looking at a different version of himself. He was looking into the vacant eyes of a brother from a different mother. It all came together in an instant, the blackmail attempt on his father, when that hadn't worked out, plan B, the kidnapping. The resemblance was uncanny. He couldn't be mistaken.

"I see the light bulb going off Brother," his lips twisted bitterly. Turning to Dave he said, "Which one of us is better looking?"

"Shut the fuck up," Dave said. Marcus winced as Dave jerked his cuffed arms sharply.

"Why?" Kyle asked.

"Why...really you have to ask?"

"Yeah, I do."

"Why don't you ask dear old dad?" He smiled but his eyes remained void of emotion.

"I'm asking you."

"Our dear father fucked his maid, my mother, when she was nineteen years old. She got pregnant with me, then instead of doing the right thing he fired her. Told her she was lying that it couldn't be his baby."

Kyle just stood there, arms hanging down by his sides.

"She begged him to let her keep her job. She was poor with no family, nowhere to turn. You have no idea what it was like growing up watching my mother struggle to raise me alone, poor, sacrificing herself for her only son. Barely getting by from paycheck to paycheck."

"Why didn't she sue him...make him take a paternity test?"

"David and Goliath—surely you're not that insulated from reality. But then again you probably are. How do you think that would have ended? The domestic help takes on the billionaire...and all the power and connections that go with it."

Marcus continued, "Mom never told me who my father was until she was on her death bed. She died from cancer when she was forty-five years old! Died because she didn't have access to good health care, because she was still dirt poor."

"Why didn't you just reach out to me or my sister or brother?"

"Fuck you, do you know how enraged I was after holding my mom in my arms as she took her last breath? I swore revenge for her. I watched and waited. For seven years I bided my time."

"You let it rob you of your soul," Kyle said sadly.

"I let it, ha that's rich! The Bennetts took it! I was the victim. The billionaire's bastard! I managed to confiscate a bar glass with his DNA on it and had a paternity test. A look in the mirror would have proven it without the science, but armed with the evidence, I met with him. Five million would have been a drop in the bucket. He refused. He had the gall to laugh at me!"

"That's when you turned your sights on me isn't it? You tampered with my brakes. You tried to kill me."

"I wanted to destroy my father, take something from him equal to what he had robbed me of."

"Your mother."

"Yes. *And you,* in your ivory tower, buffered by more money than could be spent in three lifetimes, while I could barely get by."

All the anger had drained from Kyle and he felt an enormous loss for what could have been a completely different story. He had lost a brother before he'd ever found him.

inn was sandwiched between Kyle and Ella on the ride home. The police had taken a brief statement, but Kyle was expected back at the station after he got Finn settled in. When they pulled up to the front doors, Kyle saw that his father's car was still parked there.

Ella said, "I'll put Finn to bed to give you some time with your father."

"Grandpa's here?"

"Yes, but you need to go straight to bed."

"I want to say hi first."

Ella met Kyle's eyes and shrugged. "Just for a minute then you're off to bed," Kyle said.

"Okay."

"Grandpa!" Finn ran to his grandfather who was sitting at the kitchen island drinking coffee and talking with Richard Drake.

James Bennett's eyes glistened with tears. "Finn,

thank God you're all right!" He squeezed the child in a tight bear hug, the tears escaping and slipping down his cheeks.

"Yeah, my nanny took me to spend the night with her accounta dad being busy, but then there was this bad guy there. It was weird but I wasn't scared."

Everyone's eyes were suspiciously bright as Finn proudly announced his bravery. "That's good. You're a Bennett through and through. You were very brave."

"I kept asking Lindsey to take me home then that guy yelled at me. Ella, we saw him at the place where we bought those toys, remember?"

"I remember."

"He was kind of weird and mean but I knew Lindsey liked him, so I figured he wasn't taught his manners."

They all laughed with relief that Finn seemed to come out of this unscathed. It appeared as if he never knew he was in any danger until the rescue.

"Come on Finn, I'll put you to bed," Ella said.

"Will you read me a story?"

"Absolutely."

"Night everybody," Finn said walking to each person and giving them a hug.

"I'll be heading back to the station after I talk with father," Kyle said quietly to Ella.

"I'll be here. I'll probably crash in Finn's room until you get back."

"I'll come get you." He leaned down and kissed her.

After they left the room, Richard got up and cleared the counter, then said goodnight, leaving father and son alone.

Angrily Kyle said, "You destroyed two lives, one of which was your own flesh and blood and the other the mother of your child! How could you? How do you sleep at night?"

"Frankly, at the time, I didn't believe her. She was a flirt and a seductress. I had a weak moment and gave in to temptation. One time, one mistake."

"You're telling me that she seduced you? You expect me to believe that a nineteen-year-old threw herself at her rich boss?"

"It's what happened, you can believe it or not. I know what you think of my parenting skills and I don't blame you for that, but you were on easy street compared to how I was raised. I may have been distant, but I never laid a hand on you kids. You have no idea what your grandfather would have done had I disgraced the family name by getting a maid pregnant. Your mother and I were engaged to be married."

"I don't give a fuck! Nothing excuses your cowardice."

"Until you've walked a mile in someone's shoes...as the saying goes."

"I have walked in your fucking shoes and I hated myself! I had become everything I detested about you. I buried myself in my work, using the excuse that I was providing, and yet my child still loved me, forgave me, ran to greet me every chance he got..." Kyle choked up. "The way I loved you. I used to pray that you'd throw a ball to me, praise me, hell... just acknowledge that I existed."

"I wasn't raised that way...I'm sorry son, I do love you, I've always been proud of you. I didn't want you to grow up with a big head. I didn't want the privilege of money to create little monsters."

"Every child needs love to thrive. I needed a father, not a shareholder."

Sadness clouded his father's features. "I'm sorry Kyle. I couldn't give you what I'd never been taught. I hope you'll forgive me one day."

"What about Marcus?"

"What about him?"

"When did you finally believe that his mother had been telling the truth?"

"When I met with him. I took one look at him and there was no denying that he was a Bennett."

"Then why didn't you pay him the money he deserved?"

"Give in to blackmail? Never! What I did do was decide to set up a ten-million-dollar trust account in his name. He hadn't been notified yet... it was still in process."

James Bennett buried his face in the palms of his hands. Kyle had never seen his dad look anything other than powerful and his chest felt tight seeing him so vulnerable. He walked over and draped his arm across his shoulders.

"I forgive you Dad, now you'll have to learn how to forgive yourself."

"I'm sorry Kyle."

"I love you dad. You're my father."

"I hope I can make it up to you kids. Family vacations, I want to know my grandkids. It took almost losing you, then Finn, to realize how walled off I was from my own family."

"We'll work on that. Listen dad, I have to go back to the station, why don't you sleep here tonight and have breakfast with your grandson in the morning."

"Yes, I'll stay."

"I'll get Rich to prepare your room."

"I'll see you in the morning."

"Get some sleep Dad, you look like hell."

"After I call your mother. I have a lot of explaining to do. I hope she can forgive me."

Kyle's eyes were misty as he said goodbye and left to find Rich before heading downtown to the precinct.

66

"Grandpa look what I taught Charlie to do," Finn said. He'd been sitting on the floor with the puppy on his lap, but now he placed Charlie on the ground and kneeled in front of him.

"Charlie, sit." The puppy promptly sat, looking pleased with himself. "Good pup! Now Charlie shake." He lifted his paw and Finn shook it; a huge grin plastered across his face.

"Good boy." Handing him a treat, Charlie gobbled it without chewing.

"He's a smart one," James said approvingly.

Lucy, feeling left out, nudged Finn's hand for a treat. "I'll have to work on that with you Lucy."

"Yes, I'm feeling guilty, I haven't taught her anything," Ella confessed.

"I'll teach her, don't worry."

Kyle placed the mound of pancakes on the island

next to the pile of bacon and pitcher of orange juice. "Everyone dig in, don't be shy."

Finn climbed up to sit on the stool next to his grandfather. "Grandpa, I don't remember if you've ever eaten with us at the house before, have you?"

"I don't remember either, but we'll have to change that won't we?"

"That would be great, and Ninny too."

"Yes, she is flying in this afternoon."

"Sweet!" Finn said with a mouthful of pancakes.

"Finn don't talk with food in your mouth," Kyle admonished.

Mouth still full he said, "Sorry."

James chuckled. "Mini-me. Reminds me of someone."

Kyle came up behind Ella, who was perched on a stool taking her first bite of bacon and wrapped his arms around her. He whispered into her ear, "I love you."

She looked up at him and smiled. "Me too."

"I'm wondering if Finn might like to stay with his grandmother and me at the hotel tonight?" James said.

"YES!" Finn pumped his fist in the air. Ella caught a private look passed between Kyle and his father.

"Why not? I'm sure Mom will be thrilled," Kyle said.

"Finn can go with me when I pick her up from the airport. Make sure he has a bag packed before I have to head out. Her flight arrives at three o'clock.

"Faye and Griffin are coming over tomorrow night for dinner. It will be a reunion of sorts. You and Mom have to come."

James eyes flickered with doubt then he straightened and said, "I'd like that."

Ella didn't know what had transpired between Kyle and his father since she had been fast asleep when he had returned the night before, but she knew it had been epic.

"I hate to leave the party, but I've got to get ready for work," Ella said.

"Don't go," Finn said.

"I don't want to but unfortunately I have no choice."

"You know we're in the market for a new full-time nanny," Kyle said.

Finn's eyes widened then a smile spread across his face. "Why didn't I think of that?"

"It was only a matter of time. I'm going to walk Ella to her jeep. I'll be right back," Kyle said.

Kyle pinned Ella to the jeep and covered her mouth with his own.

"You give me life," he said against her lips.

Her arms locked behind his head, she answered breathlessly, "Same."

"Spend the night tonight?"

"Sounds good, I have to pick up Lucy anyway."

"I'm going to make love to you all night long."

Ella's body throbbed in anticipation. "I hope I can get through work today."

"I'll see you tonight."

She got into her jeep and pulled away, watching him in her rearview mirror.

After all that had transpired in the last twenty-four hours it seemed surreal to be returning to work. She felt like she had been forever changed. All she knew for sure was that everyone was home and safe. Thank God!

67

When Ella entered the house, she followed the faint notes of piano music and found Kyle bent over the keyboard, forehead creased in concentration. He was shirtless and barefoot, wearing low-slung gray sweatpants. His hair had grown out slightly, which brought out the natural curl. A dark lock fell across his forehead, begging to be brushed away from his brow. Engrossed in the song, she was able to observe him unnoticed.

Her heart ached; she loved this man so much. *Perfection.* His strong tanned back and broad shoulders, the muscles of his forearms sinewy and pronounced as his fingers slipped across the keys, made her hot with desire. Like everything, he did nothing half-way. He was an accomplished pianist and every chord he played was filled with passion.

He saw Ella standing there and his eyes lit up. He segued into another song and the opening notes from

Rhianna's hit *Stay*, floated and hung in the air like a kiss. Then he began to sing in that sexy warm tone of his and her legs suddenly felt wobbly. She moved to stand behind him, lightly resting her hands on his bare shoulders. His words touched her like a lover's caress. A soulful song about a lover who'd been saved and brought out of darkness now pleading for them to stay.

When he had laid down the last note, she slid her hands from his shoulders down the front of his hard chest and kissed his neck. The emotion still lingered in the air. Ella felt like Kyle had just made love to her. He stood and took her hand in his and without a word, he led her down the corridor, up the imposing spiral staircase and into his bedroom suite.

His cobalt eyes burned with intensity as he studied her, almost as if trying to burn her image into his memory. She felt consumed by him. Tracing his sculpted lips with her fingertip, she trailed it all the way down to his navel, only stopping when she reached the waist of his sweats. She pulled them down and since he was commando his cock sprung up bouncing against his ripped stomach. He stepped out kicking them aside, then Ella backed him up until his knees hit the club chair. She gave him a little push and he fell onto the soft cushion.

Kyle watched as Ella tugged off her own tee-shirt and threw it aside. The bra followed. She pulled her pants off then the lacey panties. Kyle's eyes were glazed as his gaze roamed over her body lingering on breasts.

Ella kept eye contact with Kyle as she knelt on the rug in front of him. She stroked his strong thighs, enjoying the sensuous feel of his soft hair against her sensitive palms.

She kissed and licked the tender skin of his inner thighs then her tongue teased him until he was writhing. Kyle groaned and spread his legs wider. Cupping him in one hand then wrapping her fingers around the base of his shaft, she took him into her mouth as she glanced up at him through her lashes. His head was thrown back, eyes squeezed shut, and his hands tightly gripped the armchair. It made her wet and crazy with desire to see him aroused.

She massaged as she let her lips and tongue move up and down his shaft. Kyle panted, close to losing control, his pelvis thrusting as his passion rose to an unbearable level. He pulled her up onto his lap, kissing her wildly as he climaxed.

As Kyle shuddered in the throes of his orgasm, she rubbed herself against him, moving faster and faster until she was on the precipice of her own release. Kyle reached up to cup her breasts, squeezing as he rolled her nipples between his fingers. She rocked against him, moaning as he tugged and teased. She arched her torso, throwing her head back in abandon. Ella trembled, vibrating as she surged toward release. She cried out and shuddered, leaning forward to lay against Kyle's chest as he held her tightly against him murmuring endearments.

Her limp body lay sprawled on top of Kyle, a perfect fit, her erect nipples teased by the hair on his chest, her wild mane of hair trailing across his neck and shoulders, their hot sweat mingling, she wanted to stay like this forever. He kissed her temple, whispering the bars of a line from the song that got them started earlier, "Stay..."

Ella smiled against his chest, nipping him with her teeth. His hands were now splayed cupping her buttocks in his palms. When she bit him again, a little harder this time, he playfully swatted her behind.

"I'm hungry," she said.

"So am I," he said, his eyes burning leaving no doubt he wasn't talking about food.

"I mean it. I didn't eat any supper. I wanted to get here faster. By the way, I owe Richard big time for watching my pup today. We should get them out of their crates and take them outside."

"I let them out right before you got here but you're right. We'll move their crate into our bedroom tonight. They can sleep together."

"Hopefully they've played themselves out."

"Yeah, Charlie usually sleeps with Finn, so they'll have each other tonight."

"What cha' got to eat?"

"Leftover Chicken Cordon Bleu, some parmesan lemon orzo, and steamed broccolini with goat cheese."

"I take it chef Jacques cooked this evening?"

He grinned and said, "Would you believe me if I said otherwise?"

"No."

"Here, just slip on one of my tee-shirts." She did and it came to about mid-thigh on her...perfect.

68

*S*everal hours later, after Ella had devoured the leftovers and tended to the pups, they decided to take advantage of the hot summer night and a sky full of stars. Slipping out of their clothes, they took a quick dip in the pool. It was a luxury to be able to swim naked since there was seldom a time when there weren't workers or a six-year-old running around. Ella wrapped her legs around Kyle's waist while he held her, their slick skin feeling like silk against one another. Kyle was hard again, and Ella's flesh responded immediately.

Being weightless in the water made Ella feel light and free. She leaned back and let her upper body float while gripping Kyle tightly with her thighs. Her breast bobbed to the surface and her long hair fanned out in the water. Kyle leaned down and kissed her belly then blew a raspberry against it making her scream with laughter. "That tickles!"

She released him and swam away, he quickly caught up with her grabbing her from behind, pulling her tightly against his chest. He cupped her breasts in his hands and sucked on her neck.

"Kyle, you're going to give me a hickey."

"Your point?"

"That will look great at work. We're not teenagers you know."

"I feel like one. I need to mark my territory. Me Tarzan you Jane."

"Did you really just say that?"

"Yes, see what you've done to me?"

Laughing she said, "Let's get out and go to bed."

"I thought you'd never ask."

⁓

Kyle returned to bed after brushing his teeth, and stood naked over Ella, his expression soft and warm. She lay there relaxed and comfortable... her body sated, at ease in her own skin. She felt unhampered by self-consciousness, she was under the spell of one Kyle Bennett. Her responsiveness to his lovemaking was one of the greatest gifts. He played her like she was a fine-tuned instrument, and she was responsive to his every touch.

He sat at the end of the bed and picked up one foot and began to massage it. Pulling on each toe and stretching it before kneading the sensitive sole with strong hands. Ella practically purred. "Don't stop," she said.

He picked up the other foot and gave it the same

attention before moving up to her calves, then her thighs. When he reached the apex, he gently spread her thighs apart and dipped his head between her legs, lapping at her sweet spot as her body contracted, the sheets bunched up in her tight grasp.

He teased her with his tongue, feathery light flicks until Ella squirmed under his attention, demanding... begging... He sucked softly as she writhed under his skillful lovemaking.

"Please, I need you inside of me now," she begged.

He quickly donned a condom and slipped inside of her. He bent her knees allowing him to penetrate deeper. His hard length filled her completely and at first, he didn't move waiting until she started to writhe in agony beneath him before he began to ride her like a mating animal.

Wild, almost savagely, he plunged in and out, his hips thrusting faster as he rode her. His eyes were ablaze with passion, and she bit her bottom lip, panting as she cried out "Yes!" She contracted around him as she orgasmed. Feeling her tightness pulsating against his hardness sent him over the edge and he came hard and fast.

Ella's labored breath slowly returned to normal. She held Kyle's head to her breasts as he suckled her nipple, sending more tremors through her core as her orgasm slowly abated. She didn't want him to move. She loved having him inside of her. His warmth and weight on top of her felt like a cocoon, warm, safe, sensual. He smelled of sex... musky and manly, with a hint of expensive aftershave. Kissing the top of his cradled head, she whispered, "You are an amazing lover."

"You are easy to love. Your taste, your smell, your responsiveness...I will never get enough of you Ella." Ella pulsated against his softening shaft, like the tremors after an earthquake.

Kyle rolled onto his back, taking her with him, slipping out of her as he pulled her on top. She felt a moment of loss as his warmth withdrew from her womanhood. She licked his neck, *mmm salty*, and nuzzled him as she sprawled out full length, covering his body with her own.

They both fell asleep like that. In the early hours of the morning Ella awoke spooned against Kyle's chest, his arms wrapped around her. She wrapped her arms over his and snuggled closely against him.

"Are you awake?' he murmured into her ear.

"Barely."

"I love you, Ella Palmer."

She nestled her butt against him. "I love you too, hot stuff."

"Is hot stuff still a thing?"

"Most definitely."

"Are you ready to hang out with my entire crazy family tonight?"

"Yes, the only one I haven't met is Griffin."

"Warning, my mom, will be all over you."

"I can handle it. What's Griffin like?"

"He's the baby of the family and it's obvious. Doesn't take anything too seriously. Playful, a big flirt, charming, most women would say movie-star handsome, but don't get any ideas," he said, eyes narrowed.

"I would have a hard time believing anyone could be more handsome than you."

"Good answer. Let's hop in the shower," Kyle suggested.

"Do I really have to move?"

"Yes, my parents are early risers. They could show up anytime, plus we need to get the pups out of their crate."

"They slept through the whole night. Amazing considering the rodeo going on right next to them," she said, grinning.

"Come on, get up," he pulled her along and they quickly showered and dressed. They headed downstairs carrying two squiggly bundles who were raring to go.

"I love puppy breath," Ella giggled as Lucy licked her face.

"You want to take them outside while I throw breakfast together?"

"Sure," Ella said.

"Hurry back," his knuckles grazed her cheek. Then the puppies happily trotted behind her to the great outdoors. *Life was good...no—life is great!*

69

The chef was in the staff kitchen with his assistant, busy preparing hors d'oeuvres for the party. Richard had brought someone in to decorate the pool area festively. The large covered outdoor table was set, adorned with a bright red tablecloth and vases filled with colorful fresh cut flowers. Music streamed through the sound system as the decorator lit the candles inside hurricane lamps that hung from shepherd hooks scattered around the patio.

The decorator's assistant leaned over the pool, placing floating battery-operated lights made to look like lily pads in the water. The outdoor gas fireplace had been lit purely for ambience since it was turning out to be a beautiful summer evening. The only thing missing were the people, who would arrive shortly.

Ella had decided to wear a gauzy white floral print with an alluring lace-up back and V-neck front. It had a wrapped maxi skirt with a high-low hem. At the last minute she remembered to put on the pearls Kyle had given her, in what seemed like years ago. How far they'd come.

She glanced over at Kyle, desirable as hell in his cream linen slacks and tucked black tee-shirt. He wore his hair slicked back and a relaxed smile as his eyes did a last-minute sweep over the patio. Catching her eye, he winked and said, "Are you sure you're ready for this?"

"Absolutely!"

"Don't say I didn't warn you."

"Warn her about what?" A man stepped out through the French doors with a martini in his hand. His hair was dark brown, worn shaggy and slightly long; even without the introductions, his cobalt blue eyes were a dead giveaway that he was Kyle's younger brother, Griffin.

"Well, well, well, I always knew you had exquisite taste. You must be Ella." He took her hand and leaned over to kiss the back of it. Holding on to it a little longer than necessary, his eyes boldly sparkled with curiosity.

She found herself slightly breathless from the spell he wove. Kyle saved the day, protectively putting his arm around her and hugging her tightly against his side. "Down boy, she's already taken."

"Hey, a guy can fantasize, no harm in that," he winked at her wickedly.

"I guess no introductions are necessary but for manners sake, Ella this is Griffin, Griffin, Ella."

"You are as magnificent as everyone has said. Why don't you dump this shmuck and run away with me? I'm the handsome and charming one of the family.

Plus, I like to have fun; my brother can be a real stick in the mud."

Ella laughed at his audacity. "He's pretty charming as well, and I'd say he's learning to loosen up a bit."

"Finally, a woman who can rescue my workaholic sibling from himself. Sweet!"

"Daddy, Ella, I'm back! Hey Uncle Griffin," Finn said, running to hug each of them. "Where's Charlie and Lucy?"

Ella pointed to the round fenced-in area off to the side of the patio. He raced to the gate to let them out. Finn sat on the grass letting the puppies maul him, laughing as they competed for his attention. Kyle went over to Finn and squatted down, having a conversation with his son as Finn nodded thoughtfully.

"My nephew is growing up fast," Griffin said. His eyes lit up when Faye stepped outside. "Sis!"

Faye ran over, throwing her arms around her brother. "Where have you been, naughty boy. I never see you anymore."

"Golfing, wining and dining beautiful women, you know the usual."

Faye rolled her eyes at Ella. "My dear brother, mark my words, you're going to meet someone someday that gives you a run for your money and you won't know what hit you."

"Doubtful," he grinned.

"Hi Mr. and Mrs. Bennett," Ella said as they joined them on the patio. A waiter appeared and discreetly took their drink orders.

"Please, *ma chéri*, call us Giselle and James, we insist," she said warmly.

"Okay, thank you."

James Bennett nodded his head stiffly, but his smile actually reached his eyes today. He and Giselle were holding hands, they'd apparently moved past the long ago transgression, and were still in love after all these years.

"Mr. Bennett—I mean James, how was Finn's overnight stay?"

"We enjoyed him immensely. He is a delight."

"Yes, he is. Kyle and Jemma have done a great job," Ella agreed.

Another waiter appeared holding a tray of finger foods, everyone piled their napkins with the sumptuous fare. Kyle rejoined the group and they all made small talk. Giselle pulled Ella aside, her curiosity getting the better of her. "Tell me, are you in love with my son?"

Ella's eyes widened and her mouth fell open. "Um, actually, that would be a yes," she said recovering from her surprise.

"Good, that's settled then. *Mon trésor*, I have never seen him so content. He is so in love, no?"

"I want your son to be happy. I love him."

"*Ma belle*, you can make babies, so Finn has little brothers and sisters, no?"

Ella's cheeks turned pink as she laughed, remembering Kyle's warning and understanding a little more clearly what he had meant.

"Mother, you're making Ella blush," Kyle said walking over catching the tail-end of the conversation.

"I just said Finn needs *un petit frère ou une petite soeur*."

Kyle laughed out loud. "Mother you never give up do you?"

Richard appeared with Ella's best friend Deb following, full wine glass in hand. Ella shrieked, "Deb! What are you doing here?"

"Your charming boyfriend invited me."

Ella gave her friend a big hug. "You're just in time for dinner."

"That was my plan."

The chef, in traditional chef's uniform, right down to the toque blanche, a white chef hat, had fired up the large gas grill and was throwing shish kebabs, skewered cubes of beef and bell peppers, onions, mushrooms and bacon, onto the flames.

"Shall we move to the table?" Kyle suggested. He tucked his hand in the small of Ella's back as they made their way to their seats.

They all took their places around the table with much talk and laughter. Ella was enchanted with the whole tribe. They were all so interesting and had great stories to tell. Deb seemed to fit right in. Finn was doing his best to keep them entertained as well. She couldn't help but fast forward to his teenage years; she thought he might have inherited a little bit of his Uncle Griffin's charm. After dinner a traditional French dessert was served, *Crème au Caramel*, absolutely to die for in Ella's opinion.

Kyle suggested they move to more comfortable seating around the pool, which they did. Drinks were flowing and everyone seemed to be relaxed and enjoying themselves. Ella slipped off her heels and wiggled toes that were happy to be free. Faye had kicked hers off long ago. Finn got up and ran into the house yelling, "I'll be right back, nobody move." Causing them all to laugh at his dramatics.

When he returned, he was pulling Richard Drake along with him and Finn had a huge grin on his face. Kyle stood up and tapped his glass with a spoon, the tinkling sound capturing everyone's attention.

They all looked at him expectantly, and Ella's eyebrow's rose when he turned towards her. Getting down on one knee in front of her, she suddenly understood what was about to happen. Eyes wide, she covered her mouth with her hand. She searched Kyle's eyes, which were blazing with emotion. Finn stepped next to his dad and importantly reached his hand into his pants pocket and pulled out a ring box handing it to his father.

"Ella, you are my heart, my love, l'amour de ma vie, my other half. Will you marry me?"

With tears spilling out and down her cheeks she nodded her head yes. Holding out her hand, she watched as he slipped the huge diamond solitaire onto her finger. The group, who had been in on it the whole time, cheered. James clicked his glass with a spoon, saying, "Toast."

They all turned toward him, and he said, "Ella, welcome to the Bennett family. You are an answered prayer for us. We never thought we'd see our son happy again. Our grandson adores you and so do we. May you have a lifetime of joy and happiness together."

Finn wrapped his arms around Ella and said, "I love you to the moon and back."

"My turn," Kyle said. He lowered his head and kissed her passionately to the delight of everyone.

"See what I have to go through?" Finn said, grinning happily.

Laughing Giselle said, "One day *mon mignon*, you'll kiss a girl like that."

"No way, gross!"

Ella looked around at her family...*her family*. Finally, she had the one thing she had been longing for since she was a child. More importantly she had found her mate, the person she wanted to wake up beside for the rest of her life. She couldn't wait to have little munchkins running around the now empty halls of this mansion. It would be filled with love, joy and laughter.

The End for Now...

Thanks for reading Seduced by a Billionaire! I hope you enjoyed it. Below are the links for the rest of the series. For a deep dive into family, life and love read my Triple C Ranch Series.

Happy Reading!

Please consider leaving a rating and review on Amazon. They are very helpful and greatly appreciated!

You can find me on Facebook under Author Jill Downey.

Here's the link to The Carolina Series:

https://mybook.to/SeducedbyaBillionaire
https://mybook.to/SecretBillionaire
https://mybook.to/Playboybillionaire
https://mybook.to/billinairexmas

Links to The Triple C Ranch Series:
https://mybook.to/cowboymagic
https://mybook.to/Cowboysurprise
https://mybook.to/cowboyheatTripleC

Here's the universal link to the Heartland Series
box set:

mybook.to/BoxSetHeartlandSeries

Here's a link to my Facebook readers group:
https://www.facebook.com/groups/179183050062278/:

ACKNOWLEDGMENTS

I'd like to thank April Wilson for sharing her wisdom and hard-earned knowledge.

Thanks to my other April... April Bennett, my editor and guide. Her empathy, humor and smarts are everything I could ever have asked for.

I am so lucky to have Julie Hopkins as my interior book designer and Maria from Steamy Designs for my fabulous covers!

I'd be floundering without the constant and unwavering support of my core team Sandy Kiss, Julie Karlson, and my mom, Vera!

BOOKS BY JILL DOWNEY

Books by Jill Downey

The Heartland Series:

More Than A Boss

More Than A Memory

More Than A Fling

The Carolina Series:

Seduced by a Billionaire

Secret Billionaire

Playboy Billionaire

A Billionaire's Christmas

The Triple C Series:

Cowboy Magic

Cowboy Surprise

Cowboy Heat

Cowboy Confidential